Jared's Promise

Jason rounded the corner toward the huge foyer with its polished floor and marble walls and looked toward the door of the office that had been his grandfather's. *What had it looked like inside?* Probably neat and orderly, like everything else in Dr. Jared Fowler's world, a place where he could sit with students and work out their problems.

There was a woman standing outside the office door. She was petite and trim, neatly outfitted in a dark blue suit and simple navy pumps. Her hair touched her shoulders; her hands hung at her sides. What intrigued him was that she didn't move, just stood very still.

Deciding not to bother her, he began to walk toward the outside double doors. As he reached them, he looked behind and saw she had remained motionless.

Turning back, he said, "Excuse me, may I help you with something?"

It was Joanna Ransome. He recognized her as soon as she turned. He was totally unprepared for her reaction, though. The color drained from her face as her eyes widened and he heard a sharp intake of breath.

"Oh, my God," she muttered, meeting his eyes. "Oh, my God."

What They Are Saying About
Jared's Promise

"The emotions are gripping and the beauty of Ms. Howard's words makes this a work of art in women's fiction. There are a few surprises along the way that stun the reader, bring a tear to the eye and touch one's heart. This is a story that is passionate, totally emotional and which will reinforce the bonds and feelings of family, make you cry and keep you enthralled from beginning to end.

A story of love, compassion, forgiveness and family, add to that a talented writer and it is a perfect addition to one's keeper shelf."

—Tracey West
Road to Romance Senior Reviewer

Jeanne Howard writes a poignant story about Dr. Jared Fowler's emotional ups and downs, and a life full of love and denial, and how it affects everyone in their families. Had he truly hoped that one of the family would follow the clues and solve the complex mystery of the stranger in their lives? Why had her father left so many clues for his daughter to follow?

As Jared's family discovers, old secrets never stay hidden forever.

—JoEllen Conger
Cinderella and the Stripper

Jared's Promise by Jeanne Howard, is a compelling, thought-provoking look at a subject many would rather not contemplate. The tenderness and compassion this writer has passed on to readers is a highly moral stance. It speaks of goodness and gives the reader a sense of hope, even in trying times. All too often in books evil triumphs over good, but in *Jared's Promise* good not only triumphs, but is raised to an alleluia.

I was able to identify with Jared's grandson immediately. The interaction of the characters is genuine. I look forward to more of this author's works. 5 on my mascara scale (you will cry)

—A. Dee Carey/*The Fox Lady*
www.adeecarey.com
The Fox Lady
Fox in the Mist, Mark of the Fox and
The Fox and the Swan - Wings-Press

Jared's Promise

Jeanne Howard

A Wings ePress, Inc.
Paranormal Romance Novel

Wings ePress, Inc.

Copy editrd by: Jeanne Smith
\Cover artist: Trisha Fitzgerald

Wings ePress Books
www.books-by-wings-epress.com

ISBN 1-59088-544-9

Published In the United States Of America

September 2006

Wings ePress Inc.
403 Wallace Court
Richmond, KY 40475

Dedication

To my grandchildren,
Nate and Adela.
I wish each of you a personal seagull
and a life filled with love.

Prologue

April 9, 2002

It was the quiet she noticed first. Usually, the sounds of surf and traffic intermingled to form a background of noise she'd long ago learned to tune out. Joanna listened hard for a familiar sound, but there was nothing save the occasional cry of a lone seagull outside her window. The bird had shown up two days ago, found a piece of piling on the edge of a dune that seemed to his liking and taken up residence, his large, unblinking eyes looking from her window to the ocean and back.

As she got out of bed, Joanna's gaze rested on the familiar photo on her nightstand. She picked it up and stroked the handsome face with her forefinger. Still holding the frame, she wandered into the shadowy den where the silence seemed to take on an ominous feel.

She sat at the computer, hugging the picture close to her chest. With one hand, she keyed in her password and waited. *Rituals. How many times have I done this? For how many years? What makes me think I'll ever hear from him again?*

There was no message.

Then, as she'd done every day for the last three months, she switched to the online *Chicago Tribune*, accessed the obituary search and typed in his name.

Her breath caught in her throat. The words danced, blurred, in front of her. The photo slid out of her trembling hand and dropped onto the carpet. *Dr. Jared Fowler, noted theater director, dies at 77.* Her head dropped to her chest, the sobs rose through her throat and escaped in low moans. *Oh, Jared!*

She struggled to read. Here and there, a phrase managed to get through ... *radio broadcasting voice ... charismatic teacher ... highly respected ...* and then this:

Dr. Fowler is survived by his wife of 52 years, Victoria M. (Vicki), his daughter Dr. Marina Buckman (Dr. Andrew), his son Michael (Ellen) and his beloved grandchildren, Jason Buckman and Sarah Fowler.

Joanna fought the urge to scream ... *no! ... he's survived by me too ... I loved him as much as they did ... he belonged to me too.*

She closed her eyes and fought off a wave of dizziness. This was what she'd dreaded. *He had known. He had known there wasn't much time.*

She walked into the great room and out the sliding glass door, mindless of the weather, of the fact that she was clad only in her nightclothes. Standing on the edge of the dunes, she felt the chilly April wind and remembered another time on another beach when Jared had promised he'd be with her always.

The seagull jumped from his perch and stood looking up at her, his wings ruffling.

"I'm going to miss him so much," she said out of her need to talk to someone. "Even though we were apart most of our lives, we shared so much and I always knew he was there, you know ... *there* somewhere. Now he's gone. What do I do?"

Joanna sat on the piling the gull had vacated and closed her eyes against the tears beginning to slide down her face. When she opened them, the bird was still standing near her feet. Shivering, she breathed deeply and made her way back inside. She took a tissue from the box on the table and dried her eyes. In the den, she retrieved the photo from the floor, stood it on her desk and gently touched the face that still smiled out at her.

Sitting heavily in the chair, Joanna lowered her head and let the sobs come, her shoulders shaking, her eyes closed tightly as she gripped the arms of the chair to keep herself upright. She cried until there were no more tears, just short, hiccupping breaths that escaped in tiny whimpers. Gradually she calmed. Jared was no longer suffering. His long struggle against the ravages of emphysema was finally over. *I can't mourn for that,* she thought. *I am only crying because now I know he is truly gone.*

She riffled through a sheaf of papers in a folder on the desk and re-read Jared's last e-mail, his final request. *Now's not the time to lose control.* Then she dialed the office of the youth center where she'd been a part-time counselor since her retirement.

"Betty? This is Joanna."

"You sound exhausted, Jo. Anything wrong?"

"I *am* tired. But I've also gotten some bad news and I'm afraid I'm going to have to take a few days off."

"Oh, no. I don't want to be nosy, but..."

"Thanks. It's just that someone very important to me has passed away. I'll be out of town for a few days."

"Gee, I'm sorry. Listen, take as much time as you need. Max can fill in with the kids if they really need to see someone.

Otherwise, I know they'll understand and be waiting for you when you get back. Is there anything I can do for you?"

"No, thanks. I'll see you when I get back."

There. I got through it. I actually said it out loud.

She should tell Steven and Abby she'd be away. Steven would probably try to talk her out of going. He would worry for her, knowing what would be waiting. So she put it off, wanting to finalize her plans before she had to face her son's objections.

She turned back to the desk and looked at the picture again. *I won't let you down, my darling.*

In minutes, Joanna was booked on a flight to Chicago.

~ * ~

Meanwhile, on Lake Michigan, in a house Joanna had only heard of, a family mourned the loss of a man they loved, unaware not only of her grief, but of the fact that she existed at all.

One

Marina

Jason is pacing from one side of the kitchen to the other, unconsciously following the pattern in the checkered linoleum.

"For God's sake, Mom! I *told* you what he wanted. Why in hell aren't you *insisting* we do it his way?" His voice is shrill; I don't think I've ever seen him this angry.

At sixteen, my son is six feet tall, still mostly arms and legs, the developing muscles just starting to harden beneath his skin. Like he often does when he's agitated, he repeatedly pushes a shock of wheat-colored hair away from his eyes.

I try to keep my tone soft. "You *know* why. I don't want to fight with you about this. Your grandmother wants the funeral service and there's no way we can go against her wishes."

"But ... but, she wasn't with Grandpa and me out on the lake. She didn't hear him say no funeral, no coffin with people staring at him like he was some weird museum specimen. He said that every time we talked about—"

Suddenly, Jason's face collapses and a muted sob escapes from his lips. As he leans against my shoulder, I put my arms around him and let him cry.

He finally steps back, looks down at the floor and swipes at his eyes with his sleeve. His tawny head still bent, he doesn't say anything right away and doesn't look up when he does.

"Sorry. I didn't mean to do that. I guess I can't stand saying 'funeral' and 'Grandpa' in the same sentence. It's so final. I'm gonna miss him so much. Even when he first got sick, I never thought the time would come that he wouldn't be here."

He raises his head and I swallow hard, fighting my own tears as I look at this younger version of Dad, watch him struggle to regain his composure.

I reach out and smooth his hair, surprised he allows this little bit of mothering.

"I'm counting on you. The next few days will be very hard for us all and we're going to miss him every minute, but we need to be there for your grandmother, even if we don't agree with what she's decided."

He turns on his heel and heads for the back door. "I need to take a walk. Are you going over to Grandpa's?"

I glance at the kitchen clock. Almost two.

"Yeah, Uncle Mike should be here to pick me up in a few minutes. We have to go to the funeral home and check everything out before the viewing. I wish I didn't have to go, believe me, but it wouldn't be fair to dump everything on him."

"You don't mind if I hang around here, do you?" Jason's hand is on the doorknob. "I've gotta be by myself for a while."

"Go ahead. I'll be back by five. Mike and I want to see your grandmother and make sure Aunt Genna's gotten in okay. Your dad's at the hospital but he'll be home early so we can meet everyone at Grandmom's to go to the viewing."

Jason bobs his head. Without comment, I follow him out the door and pull up one of the wicker chairs on the porch. I watch him walk slowly toward the street and then I sit to wait for my brother.

Jason makes it halfway up the block before Mike's car comes around the corner and pulls to the curb next to him. I can see Mike leaning across the seat, the window opened, talking to Jason. In a few minutes, Jason walks on, Mike coasts up to the house and pushes the car door open for me.

"Hey, sis." Mike leans over for a quick peck on the cheek but pauses to blot the tear that is rolling down my cheek.

"Thanks." I fumble in my purse for a tissue. "I can't believe how all I want to do is cry. I've been thinking about Dad all day, feeling so damn bad one minute and then the next minute I'm laughing over something, like those ridiculous puns he always loved or that silly nickname he had for me."

Mike chuckles. "Yeah, Dad always called you his blonde bombshell. God, how I teased you about that! He loved that expression, didn't he?"

"Oh, did he ever! It wasn't easy for me, you know, growing up with all of you brunettes. I felt like a white-haired freak until Dad told me his grandmother was fair like me and she was considered the beauty in her family. Leave it to Dad to find the right thing to say."

"Yeah, he did that for me, too. I was such a shy, scared kid with that stubborn stutter of mine. I thought everybody was making fun of me, but Dad wouldn't have any of it. He told me I'd outgrow the stutter and probably be a star debater when I got to high school. He made me believe I could do almost anything."

I smile at the memory. "He sure gave us a lot of freedom to find our way. I know how surprised he was when I told him I wanted to be a pediatrician. I think he was proud of my choice, but I know he was disappointed when I picked UMass instead of a school closer to home. It was tough for him to let his little girl go so far away."

I choke back more tears and look out the window. "Sure seems impossible he's truly gone. This is going to be so tough."

"Not only on us, but Jason too, Mare. We need to give him some extra-special attention in the next few days. He and Dad were like two peas in a pod and I'm afraid he's too young to know how to deal with the loss. He vented to me a bit just now. He's pretty angry about the viewing tonight. Did he talk to you about it?"

"Uh-huh. He says Dad was adamant about not wanting one, so nothing else matters to Jason. He doesn't understand why we're allowing it to happen. He can't see it from Mom's point of view."

"Well, he's never had death touch anyone close to him. Dad was like a second father to that kid. He idolized him, you know."

"Yeah, and that'll make it all the harder. Sometimes I wonder if worshipping Dad the way we all did was a mistake. Doesn't seem possible that one man could be as perfect as he was to us, but—"

"Hey, no one's perfect, Mare, but Dad? He came damn close."

"Have you talked to Mom yet today?"

Mike shakes his head no. "You?"

"Not today. I sat with her for quite a while yesterday and she was like a zombie. I wonder what she'll do now. What a pair they were, huh? Dad was so full of life, so positive, so ... well, you know what I mean. But not Mom. Boy, talk about two totally different people. Let me ask you something. Do you have any early memories of her? Like before we moved, when you were really little?"

He glances at me and then turns his eyes back to the road.

"Uh ... no, not really. I remember snippets of stuff, mostly about either Aunt Genna or Dad, but nothing sticks out about Mom until I was about eight. We were here by then, right?"

"Yeah. We got here in 'sixty-two. That made you about six. You started school here and I was in third grade. No memories of Yardley?"

We'd lived in Yardley, Pennsylvania, when Dad was on the faculty of Manning State College near there. I remember a lot from the days in that old two-story house on the quiet street where we rode our bikes and played with our friends. Like Mike, though, most of what I remember is about Dad.

"None," Mike answers as he turns the corner to Dad's house. "I only know Aunt Genna lived with us when she was going to college and I still had that horrible stutter. I do remember how quiet Mom was, though, how she never seemed to do anything but read. But that's all. Why?"

"Just thinking, I guess. About Dad, about how lucky we were to have him for a father. We could always count on his support."

We pull into the driveway of the house by the lake. The flag flutters gently from the front porch. Crocuses and daffodils are starting to poke their heads up in the flowerbed by the steps.

"I hate that Dad will miss the spring." Mike looks around the yard as we navigate the flagstone walk that zigzags through the just-greening grass. "Every time we talked about seasons of the year, he always said how he loved autumn but spring was his favorite."

"I know. It's infuriating really. He'll miss so many things he was looking forward to. Damn those cigarettes! In spite of how much I loved him, I'm so angry that he kept on smoking, even when the emphysema started. The doctors warned him; *I* warned him. God, I even begged him. He shortened his life, Mike. He could have lived another ten years, but he wouldn't quit."

Mike opens his door and gets out of the car.

"Well, none of that does anybody any good now. Dad enjoyed every minute of his life. He lived the way he wanted to, including the smoking, and maybe it killed him prematurely, but he had a good life. Everyone who knew him respected him. Personally, I'd like to have people feel that way about me when I'm gone."

Mike goes ahead of me into the foyer, excuses himself and heads for the powder room. There is a large suitcase on the floor by the closet door with a coat lying across it.

I hear rapid footsteps coming from the kitchen and then I'm wrapped in the embrace of my mother's sister, Genna.

"Here's my favorite niece. The taxi just dropped me a few minutes ago. Oh my, you look like you need some rest, honey," Aunt Genna scolds as she hugs me close. "Have you had any sleep?"

I don't realize how much I need the warmth and comfort of her arms until I rest my head on her shoulder and let the tears come. Finally, I stop crying, wipe my eyes and sniffle a tears-stuffy nose.

"Sleep? I've had a few hours, I guess. Mostly I've been thinking about Dad, talking with Jason and letting Andy and Mike handle everything. Honest, Aunt Genna, it doesn't matter how long you try to prepare for something like this, when you lose someone as important as Dad, it's like a million-volt shock. I still can't believe he's gone."

My gentle aunt takes my face in her hands and kisses my cheek. Her face is still youthful, the chin-length silver hair tucked behind her ears falling into a neat pageboy.

"He loved you very much, and you can take comfort in knowing you did everything in your power to ease his suffering and keep him in good spirits. You gave him Jason! I often thought that grandson of his was one of the main reasons Jared hung on as long as he did. In many ways, your father re-lived raising you and Mike through Jason, only this time he actually had fun. How is he taking this?"

"Not very well, I'm afraid, but he's trying. It's going to be hard on him what with warm weather coming and all. He'll miss having his best friend out fishing with him. I know how badly he wanted Dad to be at his high school graduation and see him off to college. He's not talking about any of that, though. He speaks of Dad in the present tense, though just before I left, he broke down and let out a little of the grief. I worry about how he'll handle the funeral."

Aunt Genna's tone turns matter-of-fact. "He's not a little boy anymore. He'll do what we all have to. He'll make it through and in time he'll begin to heal and move on with his life. And how is your mother holding up?"

"She's quiet. Quiet as always. She sits and stares into space and lets us take care of whatever has to be done. I've only seen one glimmer that she's still in control. You know how private a guy Dad was. Seems he told Jason more than once he didn't want a viewing or a funeral, but Mom insisted otherwise. She didn't give a reason, just stuck to her contention that Dad should have a full-fledged funeral. Jason's awfully upset, but of course I had to back Mom. Once she made that decision, she shut down again. It's good for her that you're here."

My mother comes into the room then, her face pale but composed. When she sees her sister, she picks up her pace. After Aunt Genna opens her arms and folds Mom into them, I back out and leave them alone.

Then, feeling at odds and not knowing what else to do, I go to Dad's den.

I sit in his chair and look out at the peaceful back yard ... the improvised putting green he made for Jason, the table and brightly padded redwood chairs we put out last week in anticipation of warmer weather. I'm sad that he won't be able to sit there and read. The new Grisham book I gave him is on his desk, the bookmark resting at chapter three. His breathing too labored to allow even the mildest exertion, Dad read when he could or one of us read to him as he sat with his eyes closed, listening.

"Sitting here with Dad?"

I swing the chair around. "Hi, didn't hear you come in. Yeah, it's like he's right here. Can you feel him too?"

Mike's eyes are teary as he looks around at the bookshelves and soft leather furniture.

"Sure. Some rooms in the house will always belong to one or the other of us. This is Dad's. I feel close to him being in here." He clears his throat and looks back toward the hall. "Has Aunt Genna gotten in yet?"

"I left her with Mom. Maybe now she'll be able to open up some, let the sadness out. We're still her kids, Mike. Do you ever remember her showing us how she felt about anything? She sure as hell isn't going to let us see her grieve."

Mike turns toward the door. "I'll go say hello and then we'd better get going. We're supposed to be at the funeral home by three."

I dread the evening, especially the first sight of my father in the bronze coffin we'd picked out. I don't want to leave, but I take Mike's hand, stand and walk away from the place Dad loved to a place no daughter wants to go.

~ * ~

At the funeral home, we sign the rest of the papers and check off all the details for the viewing and service at the graveside tomorrow. It's weird; I feel detached, like I'm going through the motions for a stranger. Flower disposal (we asked that they be sent to a hospital or nursing home), when we can retrieve Dad's rings and watch (before the casket is sealed). Hideous stuff. Mike and I can't get out of there fast enough.

~ * ~

I'd like to forget the viewing. It goes on for what seems like days instead of hours. A couple of times, I look for Jason only to find him hunched over in a chair in the anteroom, his head in his hands. I touch his arm, but he doesn't look up so I leave him to grieve alone.

Mike and I stand next to Dad, greeting the stream of people who've come to pay their respects. Aunt Genna and Mom sit in the front row. I go over to Aunt Genna and lean down to whisper.

"Why isn't Mom up there with us? She should be the first one to meet everyone."

Aunt Genna stands and steers me toward the corner. She keeps her voice low. "You know your mother. Meeting people has always been hard for her. Aside from the few members of her staff at the museum, she doesn't really know anyone here. I'm sure she's terribly uncomfortable with all these strangers."

"Strangers? But these are Dad's colleagues, the university people he worked with for over twenty years. I can't believe she wouldn't recognize at least some of them. Married over half a century and she doesn't know his friends?"

"No one can dictate anyone's behavior in a situation like this, Marina. Your mother's coping the best she can." She turns back to her chair.

I spot Judith Godwin in the line, inching her way to the front. Judith's been my friend since the first day of school after I moved to the Midwest. I reach out to feel her strong, hang-in-there grasp.

She fixes on my eyes and I know she's avoiding looking at the casket.

"I don't know if I can do this, Mare. You know how much I loved your father. He was everything mine wasn't. Don't know if I'd have amounted to much of anything without Jared's encouragement."

She's done more than amounted to something. Judith was a well-known fashion model for ten years and then started her own agency. She travels around the world and is still as beautiful as she was in her twenties.

"Dad would want you here, honey," I tell her. I take her arm and walk with her to where he lies surrounded by white satin and flowers cascading from the open cover. She draws a gasping breath, puts her hand on his, kneels and bows her head. I back away.

I resume my station and give Judith a little wave as she stands and goes over to my mother. The people keep coming.

Finally, it's almost time to leave. Most of the people who had filled the chairs and conversed quietly are gone.

From the back of the room, a woman walks down the aisle. Her steps are tentative; she keeps her eyes down. Her lips move soundlessly as she kneels on the *prie deux*. After a few minutes, she touches Dad's face and her hand jerks back. She reaches out and I think she'll touch him again. But she only lingers a moment longer, then stands and turns away.

I stop her. "Thank you for coming," I say in the mechanical way Mike and I have used all evening.

Her large hazel eyes are swimming with tears; her voice is barely audible. "Your father was an old friend. I wanted to say goodbye."

She lowers her head and walks out before I can ask her name. No one else comes in, so we tell the funeral director to close the doors. It is finally over.

Two

Jason

I can't sit in this chair another minute. Mom's already checked on me twice and I know she wants me to be with everybody, but I can't. This viewing thing is worse than I ever imagined ... Grandpa in that coffin looking like a mannequin. I wish I hadn't come so I would remember him the way he was, not like this.

I feel a hand on my shoulder and look up at my friend Scott.

"Hey, Jase, I'm really sorry about Mr. Fowler. He was such a neat guy. You know I always wished I had a grandfather like him. It's gonna be totally strange going out on the lake without him, huh?"

"Thanks. Yeah, totally strange. Have you seen him?"

"Uh-huh. Jeez, he looks like he's gonna sit up and talk any minute. This is the first time I've ever seen a dea... hey, sorry, man. It's just that this is my first viewing and I didn't know what to expect. I think he looks pretty okay."

"He doesn't look okay, you know? He looks dead. He doesn't look at all like my grandpa. Man, I sit here and close my eyes and I can hear him talking. I remember so much of what he said, the way he laughed, the silly jokes he told, the easy way he had of making me feel so special, even the way he looked so sad sometimes when he didn't know I was looking."

Scott looks surprised. "I never saw him sad."

"Okay, not sad, maybe like, thoughtful. Once when I asked him what he was thinking about, he said about how life takes us where it wants us to go, and sometimes we don't always get what we dream about. Funny he would talk that way. Grandpa sure had a great life. He was so confident, so comfortable with everybody. Guess there might be parts of some people we never really see, but not my grandpa. He was like my dad, upfront about everything and so easy to talk to. You know, I bet I knew him better than almost anybody else."

"You spent a lot of time with him, that's for sure. Hey, do you want me to hang around for a while? I'm not in any hurry to get home."

I look through the doorway and see the main room is almost empty.

"Nah, thanks anyway. I think we'll be getting out of here soon. It was nice of you to come. I appreciate somebody being here just for me."

Scott walks toward the door and almost runs into a woman I've never seen. She doesn't look up at him, but moves aside, her hand holding a tissue or hankie, dabbing at her eyes. So many people loved Grandpa; I'm not surprised she's crying.

I go into the main room and try not to look at Grandpa. Dad's standing off to one side and I go over to him.

"You okay, son?"

"Yeah, but I wish tomorrow was over. I guess we'll have to tough it out, knowing Grandpa's safe and out of all the misery he went through. Maybe he's up there with those seagulls he always talked about. What do you think, Dad? Imagine ... flying around like he did in his fighter plane, but this time with only the joy of it. If I close my eyes, I can still hear him laughing."

"Good idea. Listen for his laugh and picture him way up there, smiling down. That won't keep you from missing him, but maybe it'll help."

Three

Marina

It seems strange to see Andy standing at the kitchen counter in a dress suit, the stiffly starched cuffs sticking out of the sleeves of his jacket. Usually he's in jeans or casual slacks, ready to change into scrubs when he gets to work. He's already brewed a pot of coffee.

"Hey, Mare. How do you feel this morning? Want a cup?" He leans over for a kiss and then another.

"No, thanks. I'm okay, but I don't feel very rested. I guess I must have dozed off at some point because the alarm clock woke me. Last night seems like a bad dream, you know, all those faces, the smiles, the sympathy."

"I know what you mean. It was surreal. And, of course, there was Dad. God, he looked like he was only sleeping."

"I tried to turn away so many times," I say, "but his face was always there. You know, he would have been upset over how hard the viewing was on all of us. He never wanted to hurt anyone and I know he would have hated the whole, barbaric thing."

He finishes his coffee and dumps what's left in the carafe into the sink.

"We've got to get over to the house. The funeral home cars will be there pretty soon. I'll go call Jason."

We'd vigorously opposed having limos call for us, but the director suggested we might not want to drive home from the cemetery. He said the courtesy often proves wise. I think of all the funeral processions I've seen. Stopped at intersections to let the cars drift by, I used to wonder about the black-clad occupants and the person they mourned. Today will be my turn in the car.

~ * ~

At the house, everyone's standing around, not saying much. I guess we're all trying to get mentally prepared for the rest of the morning. I hug my mother and Aunt Genna, Mike and his wife Ellen. She's five months pregnant and pretty big already. I ask how she's feeling.

"Not as good as I did with Sarah." She pulls my eight-year-old niece close. "This one was a joy; her baby brother's making my life miserable."

I only have a chance to give Sarah a quick hug before the cars arrive. We file out of the house and take the short drive to the funeral home.

We're alone with Dad for just a few minutes when the director opens the door and people come in again. Dad's friend Dan Kearney and his wife Pam reach us first. Without saying anything, they move to the casket. Holding hands, they stand with their heads bowed.

After a few minutes, Dan wraps me in a gentle bear hug and I feel his wet cheek against my face. Dan has aged as attractively as Dad, his sandy hair thinned only a little at the forehead, his dark eyes as hollow as mine.

"This is a terrible loss," he says, still holding me. "I wish I had spent more time with him, but I'll always remember him as the best friend I ever had. Jared was a very special man and I owe him all the good things I have today."

I know he's talking about the friendship he and Dad shared back in Manning, how they stayed in contact even after we moved out here. Dan spent a lot of years mourning the death of his first wife, but then Dad encouraged him to take the job in Chicago that brought him to prominence as a scientist and newfound happiness in his marriage to Pam.

He says something to Mike, leans over to Mom and gives her a kiss on the cheek. Pam does the same. Then they take a seat at the rear next to Judith. I'd like to introduce them. Maybe later I'll get a chance.

"Mare, the director says it's time."

Andy puts his arm around my waist and gently guides me toward the casket.

When we walk up to Dad to say our goodbyes, I hold Jason tightly; his chest is heaving with silent sobs. He doesn't want to be led away. We walk down the side aisle toward the door and the waiting cars, Jason between Andy and me, Sarah gripping her parents' hands, then Mom and Aunt Genna.

And then I see her standing in the back of the room, the woman who was last through the receiving line last night. Dan has just spoken to her. Her eyes meet mine for an instant. I'm struck by the sorrow I see there and I want to know who she is, but there's no time to ask.

When we arrive at the cemetery, people are leaving their cars to assemble around the casket as the pallbearers slide it into place, flanked by layers of floral baskets. I remember how Dad loved flowers, especially roses. He was partial to red ones. I could always make him smile, though sometimes I thought I saw a touch of sadness, by giving him a single red rose for a special occasion. I have one for him today. My hand is shaking in anticipation of how it will feel to put the flower on his casket instead of handing it to him to be rewarded by his gentle smile.

The minister prays for all of us, and he prays for my father who never hurt anyone in his life. We are all numb and silent. When it's over, the director passes among the family, giving each of us a pink rose to place on the casket.

"No, thank you," I say and I reach out my single red one and lay it down. Mom and Aunt Genna go next and then they step off to the side, my mother's eyes glassy as she leans heavily against the arm of her sister. Jason and Andy place their pink ones and then we hold hands and watch everyone file by and lay their flowers on the glittering bronze. Judith's eyes are red-rimmed as she passes.

Off to the side, standing alone ... she's here too, the woman who described herself as an old friend. Her arms are stiff at her sides, her head is up and her eyes are focused on the casket. Like me, she has a red rose in one hand. She doesn't know I'm watching her; her gaze never wavers. As we turn away and move slowly back to the cars, I look back and see her approach the Astroturf sheet that covers the mound of dirt around the open grave. She wobbles unsteadily as the heels of her shoes dig unevenly into the grass. As we are escorted into the car, she is standing there with her hand on the casket, laying down the rose. I look out the window as we pull away and she is still there. I try to think of who she might be, but it's too hard to concentrate.

~ * ~

The rest of the day passes in a fog.

"It seems this house hasn't been empty for a minute," Judith says. "It's been wonderful hearing all these people telling such great stories about Jared."

I know what she means. The atmosphere is more festive than mournful. At times we almost forget why everyone is here; we expect to see Dad stride into the room to greet his guests. Then reality hits us anew that he won't ever do that again and the mood sobers.

"I'm so glad I could be with you," Judith says. She stays close to me until she has to leave. She'll be flying to Brazil in a few hours for an opening, some designer's show of his exotic fall line. She says she'll call when she comes back.

Every time the door opens, I look to see if it's the woman from the cemetery. She never comes, and I figure maybe it isn't all that important anyway. There are so many people who admired my father; she's probably one of any number of former colleagues or students. I think of her tears and the look on her face and I know exactly how she feels.

~ * ~

Everyone has gone and at last we're alone. We pick at the leftover food, conversation sparse. I'm talked out. Jason isn't here. I see him from the kitchen window outside standing on the dock. Then he sits, his feet dangling inches above the calm lake waters. I know where his mind is; he's with his buddy, and my heart aches for him.

Mike says Ellen needs rest, so they say their farewells and leave. Mom heads for the stairs and waves off our offers to accompany her. She looks exhausted and we hope she'll get some sleep. Andy has disappeared. I guess he's in Dad's study or on the phone to the hospital.

Aunt Genna looks at me with concern in her eyes. "Are you okay, honey?"

"I suppose so. I know the enormity of it hasn't sunk in yet, probably won't for a few days, but right now I'm just plain wrung out. I want to go into the den and have a long talk with Dad, have him make everything all better."

She smooths my hair, like she did when I was little.

"Your father always put you and Mike first, you know. There was nothing he wouldn't have done for you. You can live with the knowledge that you were both loved very deeply. That's a marvelous legacy for any parent to leave his children, don't you think?"

I feel the tears starting again. This time, I grab a tissue from the box on the counter and take a deep breath, forcing them to stay unshed.

"Oh yes! Mike and I have such wonderful memories of all the good times we had with Dad."

I turn to hug her. "How long can you stay?"

She puts her arm around my waist as we walk into the family room. "A couple of days. I'll probably go home on Saturday or Sunday. There's no hurry. Polly and George, good neighbors that they are, are feeding the cats, and the library has plenty of volunteers to take over until I get back."

"I'm glad. You'll be a comfort to Mom, and I love having you around."

"The turnout for your dad was amazing," Aunt Genna says, settling on the sofa, patting the cushion next to her. "I knew he was well known, but nothing prepared me for that many people, even some faces I recognized from *People* magazine."

"I wasn't surprised. Many of Dad's students made it to the big time. And up until last year, he drove to the university at least a couple times a week. He said he had friends to visit and he didn't want to lose touch. He was one of the most respected people I've ever known, but then he deserved to be."

Aunt Genna watches me closely.

"You adored your father, didn't you? I don't mean you loved him ... you adored him."

I feel a bit childish, hearing it put that way. "Yes, I guess I did. Silly, isn't it? It's just that for as long as I can remember, it's been Dad who's been my teacher, my nurse, the family cheerleader, a larger-than-life person. He was simply perfect."

She squeezes my hand. "I understand. In many ways, Jared was more like a blood brother to me than an in-law. When I had to make the choice of moving to Florida to live with Mother and Dad or starting college in Pennsylvania, there was no hesitation from Jared. 'Come live with us, Genna,' he'd said. He knew your mother would be happier with me there and he certainly needed…"

Her voice trails off.

"He needed what?"

She looks down at her fingers and then out the window. "Uh, well, he needed some help around the house. You and Mike were a handful, you know, and he was very busy with his teaching and directing at the college. I was glad to pitch in."

"I have a lot of vivid memories of living in Pennsylvania, even though I was so young," I say. "It did seem like you were with us an awful lot. I particularly remember you and Dad teaching Mike and me to ride our bikes and you taking us out trick or treating on Halloween. The memory that's strongest, though, is how scared I was when Mom told us we were moving to Chicago and you weren't coming. Dad seemed simply furious with her that night."

Aunt Genna doesn't comment, but I'm not willing to leave it alone. "Dad and Mom had some very serious trouble back then, didn't they?"

I'm not sure why I'm asking that. Something vague's been nagging at me all day, though, and the question simply tumbles out of my mouth.

It takes Aunt Genna a few seconds to reply. "Well, yes, I suppose they did. Nothing is ever one hundred percent smooth in any marriage, is it?"

I laugh, thinking of the spats Andy and I have had over the littlest of things.

"No, it isn't. What do you think Mom will do now? She's spent a lot of time volunteering at the museum store, but when I ask when she's going back, she shrugs and doesn't commit. I'm worried she's going to just sit here and grieve. Has she said anything to you about her plans?"

"Not yet, hon. You know your mother ... she's never been the most communicative person, and I'm afraid this will push her even further into her shell. I'd like her to visit me for a few weeks. Some time in the Florida sun might be what the doctor ordered. Why don't you and Mike encourage her?"

It's a good idea. After my grandparents died, Aunt Genna stayed on at their beach house on the Gulf and I know Mom loves being there. It's such a relaxing place, with spectacular sunsets and cool breezes. We visited often when I was a child, usually on the spur of the moment. Mom would come right out and announce that we were going to see Gram and Papa, and the next thing we knew, we were on our way. As much as I loved being with them, I was always torn between wanting to go and wanting to stay with Dad. I don't think he ever went along. He pleaded work, saying he couldn't get away.

~ * ~

It's almost Christmas. I'm about seven. I think Daddy's going with us to Florida, but at the last minute, Mommy tells us he can't. I hear them arguing in the kitchen. Daddy wants to go with us, but she won't let him. She's shouting about not wanting him there, saying she'll be better off without him for a while. I'm really scared and I decide not to go if he doesn't. Mike hangs onto Daddy's leg, crying and begging him to go with us. Nothing works, though. Daddy explains how nice it will be in Florida with our friends and all the presents Gram and Papa will have for us. I don't feel any better, but what Mike and I want doesn't matter. We leave the next day and Daddy stays behind. The look on Mommy's face scares me.

~ * ~

"What are you thinking about, Marina?"

I come out of my brief trip to the past to see Aunt Genna, her head cocked, looking at me quizzically.

"I'm sorry. Your mention of Florida brought me back to a place I haven't thought about for a very long time. I was remembering one of the times when we were kids that we went to visit Gram and Papa and left Dad home. Do you know why he never went with us?"

"Well no, not really, honey. Maybe your mother was more comfortable without him there. She had a lot to sort out and she probably wanted to do it without your dad in the picture."

I digest this information that doesn't answer my question.

A lot to sort out? I suppose there might have been. Somehow, even though I was very young, I knew she and Dad weren't like the other kids' parents. Mom and Dad didn't laugh, hug or kiss. Mom was a vague presence, that's about the best way I can describe her. And it seemed there were a lot of times we were alone with Genna when Dad was working or Mom stayed in the first-floor bedroom with the door closed.

I remember those days with a sense of uneasiness.

"What must it have been like for Dad?"

Aunt Genna sighs. "It was a difficult time for all of us, but then you moved to Chicago and things got better."

"Nope, that's not the answer. I still remember that awful August in 'sixty-two."

"You do? Now why on earth would you be thinking that far back?"

"It may sound funny, but I think it's reasonable that some of those days still feel so fresh. After all, one day we were in our house on Main Street in Yardley and the next we were at Gram and Papa's with a lot of our toys and most of our clothes. We never took that much with us when we visited. After a few weeks, we packed up again and flew to Chicago. By the time Mom, Gram, Mike and I got there, our furniture was already in the rented house and everything was in its place. I never asked questions as a kid, but looking back, it's obvious Dad made the move alone, set up the house and waited for us to arrive. Why?

Why did he pack by himself? Why weren't we all together for something that important?"

"I'm sure there were reasons," Aunt Genna replies. "Isn't it silly to be thinking about all this now?"

"Perhaps. But I'd still like to know. Did Mom ever tell you?"

Aunt Genna stands and rolls her hands against the sides of her tailored slacks.

"Let's not get into this now. We've all had a stressful day. Personally, I didn't get a lot of sleep last night and I could use some rest. I'm sure you could too."

I wonder why she's brushing me off. I wonder what she knows that she isn't telling. Is she hiding something? He might have been her sister's husband, but he was *my* father and I won't stay in the dark. The rush of anger surprises me, but then I regret having been so pushy—now's not the right time to keep prodding for answers. I put my arm around her as we walk out of the room. I'll definitely bring it up again before she goes home.

"Okay, we'll drop it for now. Oh, I almost forgot to ask you. Did you see the woman who came into the funeral home last night just before we left? She was back this morning and I saw her again at the cemetery. She said she was an old friend of Dad's but I didn't get a name. Was she someone you knew?"

"What did she look like, honey?"

"About your age, I guess ... early sixties, late fifties. Kind of light brown hair streaked with gray ... interesting eyes. Big, greenish eyes. I think she was crying when she turned away from the casket. I was hoping she would come to the house so we could talk a bit, but she didn't."

"Doesn't sound like anyone I know, baby."

I laugh at that. Baby. I'll be forty-nine next month and she still calls me "baby."

"Well, whoever she was, she was obviously one of the hordes of people who were very fond of Dad. A lot of lives won't be the same without him."

~ * ~

First thing Thursday morning, Mike and I go back to the house on the lake. Jason comes with us so he can go out on the boat. Andy is back at work. Aunt Genna is up, dressed in a pair of jeans. My mother is nowhere in sight. I hope she's still taking it easy, recovering from the stress of yesterday.

"Well, it's certainly warmer today," Aunt Genna says. "See how the sun's rays bounce off the flagstones on the walkway to the dock? Look out there! The lake looks like a mirror, it's so still. On a day like this, your father and Jason would already be pushing off for some secret cove of theirs. Where is Jason, anyway?"

"He's out on the boat for some alone time, though he said he'll never be by himself where he can be close to Dad."

My aunt checks her lipstick in the hallway mirror. "I understand. Your mother and I are going out for a little bit to wander through the mall, be around people and away from the house. You kids mind?"

"Absolutely not. Mike and I promised Mom we'd do our best to sort through Dad's papers and get them ready for the lawyer's visit on Saturday."

We sure don't have a lot of stomach for the job, though. It seems an invasion of Dad's privacy to be rooting around in his desk, opening envelopes and reading files. But we know this important task has to be done.

I open the blinds in the den and sniff the air like a hunting hound, searching for a trace of my father's fragrance. When I was a kid, I used my allowance to give him Old Spice gift sets every birthday and Christmas, and he continued to wear it even when I stopped buying. The aftershave mingled so well with the aroma of his cigarettes. I loved the smell of him! Now, his scent is growing fainter daily. Soon it will be completely gone.

Mike's hand is on the top drawer of the desk. "I feel like a thief," he whispers. "We don't have any business poking our noses into Dad's private papers."

I hope I sound more confident than I feel. "Someone has to do it," I remind him. "Mom won't be able to handle this chore and who would he trust more than you and me?"

Mike pulls open the drawer.

"Geez, Mare, look how neat it is. He sure didn't pass that gene to me."

Everything's completely impeccable ... there are orderly arrangements of pens and pencils, rubber bands, paper clips and a large manila envelope all by itself in the middle of the drawer with a neatly typed label in the center. *To My Family.*

"Leave it to Dad, Mare. Look. Everything we'll need for Thomas is right here. His will, insurance policies and investment records ... all here."

I look at Dad's neat compilation. "He knew. He knew he wouldn't be here too much longer. As always, he did what he could to make our lives easier."

I force the tears back into their ducts, blinking fast. Mike doesn't look at me and I'll bet he's doing the same.

Mike opens the top drawer on the side. A dictionary, a thesaurus, some blank index cards. The second drawer is deeper, lined with empty awning-green hanging files.

A small manila envelope on the drawer bottom catches my eye. I fish it out, open it and shake out its contents.

"Look at these, Mike."

There are several photos. A solemn, blue-eyed little boy of about five, his hair nearly as white as mine, stares out at me in many of the pictures. In others, the photos follow the child as he grows older, probably through grade school. His hair is still light, his blue eyes reflect the smile on his face. The rest are photos of the sea in sunshine and storm, the waves boiling with froth, ready to crash onto the beach. Certainly not Lake Michigan. Turning the photos over, I see an unfamiliar handwriting. *"My view from the beach in perfect weather,"* on the one wreathed in sunshine. *"The gathering storm"* on the other. *"Steven"* is carefully lettered on the back of the little boy.

I hand the photos to Mike. "Do you know who this might be?"

He studies them, and puts them down. "Nope, no idea." Then he shrugs. "Probably from somebody Dad wrote to, maybe one of his former students."

He puts the photos in the pile of things we've decided to discard.

I retrieve them. "Don't toss these yet. Maybe Aunt Genna knows something about them."

We work a few minutes longer. It's not difficult; Dad hasn't left many loose ends for us to tie up.

"Let's save the closet for tomorrow, or whenever," I suggest, wanting to be done for today. "There's no hurry."

Mike is just as eager. "Yeah, we need to take a break. Ellen and Sarah want me at home, Sarah especially. Ellen and I aren't sure how much of yesterday she absorbed, but we think it would be a good thing for us to stick together as a family today in case she has questions or needs to talk."

I envy Mike and his little girl's single-digit age. It might be a lot easier for Jason if he weren't so aware, so in touch with the depth of his loss. I wonder about him out on the boat alone; then I remind myself he needs private time to mourn in a place where he feels close to Dad.

"Go ahead. Take your family out to lunch or something," I tell him with a quick kiss on the cheek. "You know, in a lot of ways you remind me so much of Dad. It's comforting to have you around, bro, you know that?"

Mike grins. "Thanks. How will you get home?"

"I'll take Dad's wagon. It hasn't been driven for quite a while and I know Mom won't use it."

We leave the den, tiptoeing through the empty silence in the rooms around us. Mike eases the door closed behind him as though not to wake anyone. I watch him make his way to the driveway and his car. One more wave and he's gone.

I turn back. The unfamiliar photos are still on the desk. Who would send Dad pictures of a child? And views of an ocean? Even more curiously, why would he have kept them? I tuck them into the blotter. There's no sign of the boat coming in, so I jot Jason a note. *"Gone home. Be back later to pick you up. Love, Mom."*

Dad's keys hang on the hook by the door in the kitchen. I use the remote to open the garage door and unlock the Outback. There is an unopened pack of Winstons in the tray on the console along with an empty bank envelope. I lean over and open the glove compartment. The owner's manual, some maps, the insurance card, some blank deposit slips and a couple of faded matchbooks from, of all places, a hotel in New York. The matches inside have dried and flaked away. Wonder why he kept them.

Inside the console, I find the music he listened to. I'm a little surprised by some of it; I didn't know his taste ran to Ravel, Debussy and Beethoven. Not so surprising are the digitally re-mastered CDs of Johnny Mathis' and Andy Williams' vintage recordings. A few cassette tapes sit neatly in their places. More Mathis. One unmarked. I back the car out of the garage, wait to pull onto the street and then turn toward home.

The unmarked cassette has me curious. Slipping it into the player, I'm nearly bowled over as the sound of my father's deep voice fills the car. I need to pull onto the shoulder and stop. My hands are shaking, my heart thumping in my chest. This is Dad as he sounded when I was a child, a teenager in church listening to his solo voice in the choir.

I put my head on the steering wheel, close my eyes and listen, puzzled, incredulous. He's actually crooning, his voice nearly breaking at times. I wipe tears from my face as he caresses the lyrics of "Unchained Melody." I catch and hold my breath whenever he says, *my darling*. He never used that endearment to my mother. She was "honey" sometimes, but *never* "darling."

The music goes on, the songs repeating over and over, obviously taped in sets back-to-. I feel like I'm eavesdropping on his intimacy with ... with whom? It's clear he's singing to someone.

Why is this tape here? In the vehicle only Dad ever drove? I picture him taking his thirty-minute drive to the theater, this tape playing, propelling him backwards to the time it was made. What was so powerful it followed him to the future? This discovery is almost too much to process. Questions stumble over themselves for answers. When? Where? Most of all, who?

I'm not listening to Dad anymore. I'm back to being the little girl whose trust in her daddy is total. I know him better than anyone, or so I think. There is no part of him that has been hidden. But deep inside, a niggling voice says otherwise.

Four

Genna

As usual, I can't seem to get through to my sister. After a quick, pretty much wasted trip to the mall where neither of us found any distraction, we sit on the sofa in a living room that's always been a bit on the untidy side. Vicki's not exactly a card-carrying member of the Good Housekeeping Club. When the kids were small, there was an excuse for the mess. Granted, she's gotten a little better, but I am amazed how quickly the room has reverted to such an unkempt state so soon after the housecleaners had it ship-shape for the funeral.

"Did you sleep last night?" I ask, not knowing what to expect by way of attitude or mood.

She looks around the room absently. "Enough. You know I've never needed a lot of sleep. What about you?"

I get the definite impression she doesn't care how I answer. So I don't. Instead, I say, "The kids are going through Jared's papers to get things ready for Thomas. Is there anything you think they should know?"

"No. Jared was the organized one. I'm sure he left everything in perfect order."

"Vicki," I begin. "Vicki!" I say again, a little sharper.

She turns her head my way, her eyes still in some faraway place.

"I'd like you to come back to Florida with me on Sunday. You could use a break from all this ... get some rest, a change of scene. I don't want you to sit in this house mourning day after day. I know it's only natural to grieve and you need to, but I'd like to be with you, to know you're taking care of yourself. That's too much of a burden to put on Marina and Mike. They have their own lives, children and jobs to get back to."

She's quiet for a minute then looks down at her hands. "I don't know what I'm going to do. I've lost the man I lived with for most of my life, the man I loved since the first minute I saw him. And I can't get it out of my head that he never loved me with the same intensity."

I reach for her hand but she tucks it under her thigh.

"Of course Jared loved you. He was here for you, supporting you in your work, making a home, helping to raise your children. For many years, Jared loved you."

"But not for all of them. And I'll always wonder if I truly had him all to myself, even when we moved and he was safely away from Manning. Do you think I did? Did Jared ever confide in you? Was he truly over her?"

~ * ~

I'm sitting with Jared in the kitchen. It's almost time for me to leave for Florida, for Jared to pack the house and leave too, heading for Chicago and a new job. Vicki's already gone. She's taken the kids and gone to Mom and Pop. I think she's punishing him. The house is full; packing will be hell.

His soft brown eyes are shadowed. "I'll miss you," he says. "You've been wonderful to the children and I couldn't have asked for a dearer sister. I don't know what I would have done without you, what I'm going to do without you when we're in Chicago."

"I'm sorry, Jared. I know you're unhappy. I hate seeing Vicki act like this, but I don't think she's totally in control. I think she's depressed and too proud, or too sick, to get the kind of help she needs. And this past year has only made her worse."

"You mean because of me? Because of the way we're living?"

I know he wants me to say it's okay, that he deserves to have a life with a bit of happiness in it. I can't; Vicki's still my sister.

So I hedge. "Maybe. You're not always there for her, Jared. Oh, I know it's hard. She's so inside herself, so inaccessible and so angry. But when she needs to reach out, too often you're just not there. Maybe you two should separate for a while, see if there's anything left between you to make a go of it. I know there's somebody you'd rather be with."

His head jerks up, his eyes narrowing. "Why would you say that?"

"I'm not stupid. Granted, I don't know who she is or how far it's gone, but sometimes I see desperation in your face. I've seen you hang up the phone in a hurry when I come into the room. I know how often you're gone and for how long. I live there, remember? So why don't you split up and see if that's what you really want?"

He looks like he wants to cry. As much as I love my sister, I can't help feeling sorry for him.

"I guess I want to, very much. But what will happen to the children if I leave them? In Florida, and you know that's where

Vicki would take them, they won't have me at all. Their safe little worlds will collapse. I struggle with that every hour of every day. How can I do that to them?"

He's tortured all right. I don't pry, don't try to come up with something comforting to say. This is one of those damned-if-he-does, damned-if-he-doesn't situations, and I know I should stay out of it.

"Well, I know you'll do what you think is best for the kids," I say. "You're right; they need you. But I don't think you'll be much good to them if your heart isn't in it. I don't envy you, Jared. It seems to me you lose, no matter what you decide."

~ * ~

Now, sitting with Vicki after what seems like an eternity, I don't know how to answer. Did Jared ever confide in me? So what if he did? What difference does it make now, anyway?

"No, he didn't. I know he was very concerned about your frame of mind and worried about taking the children to Chicago without me there to help care for them."

"There was more. I knew it at the time and I know it now," Vicki replies with surprising vehemence. "Sometimes I thought he would go out the door and never come back. If the children hadn't been there, I'm sure that's what would have happened. It's not a good feeling to know your husband stayed only out of obligation or a sense of responsibility to the children."

"But I thought all that changed once you got settled here, found the work you loved and built this wonderful house. You both seemed happy."

She doesn't smile and no light brightens her eyes.

"It took a long time. We worked very hard at it ... the years of counseling, the compromises. But you're right. We settled into a kind of routine, a comfortable routine most of the time. The kids kept us busy—Michael with Little League, Marina with Girl Scouts—and later with the drama club. We were a typical suburban family. And Jared was always a good husband.

Thoughtful, nothing ever too difficult or inconvenient, always glad to help out. But sometimes I felt like part of him wasn't here. I honestly don't think I ever had all of him."

She says this with her brow furrowed thoughtfully, like she's struggling to finish a difficult puzzle. And then she continues.

"I think she was always there somewhere in his mind..." She nods almost imperceptibly, perhaps fitting pieces of the puzzle in place.

I suddenly remember Marina's mystery woman, the one at the funeral. I start to mention it to Vicki, but check myself in time. Could there be a connection? Could the woman in Jared's past and the stranger at the funeral be the same?

~ * ~

The phone rings as I pass it on the way to my room. We've had lunch and Vicki is in her room. I pick up the receiver in a hurry so it doesn't disturb her.

"It's me, Marina. I *really* need to see you right away. Can you break away from Mom for a little bit?"

"Sure. I think your mother's napping. Do you want me to take her car and come to your house?"

"No, I'll pick you up. I'll be there in a few minutes."

"You sound agitated. Is anything wrong?"

"Not wrong exactly; I can't explain. I'll be right there."

I scribble a note to Vicki in case she wakes up looking for me. *Gone out with Marina. Won't be long.* She won't question anyway. At times, I think she wouldn't notice if we all disappeared and left her alone.

I decide to wait on the front porch, but haven't even gotten to a chair when I see the Outback turning the corner. Marina has wasted no time getting here.

She leans over, pushes open the passenger door and re-adjusts her seat belt. She waits while I fasten mine.

"Where to?"

"Nowhere in particular."

When I look closer, I see she's been crying. "Honey? What's happened?"

She doesn't answer, just shakes her head, fighting tears. Finally, she says, "Wait a minute and you'll find out."

We drive another block or two and swing into the parking lot of a small office complex. She goes to the end of the row and parks against a fence. Without explanation, she pushes a cassette into the tape player. I'm not prepared for what comes next. Sucking in my breath as Jared begins the first song, I feel like I can't exhale until he's finished. Then he's singing again, another plaintive, soul-jarring lyrical story of love. I hear his tears. I want to cry, too, hearing him sing like that.

Neither of us says anything. The music lasts for about twenty minutes and then, without pause, the songs begin again. Marina pushes the 'eject' button and the tape pops out. The sudden silence is eerie, uneasy.

"Where did you find this?" I ask.

Marina taps the console between us. "He had it in here with his other tapes. I was curious because this was the only one that wasn't marked. What do you make of it?"

"It's bizarre," I say, so low I'm surprised she can hear me. Louder then. "I don't know, Marina. It doesn't sound like anything he would have been doing professionally. I guess I'm thinking what you've obviously already decided. He was singing to someone, someone very special. Is that what you think?"

"I have to! Listen to him! I've never heard anything like that. When he sang at my wedding, his voice was wonderfully rich and powerful and I knew he was giving us a gift of love. You know how beautiful the music was—you were there. I've heard him sing countless times, but I've never heard him sing *to* anyone, really sing *to* a person, I mean. If he'd made this tape for Mom, we would have heard it long before now. No, he didn't make this for her, I'm sure."

I assent silently with a small nod.

She goes on. "I called Andy and told him about the tape. He thinks I should back off, destroy it and not make a big deal out of it."

"Why would you destroy it?"

"Andy thinks if word of the tape got out in the family, there would be questions raised that Dad wouldn't have wanted asked. He says Jason would be terribly upset if he were to hear his grandfather sing like this. And of course, if Mom hasn't ever heard it, she definitely shouldn't. But I can't destroy this. Absolutely not. Mainly because we don't have any other recording of Dad's voice to remember how marvelous it was. But now even more, I need to know exactly what went on back in Pennsylvania and I think this tape may be part of the puzzle."

~ * ~

I'm in Jared's old Studebaker station wagon. He's picked me up at the auto shop, the one my junker visits regularly. Lately, he's been smiling a lot. Vicki's darkness hasn't touched him like it so often does. He's sweet to the children and even kinder to me than usual. I know he's grateful for my help around the house. But he's different and I'm not sure why.

"Do you mind a quick stop at Dan's?" he asks, his fingers pushing radio dial buttons. "I need to pick up something I left there."

I settle against the seat and close my eyes. "Nope, I'll just get a little nap. I promised the kids a walk to the playground tonight after dinner. I need all the rest I can get."

He's humming along softly, a Johnny Mathis song... "Misty," I think. "I'm too misty, and too much in love," he sings along quietly. His voice is like smooth velvet. I look at him from half-closed eyes. His smile is dreamy, like he's getting ready to kiss someone. It's the kind of look I hope I get someday from the man I fall in love with. I feel like I've seen something I wasn't supposed to, so I close my eyes again. The song ends, he turns off the radio and continues humming wordlessly.

~ * ~

Now here's this tape, Jared singing "Misty" again and I can picture his face and see his eyes. I know he's singing to the same woman he was singing to then.

"Part of the puzzle? I don't know, honey. Andy's probably right. Everyone has a piece of themselves they'd rather keep private. Your dad was no different. He's entitled to some history of his own. I'm not saying you should destroy the tape, but I agree with Andy that it's probably best left without further prying."

"I wonder how old the tape is?" Marina muses as if she hasn't heard me.

"Hard to say." I'm purposely rearranging my coat, shifting my purse from the floor to the console, signaling my desire to end this. "We'll probably never know. The songs were all popular long before you were listening to music."

Marina puts the tape back in the console, carefully as though it might break.

"I was listening to music all the time when I was a kid," she retorts. "I remember many of these songs and not because they're golden oldies. This is such an odd mix, though. I've never heard the one about the willow tree."

I have. "Ah, yes, 'Willow Weep for Me.' You certainly don't hear *that* very often."

She puts the car in gear and backs out of the space.

"All I know is it's bugging me that there was another side of Dad we never knew, and I get the feeling you know more than you're letting on. Why?"

~ * ~

I'd never been in Dan's house. I had no idea how charming and isolated it was. Jared has to unlock a gate so we can drive down a narrow little lane through the woods. The house is a cabin, like I'd always imagined the one where the seven dwarves lived when Snow White happened along. Inside, it's warm and inviting. I sit on the sofa and look around while Jared hunts in the kitchen for whatever he came for. A massive stone fireplace covers the entire wall, the centerpiece of the room. I notice fresh ashes on the hearth.

"Jared, do you come here often?"

He comes out of the kitchen with a small paper bag in his hand.

"Not very, but I promised Dan I'd look after the place and keep the plants watered. Never stay too long, though."

He's not telling the truth. Not just because of the ashes. I can't explain the feeling I have, but the place has a lived-in look, like it's home to someone. Jared seems very comfortable here. He's at ease as he walks from place to place, touching the furniture possessively, as though this were his real home.

I don't challenge him. I watch as his eyes sweep the large room ... lovingly is the word that comes to mind. I think to myself, There's a side to this man I don't know.

~ * ~

"What am I keeping from you? Nothing. Look, you're blowing this way out of proportion. Face it, we all have parts of ourselves we'd rather not bring out in public."

I wonder how long she'll keep hounding me for answers. I wonder how much I should finally tell her.

"You're the only one I can ask about all this," she persists almost angrily, her eyes on the road. "I wouldn't dream of broaching any of this with Mom. I'm not even sure Mike will listen to the tape. I simply need to know what you know."

"Why can't you just let it be?"

"Because I *can't*. When I listen to the tape, I can see him. I know he's looking at someone and his words and feelings are going straight to her. Who is she? I want to know who *else* shared his life. Is that wrong?"

~ * ~

I want to know. Who does he bring to this house? We leave the cabin in the woods and get back into the wagon. The way Jared locks the door, heads out the lane and relocks the gate after we've driven through makes me feel like he's just left home.

"How long will Dan be away?"

"He's on a research team in Alaska, something about habitat study. He'll be back in September."

"Is he married?"

"He's a widower, unfortunate for a man so young. His wife, Stephanie, died a couple years ago and he built this place to get out of the city where they'd lived. Dan is a sensitive, caring man. He's having a pretty hard time trying to adjust."

"The cabin is beautiful. I can see you like being there."

Jared gives me a sidelong glance, his eyebrow raised. "I do. It's a refuge of sorts. The kids used to like to play here, but..."

"But what? Don't they anymore?"

"It's not important. Anyhow, I like the quiet and the serenity of the forest. Dan found a perfect place."

I'm still wondering ... why doesn't he bring the kids?

We're almost back to the house he and Vicki are renting. If they stay beyond this year, they'll probably buy it. We turn the corner and Jared reaches for his cigarettes. Almost at the house, I glance at him. He's tensing, his eyebrows knit, his grip on the steering wheel tightening.

~ * ~

"Well, baby, I still say some things are perhaps better left alone."

She doesn't answer but swings into the driveway. She doesn't unbuckle her seatbelt or turn off the ignition.

Her voice is flat and she doesn't look at me right away.

"I'll be back in a little while. I don't want Jason to be out too late. Andy and I decided he could stay home today and tomorrow, but Monday he's back at school and I'd like to have some time with him before then. I get the feeling there's still a lot he needs to talk out. Thanks for coming. I needed you to hear the tape to be sure I wasn't imagining the way I interpreted his tone. You agree with me then? He wasn't warming up his voice with some favorite tunes, was he?"

I get out of the car and lean around the door. "I think you're right, honey. But what's done is done, many years ago. Why try to put pieces together now?"

Without responding, she backs out, turns up the street and slowly disappears around the bend.

~ * ~

"You're back." Vicki is sitting on the porch as I come up the walkway. She doesn't ask where we went.

"Marina and I took a ride," I tell her anyway, not lying. "She needed to talk." More truth.

I see a flicker of something other than total detachment in her eyes.

"Marina seems to be having more than the usual problems with Jared's death, doesn't she?" she asks.

"Whatever 'usual' is. You know she adored her father."

"She and Mike went through a lot of his personal things yesterday. I'm sure that was very hard on both of them. I still haven't gone into the den or opened Jared's closet in the bedroom. I suppose that will all have to be done sometime."

"Not yet," I assure her. "It's still very soon."

Her voice is small, like the simple act of speaking is exhausting.

"I don't want to do anything. It's not fair to put it all on the kids, but I can't bring myself to accept the finality. Even when Jared and I separated that time shortly after we moved to Chicago, I didn't feel that was final either. I believed he would come back, to the children, if not to me. I knew by then he'd

43

found someone else, but I hoped his sense of responsibility to the kids was too compelling for him to give up on us that easily."

"And he did, didn't he?"

"Uh-huh. We'd been separated a little over a year when he came back. I always wondered if he went looking for her. Later in a counseling session, he told me they'd ended it and he never mentioned her again. We worked it out. We had a good marriage, I believe. I know he loved the kids and I believe he loved me in his own way. I'm not ready to let him go."

For a moment, I think I hear tears in her voice. I've never seen my sister cry. I was a late-life child and Vicki was already out of the house by the time I was old enough to have memories of her. Somehow, I know she didn't cry as a child, even when she fell off her bike or had her heart broken by some adolescent boyfriend.

Sure enough, no tears are shed and she lifts her chin as she stands.

"Wonder if there's any mail?" she asks.

How did they manage to stay married that long? I wonder about the two people so different. Jared, his heart on his sleeve most of the time, Jared who wept openly when he was sad or laughed a wonderfully deep chuckle when he found something amusing, as he so often did. How could he have coped for so many years with the obvious distances between them? What did he do with his need to feel, to communicate? And what will Marina discover if she keeps digging into Jared's past?

Five

Marina

Am I wrong about this? I've asked myself the same question fifty times today. Andy and Aunt Genna say I am. They want me to put the tape away and never let it be heard by anyone ... ever. I know that's probably what I should do, but I can't. I simply can't.

After I drop Aunt Genna off, I drive around for a few minutes, thinking and remembering, probing my own brain like a laser trying to find some clues, things I've probably long since forgotten, things that could help me find the truth about how my father really lived. Then I go home. The house envelopes me with ghostly silence. I stretch out on the sofa, close my eyes and let my mind drift. The ringing phone interrupts my solitude.

"Marina, how's it going?"

It's Judith, calling from who-knows-where.

"Okay, I guess. I'm glad everything's over, but it seems that a whole new situation has cropped up. I need to talk to you about it when you can."

"Can you tell me now? Maybe I can help just by listening."

It doesn't take long to summarize everything for her.

"I was pretty young. If all this happened while Dad was at Manning State, I couldn't have been much more than six or seven; we were only there a few years. I remember being scared, listening to Mom snap at Dad, knowing he'd be going out again. I was so afraid he was going to leave us I probably didn't pay much attention to the little things that might have worried me more. Maybe I didn't want to see them, even at that age.

"But, damn it, now I need to know! I can't get over the feeling that all the while I was growing up relying on my father, he had another life that didn't include Mike and me, a life that made him smile and sing until another argument with Mom drove him out of the house."

Judith hasn't interrupted. I can hear her soft breathing on the other end so I know she's still listening.

"He was working a lot then. He left before I went to school in the morning and almost always went back out after dinner or after he'd tucked us in for the night. Aunt Genna told us he was a very busy man."

"Did he direct plays there like he did at Roosevelt?"

"Oh yeah, he was devoted to the theater. Once, in spite of Mom's objections, he dressed us both up and took us to a Sunday matinee. I don't remember exactly what musical it was, one of Rodgers and Hammerstein's I think, but being on campus was quite a thrill. We went to the snack bar for a soda. I remember all the college kids and the way they looked up to my dad. He knew almost everybody and I remember feeling very important because I was his daughter."

~ * ~

My dress is pink. It has a big bow at the back and Mike is wearing a sport jacket and little bow tie. Daddy walks with us across the lawn from his office to the place he goes for coffee. He's skipping with us and then, when we get inside, he looks around the room, takes our hands and goes toward some strange people: an older lady, an older man and a pretty girl about as old as Aunt Genna. She has shiny, honey-colored hair and a friendly smile. One of Daddy's students, I think. She says the man and woman are her mother and father and Daddy shakes their hands. We can't stay, he says, and I'm very glad about that. I want to get to the theater to see all the costumes before everyone comes to get dressed. Daddy says I can try on one of the big hats. He says it will look terrific with my blond hair. Anyhow, Mike tells these people we're going to move. Daddy's hand tightens on mine and he hustles us out. He's quiet all the way back to his office and I feel like one of us said something to the pretty girl he didn't want us to say. Daddy's sad again. I wonder if I made him that way. This time, though, I think it was Mike.

He just blabbed about us moving. It wasn't anybody's business, and he erased the smile right out of Daddy's eyes.

~ * ~

"Marina? Are you still there?"

"I'm sorry ... I was remembering an incident that happened when I was a child. Strange it should be so clear. It was the feeling of, uh ... guilt, yeah, that's it ... guilt. Knowing something wasn't quite right with our family but not knowing what, so of course it had to be something I was doing wrong. I knew Mom was angry most of the time. It was an emotion you could breathe in the air in our house. Dad escaped. He ran to his work, to his students, to somewhere rather than stay and face whatever was going on, stare down the problem and deal with it."

"Have you talked this out with Andy?"

"No, he's been busy and his reaction to the tape kind of turned me off."

"Don't you think he'd understand?"

"He should. You know, his parents divorced when he was only six. His mother's always told me the divorce was so amicable and Andy accepted their split easily. He 'adjusted,' is the term she used. She loved to brag about how civilized her divorce had been."

"Well, I guess some people can manage to deal with the anger and make a divorce work," Judith says.

"Yeah, but that isn't how Andy tells the story. He remembers name-calling, phones being slammed down and tightly controlled fury whenever his parents needed to interact. He said he felt like a ping-pong ball, flung from parent to parent, afraid to please one lest he offend the other. He's still paying for all of that."

"How so?"

"You know him, you know how insecure and uncertain he sometimes is. I often think his joy in Jason comes from his own unhappy childhood. I have a hard time even remembering any time Dad made me sad."

~ * ~

On the ride home, Daddy is still quiet. He turns on the car radio, which means he doesn't want to talk. Mike's head is down. We pull into the driveway at the back of the house and Daddy turns off the engine. Mike doesn't move.

"Let's go, Michael," Daddy says, opening his door. "Come on ... I need to get back to work."

Mike still doesn't move.

Daddy comes around to Mike's door and opens it. Reaching inside, he takes Mike's hand. "Let's go, son. Marina can't get out if you don't."

Mike lets Daddy help him from the car. Still holding Daddy's hand, he starts to cry. "I'm ssssorry, Daddy," he sobs. "I'm ssssorry."

Daddy kneels down and hugs him. "For what, son? What could you be sorry for?"

"I mmmade you sad. I said something that mmmade you sad."

Daddy holds Mike tight and motions for me to go into the house. Then he changes his mind.

"No, Marina sweetheart, you stay. I need to talk to you both. Michael, Marina ... remember once you asked me why I was sad? I told you grownups sometimes get that way because something is wrong they're having a hard time fixing? I hoped you understood. How foolish I was! You're children! Of course you can't be expected to understand the wacky, stressful world of adults. Daddy gets down in the dumps every now and then because I have a lot on my mind and some of it isn't cheerful. Michael, honey, you didn't say or do anything to make me unhappy. I was so very proud of you today. Meeting people and going to the play were something new for you, and you were a perfect gentleman. And Marina, you were a perfect little lady. Don't worry about the times I frown or seem unhappy. But I want you to know you aren't the reason; you're never the reason. Okay?"

~ * ~

I tell Judith that story and remembering the incident, something else strikes me.

"The girl was backstage with Dad during the play and in his office when it was over. There was something comfortable and easy in the way he talked to her. She walked us out to the car when we were ready to go home. Dad told her he'd be right back. She said everyone would be waiting. But, you know, it sounded more like *she* was the one who would be waiting."

"Gee, I don't know what to tell you," Judith says. "I'm sorry this is giving you such a hard time. It's more stress you have to deal with so soon after losing your dad. I hope you get some answers so you can set your mind at rest. Either that or you drop it and move on. Maybe some things *are* better left alone, huh?"

Sounds like Aunt Genna. We hang up and I go back to the sofa. Now that I've brought back the visit to the campus, I close my eyes and try hard to remember something, anything, more. It feels like I'm almost there, like all I have to do is blow away some smoke and the scene will be clear.

Shiny, honey-colored hair. Smiling face. I'm at eye-level with her as she sits in front of me, looking up at Dad. Her eyes are almost green, lively and sparkling. Mike says we're moving to Chicago soon and the sparkle goes out. For a moment, the eyes are sad ... sad, hazel eyes. The woman at Dad's funeral. Hair still light brown but flecked with gray ... large, sad hazel eyes.

I jump up and grab the phone. I'm caught off guard when my mother answers.

"Hello, Marina, is everything okay?"

I lie, nearly stumbling over my words, anxious to get Aunt Genna on the other end. "Sure, Mom. Did you get some rest?"

"I'm fine," she says in her familiar monotone.

"Is Aunt Genna around?" I feel sheepish pushing her off so quickly.

I hear her cover the receiver and call for Genna.

"Just a second; she's coming in from the back yard. Here she is ... I'll see you later."

Without waiting for my response, she gives the phone to my aunt.

"Marina?"

"Aunt Genna, the woman who was at Dad's funeral. I remember seeing her with Dad on the college campus when I was a little girl. She must have come all the way from Pennsylvania. I need to tell you about it ... Genna? Aunt Genna, are you still there?"

"Yes, yes, I'm still here. Of course I can come over for dinner, thanks for asking. Your mother needs to spend a few hours at the museum this evening, so why don't I come over when you pick up Jason?"

"Is Mom there right now?"

"Yes, sounds good to me."

"I understand. I'll be over soon; I really need to talk."

~ * ~

I ride out to the house on the lake and find Jason and Aunt Genna waiting for me. I'm so anxious to tell Aunt Genna about the woman, I barely listen to Jason. He's talking about being on the lake and something about a seagull, but my lack of response discourages him and he falls silent for the rest of the short ride. At home, Jason goes right to his room. Finally, I can pour out the story to my aunt.

"Marina, why would you come up with a memory from that far back, and how can you be sure you have it right? Children experience things that are bound to get twisted and distorted as they grow up. How can you be sure?"

I find myself using the same patient tone I often employ when explaining something to Jason. "Because. Because of what happened when we left the college. Dad seemed so down, even after the play was over and everything went so well. He was still quiet and inside himself. Mike thought it was because of something he said to this girl and her parents. Mike was crying and Dad reassured both of us nothing we could ever do would make him unhappy. It took him a long time to calm Mike down, I remember, but even though he had promised this girl he'd be right back, he stayed with us until we were asleep. It was an experience I never forgot, but now I have a new reason to remember as clearly as possible. Good God, why would someone Dad knew forty years ago be at his funeral?"

Aunt Genna hesitates and then, her voice low, she says, "Perhaps she's known him all along."

"Well, that's certainly not what I want to hear. Are you saying Dad and this woman had a relationship all these years?

Come on, that's what sappy novels are made of. People with that kind of connection either wind up together or they don't. They couldn't have stayed involved for forty years with no one knowing it. Could they?"

"I wouldn't know. You're talking to someone who couldn't stay in a relationship for a month, let alone forty years. Face it, how could we know? And, more importantly, why would we need to know? You say you met this girl before the last of your dad's plays at the college. That was in 'sixty-two. And you moved a few months later. Any relationship he might have had with her obviously didn't survive the separation. No, I think this is definitely something you should take your nose out of ... move on with your work and your family."

I hear her. And I wonder why she's working so hard to send me off track. If I'm being so foolish, why doesn't she just laugh at me so I'll forget the whole thing and back off?

~ * ~

It's been snowing hard. Mike and I make angels in the drifts in front of our house. Daddy comes out and builds a snowman with us. He's going to his friend's house to be sure the heat is on and everything is all right after the big storm. He says Mike and I can go too. We love the house in the woods, even though it reminds me of where Hansel and Gretel met the witch. We sing all the way there. It takes Daddy a long time to clear a path to the gate; the snow is so deep and his shovel is small. The car plows through the driveway and piles of snow block the front door. His face is red from the cold when he finally has the walk cleared enough for us to use.

We bound into the house, lots warmer than outside and so cozy. Daddy usually makes hot cocoa and we play while he takes care of the plants. We shed our coats and run around the big room.

"Daddy, Daddy ... make a fire in the fireplace!"

Daddy is standing in the doorway from the kitchen, looking around. He looks strange. He goes into the kitchen, puts down the watering can and tells us we have to go home.

Mike starts to cry. "But why, Daddy? Why can't we stay here and play in the snow?"

"We can play in the snow at home, guys," he says, picking up our coats from where we'd dropped them. "Let's go."

It's not fun there anymore. Daddy isn't smiling. He's looking around like he can't find something. Mike and I don't talk all the way home. Daddy doesn't even turn on the radio. We never go back there again.

~ * ~

I decide to try another tack. "Aunt Genna, did you ever go to Dan Kearney's house with Dad?"

"Uh-huh, I remember going there once. He needed to pick up something he'd left and we went by on our way home. Why?"

I tell her about the feeling I had in the house when Dad was so anxious to get us out.

"I felt like we'd intruded there. Like we weren't supposed to be there. Even when the weather turned nice and it was the perfect time to play outdoors, Dad never took us back."

"He must have had his reasons," Aunt Genna says. "I know your father was always very busy, what with getting ready for the play and then planning for his new job. He probably didn't go there himself for more than a few minutes to water the plants."

This time I know I'm not imagining it. She sounds like she's trying to convince me what she's saying is true and she's trying way too hard.

"That brings me right back to my question from yesterday. Why didn't we stay and move together? Now I wonder what Dad did those couple months after we left. I wonder if he stayed at Dan's and if so, if this mysterious woman was there too."

Now Aunt Genna's tone is impatient, almost commanding. "I'm telling you, Marina, let it be! Nothing good can come from this incessant questioning. Your father was your father. He was a good man. Why can't you leave it at that?"

"Why should I? Something isn't adding up here. I want to know what he kept hidden from everyone. Or *who* he kept hidden."

A little nagging voice in my head is warning me I'm not going to like the result if I keep probing. I'm also not making much headway with Aunt Genna. Clearly, she's not going to tell me anything more. Maybe that's for the best. Sometimes knowing is worse than staying comfortably in the dark. So I tell myself ... *let it go, Marina. Remember Dad for all the good things and the good times. Let it go.*

~ * ~

After dinner, Jason retreats to his room to study. He's going back to school Monday. His friends have been very good about keeping track of homework assignments while he's adjusting to the loss of his grandfather.

Andy gets a call from the hospital emergency room. He's needed to repair a broken arm. He's shaking his head as he puts down the phone.

"You'd think these kids would learn to be more careful climbing trees," he says.

"Didn't you climb trees when you were a boy?" Aunt Genna asks.

With a smug smile, Andy says, "Sure. But I never broke anything doing it. I was a careful climber!"

I'm laughing as I kiss him goodbye.

"I'll be a couple of hours at least," he says, turning toward to the door. "You two have a good visit. And, Aunt Genna, try to get Marina to cool it with her hunt for Dad's past."

"He makes it sound like a movie ... *The Hunt for Dad's Past,*" I say with mock drama.

We sit in wing chairs facing each other.

"You have such a beautiful home, Marina. It's so cozy and warm."

"Thank you. I do love the house. We were very lucky to find this old Victorian when properties off the lake so near Evanston weren't selling well. We wanted to buy something that was close to Mom and Dad while Jason was growing up and we could afford this."

Frankly, it had been wonderful having a dependable babysitter like Dad. We never worried about Jason; he was safe with Dad. I feel the tears starting again.

"When will you go back to the clinic?" Aunt Genna asks.

Her question steers my thoughts away from my sadness.

"Probably Monday. We'll meet with Thomas tomorrow, he'll read Dad's will and then we can all try to go on with some kind of routine. Have you talked to Mom about spending some time with you in Florida?"

"We kind of explored the idea last night. I honestly think she may give it serious thought. Your mother's at odds right now, and I think she roams that house wondering what it'll be like when I'm gone, you and Mike are back at work and she's by herself."

"I'm sure Jason will be there a lot."

"Are you? I'm not. Jared was the reason Jason spent his time there. Oh, he might go out on the lake occasionally to do some fishing or some thinking, but he's growing up quickly, and I suspect there will be other interests to occupy his time. I think Vicki is going to have a difficult time adjusting and a trip to Florida might be what she needs."

"We'll all have adjusting to do. Jason will need some extra special loving ... he has a hole in his life, but he'll keep busy with the band and schoolwork. Andy will miss Dad too, but his work is all-consuming. Sometimes it's like Jason and I don't even exist in his busy world. And then there's Mike ... be fine, especially with the new baby coming."

Aunt Genna smiles. "Mike's a lot like your dad that way. His philosophy always was whatever life throws at us, we need to pick ourselves up, adjust our attitudes and move forward. Mike seems to be able to do that too, and I'm certain he'll apply it to this loss as well."

I feel the sadness again, tinged this time with self-pity. "That leaves me. Now that Dad's gone, I feel lost. Jason has about a year and a half at home and then he'll go off to college somewhere distant and strange and he'll rarely come home again, at least not as the same boy we knew. He's practically a man. I know I have my work, but I don't want to make my job my whole life. Sometimes I wish I had been able to have more children so the nest wouldn't be empty quite so soon."

"Listen, honey," I cock my head and hear Dad's voice. *"Give yourself happiness first. The trek through life can be lonely and difficult. Don't tie yourself to a career that demands too much. Find someone to share the journey, someone who can make it a joy. Once you do, never let go and never put anything or anyone ahead of treasuring that joy."*

"Ah, baby, don't cry!"

I feel the tears splashing out of my eyes, even though I'm not aware of weeping. Aunt Genna gets up, crosses to my chair and puts her arms around me.

"No, forget I said that. Go ahead and cry. Let it all out, baby."

So I do. I'm crying my heart out and I can't stop.

~ * ~

"Why do we have to move, Daddy? Mommy says we're leaving Aunt Genna and I have to go to a new school. Why, Daddy? Why can't we stay here?

"Mommy's mad, isn't she, Daddy? I heard her yelling at you. Why does she yell? Why can't you both just be happy?"

It's dark and scary in my room. "Daddy? Daddy?" I call louder still.

The hall light snaps on, flooding my doorway with brilliance that hurts my eyes for a minute.

"It's okay, Marina, Mommy's here."

"I want Daddy!" I'm still crying.

"He's not here; he's out again. Now go to sleep and maybe he'll be home when you wake up in the morning."

She turns out the light without coming to me. I lie awake for I don't know how long. Finally, I hear his footsteps coming up the stairs.

"Daddy?" I need to whisper; I only want Daddy to hear.

He doesn't turn on any lights. He's kneeling by my bed, his hand pushing the hair back from my eyes.

"What is it, my beautiful little blonde bombshell? Why are you still awake?"

"I don't know, Daddy. I think I had a bad dream, but when I woke up calling for you, Mommy said you were out. Where were you?"

"I was working, honey. You know Daddy works a lot."

"Will you take us to the park after work tomorrow?"

"We'll see, honey. Now, it's very late. I'll sit here with you for a few minutes while you get back to Dreamland where you belong."

He kisses my forehead, rearranges the blankets and sits on the floor by the bed. I'm safe now.

~ * ~

"I'm not sure why I'm crying," I tell Aunt Genna as she hands me a tissue. "Is it because Dad's gone or because I'm feeling so alone?"

"Both," she answers. "Both. Imagine your son's grief if anything were to happen to you. He relies on you more than Andy. Think of how devastated he'd be and he's only had you for sixteen years. You had *your* father for nearly fifty years!"

"I keep remembering bits and pieces from my childhood," I tell her, dabbing my eyes, imagining mascara running amok.

"That will happen for a long time, I'm afraid. Those were the years that made the greatest impression, even though it didn't seem so at the time. Everything you experienced was carefully stored away. Now, whether you want to or not, you're going to have flashes from those times, the good and the bad. When they come, savor them but don't dwell on them. Put them away and eventually they won't intrude as often."

I try to lighten the mood. "Is this my Aunt Genna, the family shrink, speaking? Are you analyzing me?"

She shakes her finger in my face. "I may have wanted to be a psychiatrist," she says with mock sternness, "but school teachers are almost as good at reading people's emotions."

"*Were* almost as good," I remind her. "You retired early, remember? Something about burnout? So why start in on me?"

"Because I love you enough to give you some Aunt Shrink advice. Don't try to put down the grief, baby. Treat the sips of memory as they come like fine wine and take the time to taste them. Believe me, the day will come when happy memories are hard to dredge from the flotsam and jetsam of your life!"

~ * ~

"Grandpa told me about flotsung and jetsung today, Mom!"
"About what?"
My father strides in through the garage door, places the tackle box on the shelf and stands the fishing poles against the wall.

He chuckles. "It's flotsam and jetsam, Jason. I told Jason about the floating debris that's found on bodies of water sometimes, especially the oceans and harbors. There was an old poem I knew once that talked about it ... flotsam and jetsam. It came to me today."

He stands still. He has a faraway look in his eyes.
"Flotsam and jetsam," he repeats.
"Grandpa, can we go fishing again tomorrow? Grandpa?"

It seems to take a minute for my father to remember where he is, to come back to the here and now from wherever he had gone.

"Sure, my man. Tomorrow after school, I'll have the poles ready and I'll go to the bait shop before you get here."

~ * ~

Aunt Genna laughs when I tell her about hearing those words that day. "Your father loved poetry, didn't he?"

"Oh, yes. He read nursery rhymes and poems to us all the time when we were kids. We heard some of them so many times we memorized them. He'd trick us by putting the wrong word in a line and he'd wait for us to correct him. That reminds me, there are a couple of his books of poems I've always wanted to read. I often found him absorbed in one or the other of them when I'd stop by his den on the way to my room. I wish I had asked him to read some of them to me."

"You can read them now; there's no time like the present," Aunt Genna says, standing. "Or if I may coin a phrase ... better late than never!"

"Gee, that's really catchy! Wonder if anyone will ever remember it?"

We walk toward the front door and she gives me a withering look.

"You'd better not disrespect your elder, young lady!"

We're laughing like schoolgirls as we walk up to the car.

"I'm sure gonna miss you when you go home!" I call across the car roof.

~ * ~

Mom's not back yet. I'm surprised she's stayed out this late. Aunt Genna goes to her room to sort her clothes for packing. I go to Dad's den and the feeling of sadness hits all over again. At least this is one place where he still lives.

The shelves are filled with scripts from plays, books on the theater, drama, acting and directing. A few bear his name as author; he is a contributor to many others. There is no rhyme or reason to the way the books are arranged. I find a couple of poetry anthologies but pass them up. This is what I'm looking for. Two slender volumes, their covers worn. I remember the name of the poet, Walter Benton. Taking them off the shelf, I sit at Dad's desk and open *This Is My Beloved*.

~ * ~

"Daddy, will you read to me?"

"Sure, honey. As soon as I finish this page."

"What are you reading?"

"Poems, Marina. Beautiful poems about a beautiful lady."

"Did you know the lady, Daddy?"

"Once upon a time, sweetheart, once upon a time."

He closes the book and places it on his desk. "What would you like to read, honey?"

~ * ~

There were many, many times like that, when my father dropped whatever he was doing to spend time with me.

He was right. The poems are beautiful. Sensual, graphic, filled with imagery. He has phrases underlined, asterisks in the margins. They are plaintive and sad one minute, love-filled and joyful another. It doesn't take long to read them all. I'll go back one of these days and read them again, take time to study them to find the fascination they held for my father.

I'll wait to read the other one, I decide. I open the cover and see an inscription:

June 27, 1962

Dearest Jared,

When you are far away, let Mr. Benton keep me close to your heart until we can be together again. I will love you always. Joanna

Honey-colored hair, sad hazel eyes. Joanna?

Aunt Genna comes into the room as I read the inscription again and again. I hand the book to her.

"Read this. She gave it to him on his birthday just before we moved to Chicago."

She reads the words, looks up at me and then lowers her eyes with a sigh.

"All right. I'm going home Sunday. At least I can tell you what I know if it will help you put this matter to rest. It isn't much, but I guess I owe it to you to tell you about your father and Joanna."

She sits in one of the leather chairs by the desk. The book of poems is in her lap. I realize I am holding my breath and I feel the anger again. After all my anguish, now she says there's more she could have told me? I want to lash out at her, vent my resentment at her deception, but I'm afraid she'll clam up and I won't find out any more. So I stay quiet and don't interrupt.

"It isn't much, I've already said that, but I'll start at the beginning and tell you what I remember.

"When I came to live with your parents, your mother was deeply depressed. Jared and I believed it happened after Mike was born and kept getting worse. He couldn't do anything to make her get help; neither could I. So we divided the household stuff that had to be done, like laundry, meals and everything else and kept going, hoping she'd snap out of it on her own. He spent all of the time he was at home with you and Mike. When you were in bed, he usually went out, back to his office at the college, he said."

She stops. "Are you sure you want me to tell you all this?"

I throw my arms up and lean forward in the chair. "How can you ask that? Haven't I been begging for what you know ever since Dad's funeral? Just tell me. I'm a big girl, for God's sake!"

She seems surprised at my angry outburst. "Ohhh-kay. It was the last year you were there. He started staying out overnight once in a while. He hummed to himself a lot and laughed with you kids. I'd never seen him like that."

"I remember times like that too," I comment, and immediately regret the interruption, hoping it doesn't sidetrack her.

"Anyhow, when you told me about the time you went to Dan's house with your dad and then left so abruptly, I knew exactly what you were talking about. He and I stopped there one day and I always wondered after that what the house actually meant to him. He was completely at ease there, relaxed and happy. We only stayed for a few minutes and it seemed the closer we got to home the more tense he became. I couldn't shake the feeling that somehow Dan's house was where he really wanted to live.

"Then right after we got home from Florida after Christmas, the letter from Roosevelt came offering your father the new job. I know he was torn between needing to make the upward career move and wanting to stay at Manning State. I suspected it wasn't only the work and the college he would miss and I was right, although I didn't actually know that until you, Mike and Vicki had already left for Florida. We had an honest talk, your dad and I.

"Jared admitted his reluctance to make the move. Brash as always, probably downright rude, I asked him why, if he was so unhappy with your mother, he didn't just leave her, let her move to Florida and go to Chicago alone. I told him then I thought he was in a no-win situation and I knew there was someone he'd rather be with. I guess I surprised the hell out of him, but he didn't deny it. He said he didn't know how he could go off like that and leave you and Michael. It was you he was thinking of, in spite of his own desire to break away and start all over again. I remember how sorry I felt for him. He didn't talk to me about the woman. I assume it was this Joanna, and once I'd moved back to Florida and you were all here, I never spoke of it to him again. It didn't seem necessary. Even though your start here was sort of rocky ... okay, very rocky ... your parents decided to try again after their separation and they both worked at it until the problems were solved."

I'm digesting this revelation. Dad wanted to leave Mom. He was unhappy about moving to Chicago with her. There was someone else he wanted to be with. But he went because of Mike and me.

~ * ~

"Daddy, are you crying?"

He's not looking at me, but I see tears on his face. He quickly wipes his eyes.

"Daddy's just a little glum tonight, that's all, honey. Everybody gets that way now and then, even you, right?"

I curl up close to him.

"Can I make it better, Daddy?"

"You always make it better, Marina. You and Michael are the most important people in the world to me. I love you both very, very much."

~ * ~

Oh my God! It was true. Whoever Joanna was or what she meant to my father, he left her behind and stayed with us. I suddenly feel a confusing combination of anger, guilt and compassion.

"Are you okay, Marina? I know all this can't be pleasant to hear, but you'd have kept digging until you got to the bottom of it. I hope you're not thinking any the less of your dad because of this part of his life, or of me for trying to conceal it from you. He was a wonderful father, someone who struggled to do what he thought was right, and you should remember him that way. Truth be told, if your mother had been okay, I think he might have stayed with his Joanna and tried to keep you and Mike in his life as much as possible. But the thought of leaving you with Vicki while he built a new career in a new place was more than

63

he could stomach, I guess. He followed his conscience and kept his family together."

She hands the book back to me.

"There. Your father and Joanna must have shared a love of these poems. I don't doubt that for the rest of his life he read them and maybe even thought of her. But he stayed here with you and worked hard at his marriage. In the end, I think nothing else counted."

"Okay, I guess I can understand why you didn't want to talk about it. You were trying to protect me from hearing about Dad's other life. He must have gone through some times when he felt very much alone. How I wish I'd known all this then so I could have helped him."

"I'm sure he did, sweetie. But it wasn't your job to help your father through his personal crises. It was your job to be a child and his job to try to shield you as much as possible from the conflict. That you have only vague recollections of some of the unhappier times shows how successful he was. You had a beautiful childhood, didn't you?"

"Most of the time, yes. I remember being afraid when they'd fight, or Dad would go out and I'd worry he'd never come back. He took a trip to New York right after the play and I remember how terrified Mike and I both were. It wasn't like Dad to be away from home for such a long time."

As I say that, I remember the matchbook I found in Dad's car. Did he keep it as a memento of time spent there with Joanna?

"Speaking of childhoods, any idea who this might be?" I reach in the drawer and retrieve the photo of the boy.

"No, I don't have the slightest," she answers, turning it over to read the name on the back. "Steven? Doesn't mean anything to me, but he sure does look a lot like you did at his age. Blond as blond could be. Where did you find this?"

"Dad had it in an envelope at the bottom of his file drawer. Looks like the envelope slipped out of a folder and he forgot it was there. I thought you might know who it is."

"Sorry, baby, I—"

"What are you two doing here in this dark room?" My mother's voice has a strange lightness to it.

I put the books on the side of the desk, tuck the photo under them and stand.

"How are things at the museum, Mom?"

"Okay. I'm glad I got to see everyone before I leave."

"Oh, you're going to Florida? When did you decide?"

"I don't know. Genna's idea makes sense. I need to get away. It won't be for long, but I could use a change of scene. These last months have been very hard."

"Wonderful. You can catch up on your sleep, visit some old friends and enjoy the sun. We'll look after things here on the home front. Have you told Mike and Ellen?"

"I'll go call them now and then I have to pack. You and Andy can look after the house while I'm gone. Jason will probably spend a lot of time here anyway. I won't stop the mail or cancel the newspapers. You kids can see to things..." Her voice trails off absently as she leaves the room going toward the staircase.

After Mom leaves the room, I resume the conversation.

"Do you have a problem with my sharing what you told me with Mike and Andy? I think knowing everything will help them both to see the larger picture. Of course, I'll never say a word to Jason. He's too young to know there was a side to his beloved grandfather he never saw."

"I'll leave that up to your good sense."

"Thank you. Thanks for finally leveling with me. But I'm not so sure about how hard Dad tried to keep his secret. Didn't he leave the tape in his car and these books of poetry on the shelf? It hasn't taken a lot of smarts to find them and put two and two together, has it?"

~ * ~

I don't see Mom or Aunt Genna on Friday. Andy's at work; Jason hangs around the house and then goes out with some of his friends. I need the time to relax, try to put the stress of the last three days behind me. We go out to dinner and it's almost like we're a normal family having a normal evening. Occasionally, one of us falls silent when a memory crosses our consciousness. It's good to be together, though. I make a decision not to talk to Andy about the poetry and the information I've gleaned from Aunt Genna. Not yet anyway. He's working so hard these days; he doesn't need what I know about Dad's secrets to add to his burdens.

While he's in the shower, I decide to check out one more thing in search of some answers. I go downstairs to the den and take Dad's address book out of the drawer. It's the first time I've looked in it since we had to call everyone with the news of his death.

The phone only rings twice and Dan answers.

"Marina, how nice to hear your voice. Is everything okay?"

I assure him everyone's fine and then I ask, "Dan, at the funeral home on Wednesday morning, before we left for the cemetery, there was a woman whom I've never seen before."

He laughs. "Good God, that room was filled with people I'd never seen before. Jared certainly had more than his share of admirers. But I'm not sure whom you're asking about. What did she look like?"

I describe her as I did for Aunt Genna. "She was talking to you," I added, "and I thought you might have known her."

I don't hear any hesitation in his voice. "I do know who you mean, but I'm sorry, I don't know who she is. She dropped her purse as she passed my chair and I was simply handing it back to her. Why do you ask?"

"Nothing important. I wanted to jot a few thank you notes to people who came but no one seems to know who she was. Probably just a former student."

"I suppose," Dan says. He asks about Mom and Jason, we chat a moment more about the trip he and Pam are planning and then I hang up. I think Dan would have told me if he knew anything about the woman. He was Dad's best friend, and surely he would have known if Joanna and Dad were still in contact. It's a reassuring thought. That night, I sleep soundly for the first time since Dad died.

~ * ~

Thomas reads Dad's will in a quiet monotone. It must be difficult for him to perform this so final a chore for his friend. There are no surprises in it. He leaves everything to Mom ... all his assets, the house, the insurance policies, the usual estate stuff. He makes provisions for Jason, Sarah and the new baby with modest trusts. My parents were never wealthy, although Mom and Aunt Genna inherited generously when Gram and Papa died.

When Thomas is gone, I sit at Dad's desk and touch its smooth surface.

"Dad certainly knew what to give each of us, didn't he?" Mike says, holding some of the CDs Dad kept near his player on the bottom bookshelf. "He knew I'd love these, all those old record albums and his tools. I'm glad now he kept the turntable and amplifier. I'll enjoy listening to all this old stuff."

"I understand. I was going to ask Mom for this desk someday if she ever remodeled the house, but he gave it to me, knowing how much I love it, how many memories of time spent with him it holds. And his books? I've been sitting here mentally placing the ones I want to keep on the shelves in my den."

"Dad did well," Mike says. "Did you see the expression on Jason's face when Tom read his bequest? Can you think of anything that kid would rather have had than the boat, the tackle box, Dad's university ring and his watch?"

"No, I can't. Those sentimental things mean more to us than anything else he could have left."

I don't tell Mike that I listened throughout Thomas's reading of Dad's will for some mention of Joanna. Totally unrealistic, I admit. If she were some big secret in his past, why would he blow it by leaving something to her or letting on that she exists? Even though I know better, I also know Dad was sentimental enough to want to be sure she knew he was thinking of her. I'm relieved but maybe a little disappointed when her name doesn't come up.

We hang around the house for a few minutes before leaving Mom and Aunt Genna to finish packing for the trip. They've arranged for an airport shuttle so none of us has to do the transporting. Traffic to O'Hare on a Sunday can be brutal.

~ * ~

"Hey, sleepyhead, isn't it about time you were up?" Jason is at the kitchen table, an open notebook next to his cereal bowl as I struggle into the kitchen.

It is unusually late for me to be getting out of bed. Andy came in sometime during the night and is still snoring lightly when I rise quietly so as not to disturb his rest.

"Hey yourself," I tease. "Who is this big guy sitting at my table?" He's growing so quickly into the man he will soon be. I always hoped he would turn out to be like Andy and my father—strong, dependable, kind and compassionate. These are qualities I've have always admired in both of them. I also want him to be as honest. Dad and Andy speak their minds, not in hurtful or argumentative ways, but with a candor I always rely on.

Now I wonder, though, whether Dad was always truly honest. What if all those years we were sharing him with someone we didn't even know?

Thoughts like this make me weary. I don't want to admit them back into my consciousness. Last night I was planning the placement of Dad's desk, not worrying about that woman he might have known so long ago. Now she's back, and I realize she'll stay with me until I find out what she was to Dad and why she was here for his funeral.

"What're you up to for the rest of the day?" I ask Jason as he takes his nose out of the notebook long enough to eat a spoonful of cereal.

"Dunno. The weather's not nice enough to go out on the boat. Scott said something about hanging out to watch videos or maybe I'll go down in the basement and practice."

In addition to his good looks, Jason has also inherited Dad's musical abilities. He's been playing drums since he was about ten and we encourage him to develop his talent.

I look out the window and see what he's talking about. The sky is overcast and the wind's blowing up an April rain. A perfect day for hunkering down with a good book.

"Sounds good to me, hon," I say as I reach over for a quick peck on the cheek. "I think I'll go over to Grandmom's and pack up some of Grandpa's books, sort through them and see what I want to keep."

"What'll you do with the ones you don't want?" he asks, his eyebrow raised like Dad's did.

"Probably donate them to the library or the university. You know I could never destroy any of them, no matter how little interest they hold for me. But I know I'll want his poems, his plays and the textbooks he wrote, those sorts of things. I'd kinda like to be able to take an informal inventory while Grandmom's away."

"Okay," he says, back to the notebook and cereal. "I'll know where you are if I need you. Be back for dinner?"

"Sure. There's still a lot of food left at Grandmom's. I'll bring something home for us tonight."

I hear Andy moving around upstairs and go up to say good morning. He looks exhausted as he makes his way into the bathroom. I quickly start making the bed.

"Hi! I hope I didn't bother you when I got in last night," he says, leaning over for a kiss. "I had two emergencies and I stayed with the one little guy until he came out of the anesthesia and his parents had some time with him. I didn't mean to be out so late, but ... well, you know how it is."

I do, that's why I never complain when he's not around. There's a reason we both became doctors and, fortunately, neither of us begrudges the other the time we devote to our patients.

He smiles at me ruefully. "I'm sorry, but I'm going to have to go back today, for a little while at least. I need to make rounds and then file some of the reports I left undone last night. I'll try not to be out too long."

"No problem. I want to go to Dad's and pack up some of his books. I think it's a good idea to get the things out while Mom's in Florida. Maybe if she comes home to a house that's changed in at least one way she can begin to do the other things that need to be done. Dad's clothes, for instance."

"I know what you mean. As hard as it will be, she'll have to deal with all of the tough things one of these days. Are you sure you're up to digging in so soon?"

"Uh-huh. In a comforting kind of way, I feel close to Dad when I'm around his things. What time do you want me to quit and be home?"

"No time specifically. Don't stay so long you let everything get to you, that's all. Give me a call when you're on your way home and I'll set the table and start dinner. Anything special you want?"

"No, I told Jason I'd bring home some of the leftovers from Mom's. There are a few casseroles in the refrigerator and the freezer. We could live for the next week on all the meals the neighbors brought in."

"Great. I didn't feel like cooking anyway."

He goes into the bathroom and turns on the shower. Over his shoulder, he says goodbye, he'll see me later. I go out quickly, grateful he doesn't bring up the tape again. He almost sounds like he's forgotten about it all together.

I get into the Outback. The sweet smell of Old Spice and cigarettes is nearly gone. "I'll drive this car until that aroma is gone," I say aloud to no one. "Maybe I can keep Dad close for a while longer that way."

~ * ~

The house is so quiet I can hear the ticking of the grandfather clock in the dining room. I must remember to wind it while Mom's gone. I take a Coke from the refrigerator into Dad's den. I'll go through the books, put the ones I definitely want on one shelf and isolate the others for packing later.

The process goes quickly. I've spent so many hours in this room I already know which books are important to me and which can be given away, so I go through each of the shelves quickly, pausing occasionally to check the contents of an unfamiliar book before deciding on which side of the shelf it will go. Left goes with me, right waits for the packing cartons.

I push the monitor of Dad's computer out of the way so I can put a pile of books on the desk.

Dad's computer! Why haven't I thought to check and see if there are more clues about Joanna there? It makes sense. If Dad kept in touch with her, maybe I'll find some evidence of their contact. Unless he deleted everything, that is. I'm annoyed with myself that I haven't thought of the computer until now. Only one way to find out.

Moving the stack of books again, I swivel the monitor back around and boot up the computer. As I wait, I take the pictures out of the blotter and look again at the sea and the little boy. Who took the photos of the ocean? Who is the child? And why did my father keep them?

I open his e-mail account. Since I was the one who taught him how to use Outlook, I know his password. I go right to the 'Sent Items' folder to see if there's anything there. I feel a bit guilty, but all the while I'm thinking I shouldn't pry into his personal mail, I'm scanning the messages, looking for something that might be connected with someone named Joanna. I find a whole list of messages, all to the same address, so I scroll down to the oldest one. I look behind me as though I'm expecting to be caught peeking into Dad's private world and then I open the message.

It was written last August at a time when Dad was so very sick we didn't think he'd make it. The message begins, *"My darling Joanna."* I'm not sure I want to read further but it's too late now. I need to know.

> *My darling Joanna,*
>
> *It's been a long time, and I wouldn't blame you if you deleted this message without even reading it. But each day brings some wonderful memory of you, of those magical times we had together forty years ago and I had to connect with you one more time.*
>
> *Through our letters, we've shared our lives. In these last years, I've had a lot of time to think and I've recognized something about myself that has caused me even more guilt than I felt over the deception with Vicki and the children. I see my role in our relationship in a different light and I'm not proud of what I've discovered.*
>
> *Doris tried to explain it to me once, although I never told you that. You came into the snack bar just as we were finishing our conversation and we quickly changed the subject. She warned me that I would keep pursuing you, to your detriment, until I got what I needed more than anything ... your unconditional love. I think she used the word 'adoration.' I don't need to tell you I ignored what*

she said, brushed it off as so much psychobabble and then did exactly what she said I would.

You gave me that unconditional love, my darling Joanna. And I always felt adored when we were together.

But now, as I look back on the past years, I realize that, while I went about living my life, realizing my professional and personal successes, I wasn't willing to let you do the same. It would have taken courage I didn't have for me to step out of your life permanently a long time ago, to give you the freedom you gave me.

But instead, I selfishly came back time and time again, making sure you were still there to fill the emotional gaps in my life, while I knew the connection with me was keeping you from living yours to the fullest. The health thing was honest, but not completely. I was more afraid of having Vicki find out what I'd been hiding all those years than I was of finally breaking your heart. How could I have done that to you? What does that say about me?

Not a day has passed I haven't wished I were a stronger person, willing to lift the veil and reveal myself as I am. Not a day has passed, too, that I haven't wanted to break the silence and tell you how much I've missed your letters, having you to talk to, sharing your thoughts and remembrances of our shining days together.

They were shining, my darling. I could not rest if I thought you believed for even one moment that everything we shared had been a sham, or that my feelings for you were anything but deep and very, very real.

I can close my eyes and feel your fingertips on my face. I can hear Jim playing our favorite songs and see the flames dancing in your eyes. I can see Manhattan from atop our Emerald Palace and feel the spray from the wake of one of our ferries. I still see you in every season, in every kind of weather and always with love and longing. Please, please believe me.

Perhaps by now, after the way I've abandoned what we had, you feel anything but love for me. I couldn't blame you for anger, even hatred, but I pray it hasn't come to that. I still need your love and want you to know you still have mine.

In spite of the sadness, the tears and the lonely years, think of me gently and with compassion.

Remember, my darling, I love you and I always will.

Jared

I read it again and again. Who is Doris? Is Jim playing the piano on that tape of Dad's? Are those their favorite songs? What is the Emerald Palace? Oh, God, the guilt! He abandoned her? When? For how long had the relationship gone on after we left Pennsylvania? Did they ever see one another again? I am consumed with questions. I want him here in this room so I can confront him with my discoveries and make him tell me everything.

I want to scream at him. "How could you carry this to your grave?"

Did she respond? What would she have replied to this plea for understanding? If he didn't delete his messages to her, perhaps he kept the ones she sent him.

I look again at the folders we created. I remember Dad laughing when I made one called Personal Correspondence. *"It's like I'm going to get some top-secret government missives. Do you really think I need this?"*

I assured him everyone had such a file and the lesson went on. Now, I see he has used it for messages from only one source: Joanna. The one dated August fifteenth is obviously her reply.

Dearest Jared,

My prayers have finally been answered. After four years of silence, I hear your voice as I read your words and I am reborn. It's been like a death these past years, struggling with your sudden departure from my life, not knowing why you refused to use Dan as a go-between so we could stay in touch.

It has been a time of anger, frustration and, most of all, hurt, and a feeling of absolute abandonment. Add to all of that my constant worry about your health and you can only imagine how I have battled each day to get out of bed and face the world one more time without word of you.

All of my days have been filled with emptiness ... sounds strange when put like that, doesn't it? Filled with emptiness. But that best describes how I've felt. The space in my heart once occupied by you has been hollow and barren for so long it has ceased to pain. There has only been a dull ache that haunts my days and makes me roam around the house at night unable to sleep. Not even the beauty of the sea outside my door has comforted me as I spent hours sitting on the beach praying one day you would re-establish our connection. I had given up hope.

Instead, I turned each day to the death notices in the Tribune *online, scanning anxiously, sighing with relief when your name did not appear. You sounded so fearful and ill in your last letter that awful April; I worried you would not survive long.*

And now here you are. I'm so grateful I cannot find the means to be angry. Funny, I've never been angry, in spite of the way you chose Vicki's feelings over mine, the way you decided for both of us that I should no longer write with news of my world, sharing as we had done for most of our lives. Oh, I wanted to be angry; how hard I tried! But it never came—only the crushing sadness, the aloneness, the fear you would be gone without our having ever said a proper goodbye.

I have so much to tell you. Now doesn't seem the time. I simply need you to know that there is no anger, most definitely no hatred. Nothing you could have done would ever have inspired hatred. Instead, I'm simply relieved you've written. Like that time in 1965 when your letter found me already married and unable to come to you, this e-mail has left me with mixed emotions of joy and regret, the first far stronger than the second.

I will write again, my love, but only if that's what you want. This has been enough for me, enough to let me know how you truly feel and why the years of silence. Thank you for that.

Love always,
Joanna

Four years ago. Oh yes. Dad was in the hospital for a few weeks in April that time. The prospect of partial lung volume reduction surgery was being considered to possibly slow down the emphysema. He was very frightened and seemed to depend on Mom and me like he was the child and we the parents. It must have been then that he stopped writing to Joanna lest Mom discover the contact, the one she apparently believed had been severed years ago. Now it appears that for nearly forty years he'd been hiding his secret, maintaining a relationship long distance while being Dad to Mike and me and faithful husband to Mom. I read the e-mail from Joanna again.

So it sounds like Dan has not been up front with everything he knows either, covering when I asked about her. Obviously, he and Joanna have corresponded and not too long ago at that. What else didn't he tell me?

Then there's the matter of the letter she refers to. My mind is racing backwards. Dad left Manning State in 'sixty-two. When Mom and Dad split in late 'sixty-four, he moved out of our house near the Roosevelt campus. I remember the year because I was ten in May and my birthday party was marred by the hostile silences between Mom and Dad. He was already in his new apartment at Halloween, but he came back and took us trick or treating and stayed to tuck us in. That was 'sixty-five; he wrote Joanna soon after? What could he have wanted but to resume their relationship? She says she was already married by then and so he came back to us and he and Mom began to work things out.

Sighing, I come back to face the last vestiges of his other life. On August sixteenth, he has written to Joanna again.

My darling Joanna,

I had so feared you would reject my reappearance and simply leave me to suffer as I did you. Your letter reaffirms my belief in your goodness, your compassion and most of all, the love that's sustained me for all these years. Thank you, my darling, for all of it.

I too have much to tell. It just seems that using what little time we have together (I still tire so easily) catching up on trivia is a monumental waste. I want nothing more than to tell you, over and over again, how much you are loved and how I regret the pain I've caused these past years. Please don't think harshly of Dan. He argued strenuously against my cutting off contact. I finally invoked our long friendship to make him do it my way, the wrong way, I know, but at the time the only way I could.

I have built a happy family, Joanna. I love my children and their mother and my wonderful grandchildren. You loved them as though you had lived with them all these years. You were part of my family, but

I still could not bear the hurt in Vicki's eyes were I to reveal our lasting relationship. Rejecting you in the interest of preserving my image here at home was my way of coping, my vain method of running away from my own deception. We could have continued to correspond with Dan as the conduit. After Marina patiently coached me in the use of my new computer, I could have broken the silence myself. What held me back? Reluctance to open an old wound, perhaps? Fear of the magnitude of your anger, certainly. I know I've spent a lot of time working on improving my health but my efforts have only bought me a few more years, not immortality.

You were never forgotten. So often I wrote long messages to you only to delete them unsent. Finally, the need overcame the hesitancy and here I am. That you received me again with an open heart means so very much!

Tell me about your life, dear heart. Rail at me for being absent and for causing you such worry. Nag me to take better care of myself (I still cannot give up smoking); brag to me about Steven's successes, how fast Brian is growing and tell me if there is another grandchild. Take me back into your world, my Joanna. I've missed being part of it with you.

Remember I love you and I always will.
Jared

This is almost too much. I lower my head and let the sorrow take over. Someone else has lived with us throughout our childhood and adult lives. She's been a wraith in our home, a ghostly presence accompanying us through school, college, even our marriages and our careers. This woman knows us intimately, it would seem. Yet we never knew she existed. Although I want to hate her passionately, I find myself filled with a longing to reach out to her, hold her close and comfort her. I want to know more about her, like a last name, what she did at Manning, anything else that helps me get a picture of her.

Sometimes I'm amazed at my own lack of common sense. She was at Manning State with Dad. Seems like that would be an obvious place to start trying to track her down. If Joanna were someone he worked with there, perhaps her name is on a list of faculty or retirees?

I open Yahoo! and type Manning State College into the search box. It comes up Manning State University. There is a home page and I open the link. Where to begin the search for Joanna? There could be any number of Joannas at Manning. I feel temporarily frustrated. Then I search through the faculty list anyway. There is no list of retirees, but there is a Joanna Fitzpatrick. She has a page and the photo that smiles out is of a very young woman. Forget her. Dad was retired and in his late seventies, but the woman at the funeral didn't look nearly so old, so maybe she wasn't a colleague after all, but one of Dad's students? The idea is repulsive to me. Dad, of all people, involved with a student? I shudder to think of the consequences should he have been discovered. In those days, he'd have been fired on the spot.

But I open the alumni link anyway. It has an e-mail directory that is sorted according to year. My math is lousy. I know we left Pennsylvania in 'sixty-two so I start there. That would make Joanna a senior. There is no Joanna listed. I go back a year thinking perhaps she is a graduate student. There is one Joanne, one Johanna. Nothing in 'sixty either.

In 'sixty-three, I find another Joanna. A listing for a Joanna Ransome Webber. A *Doctor* Joanna Ransome Webber, no less. This has to be right. Any younger and she'd be in her teens. I exhale slowly. My God! She was obviously only about twenty when this was going on. Twenty!

Come on, Marina, I remind myself. *Back then, most women were getting married right out of college, high school even. No doubt she was a very mature twenty.*

Joanna Ransome Webber. She has a married name and she's a doctor. I wonder if the degree is academic or medical. I Google the name and come up with nothing. Whoever she is, nothing she's done merits an Internet listing and she apparently hasn't put up a personal web page. Her e-mail address gives no clue to her whereabouts, what part of the country she's in or anything more than a few lower case letters that could hook me up with her in an instant. I'm not ready for that. What could I say to her? How can I prepare myself for what she might say to me? *If she responds at all,* I remind myself. It could be that contact with Jared Fowler's daughter is the last thing she wants. Then again, maybe not.

Six

Joanna

"Gran, that bird's still here. Doesn't it ever fly away?"

The seagull squawks as I carry Brian's overnight case from his room. He's the light of my life, this darling grandson, with his mischievous brown eyes and loving ways.

"No, Brian, he doesn't seem to. I guess he's comfortable here. He likes my house about as much as you do."

In a few minutes, Abby will be here to pick up her son and take him back to Philadelphia. She's been with her mother in Ventnor, only a few miles down the beach, for the past couple of days. I'm grateful she left Brian with me.

My life has gone on pretty much as it did before Jared died. I work at the Center in the mornings, spend afternoons on the beach, enjoy my marvelous home, my writing and especially the remembering.

"Gran? Is this your book?" He comes out of the den carrying a stack of papers.

"Yep, that's it. Please, please don't drop it. Put it back very carefully where you found it."

Brian walks very slowly back into the den. "What's it about?"

"I'm writing about my life, honey."

"Why?"

"Because I want to put it down on paper while I can still remember all the wonderful things I did when I was very young." *And while I can still feel the glorious warmth of falling in love.*

My den had been transformed into a sanctuary, a repository of the past, mementos I relied on as I slowly wrote chapter after chapter, detailing an ordinary life made extraordinary by the love I shared with Jared Fowler.

"Can I read it someday, Gran?"

"I hope you will," I tell him with a smile. "You'll need to be a lot older, though, or the story won't make a lot of sense."

Ever since I've been a little girl, I've wanted to write a novel. Reading was my main passion then and I was devouring six or seven books a week by the time I was in my teens. Nothing absorbed my interest as much as a well-told tale, whether it was a mystery, a love story or a saga that stretched over many generations. Many a New Year's resolution list contained a vow to begin work on a book of my own, but inevitably something got in the way. All the usual excuses, I suppose, from being too busy to not knowing where to start. I know now, of course, that all the procrastinations meant I was too afraid to actually put down the words. Why the fear, I'm not sure, but once it was identified, I didn't have any reason to continue allowing it to rob me of my dream.

So, I sat at the computer one dreary day as the waves pounded against the beach and the wind howled outside the window and the words began to flow. Although it was supposed to be a novel about fictional people, it became obvious as I wrote that I was telling the story of Jared and me.

It began with the first time we met and worked its way through to the final letter he wrote when he was too ill to risk receiving any more from me. It was a painful journey sometimes. I often saw the words on the screen through a haze of tears, but I was compelled to keep on writing. In a way, the process was cathartic, allowing me to see how our affair dominated my life and, had I not gone through so many months of therapy, nearly destroyed me completely. I recognized in the telling of the story how much I've grown emotionally since the fragile, insecure twenty-year old girl I was encountered the man of her dreams and nearly sacrificed everything to pursue the affair. I had to come to grips with what I now recognize as the temporary mental breakdown I suffered through the more traumatic days of that final year we had together at Manning. Large blocks of time, even weeks, remain blank to this day, testimony to the ability of the mind to defend against destructive memories. Where I couldn't force myself to remember what actually occurred, I used some license to fill in the story, aware that a reader would never know. As I realized how deeply affected I am by those experiences, I thought briefly of more therapy, even hypnosis, to try to bring back the missing times. Thanks to friends who listened patiently as I battled with my need to know versus the wisdom of knowing it, I decided to leave well enough alone, to accept the gaps in memory and move on with my life.

I struggle with the contradiction between the self that others see and the inner self that is still part child, part adolescent, part dependent and needy. In the years of my counseling practice, I've watched hundreds of women like me work hard to transform themselves from insecurity to confidence. As they left our final sessions, I often found myself wondering about them—how really complete their transformation was, how truly independent they'd become. My doubts come from within, of course. I know that lying dormant under my self-assured façade is the soul of one who still harbors an unfulfilled desire for someone I could never have. In a way, it's sad that I could never embrace the positive aspects of my life long enough to break the hold Jared had on my heart.

Of supreme comfort, though, is my knowledge that Jared, despite his fame and wonderful family, never broke my hold on his heart either. His letters are poetic testament to the strength of his love. So, however weak my fantasies of Jared made me, I certainly was not alone in nourishing them.

The book was almost finished when I got the news of Jared's death and felt the incredible knife in my heart as the *Tribune* obituary popped up on my screen. I knew it was coming, but I was never quite prepared for its finality. Then I made plans to go to him, to do as he asked, one more time.

I can almost hear his deep chuckle as he wrote in the e-mail *"I believe, in spite of my personal wishes, that Vicki will insist on a funeral and a viewing. You know how I feel about that, but nothing will matter then, my darling. I will no longer be able to hurt anyone or be of comfort to you. But my need for you will not have diminished and I will wait for the touch of your hand on my face before I finally rest at peace. And then know, Joanna, know I will always be with you. I promise to find a way to reach out and wrap you in my arms once again. When it seems least possible, I'll be there, I promise. Watch for me!"*

I didn't put much stock in the "I'll be there" thing. It has, after all, always seemed "least possible." In spite of the promise he made when we were last together, I knew in my heart we would never meet again; I would never feel his embrace again. Oh yes, he's with me in spirit. I can never forget him, but in his arms? I've lost that chance forever.

Brian is racing to the door. "Hey! Mom's here."

"Hello, you two," Abby strides into the great room and hugs first her son, then me.

"Do you want to take one more run on the beach before we go home, Bri?"

"Cool!" Brian says gleefully, running out the sliding glass door. "I'll be back in a minute."

Abby sits, rests her head on the back of the sofa for a moment and sighs.

"Thanks for keeping him, Mom. I needed to have those couple days with my mom. She's been so lonely since Dad died and I know she misses our long talks and leisurely walks on the beach. I could have taken Brian, but I really needed to be alone with Mom. We covered a lot of ground."

She gives me a piercing look and plunges right in. "Now, we haven't had a minute to ourselves to talk. How are you doing, I mean *really* doing? You haven't told me what happened in Chicago. Can you talk about it?"

She's caught me totally off guard. She and Steven have always known about Jared, but I never spent a lot of time talking about him. I guess it's only natural they'd want to know about the funeral.

"Thanks, sweetie. Yeah, I guess it will help to tell someone about it. Where do I start?"

"Anywhere. How about when you first got there? Did you go to his house?"

"Yes and no. I asked the taxi driver to take me past it. Oh, Abby, it's lovely. It's right on Lake Michigan, tranquil and very beautiful, as I always pictured the home Jared would make for his family.

"You'll think I'm really a sentimental old fool, but I stopped at a flower shop to buy a red rose. I still have the old, dried-up pressed one he gave me when we visited New York for the first time. I figured it was my turn to give one to him."

"I'm sure Jared would have loved that," Abby says. "How did you manage the funeral home? It must have been very hard."

"It was. I intended to go in with a lot of other people, to melt into the crowd and maybe spend a few moments with him without being noticed. But when the cab pulled up to the entrance to the chapel, I froze. I just couldn't go in. You know, it's been ten years since I last saw Jared, but when I did, he was still handsome, mirthful and oh, so alive! I couldn't imagine him without his essence, his *life*! I wondered how I would introduce myself, whether Vicki would reach way back when she heard my name and remember who I was. Jared told her about me when they were in counseling and I was scared silly she'd make the connection. So I had the driver cruise around the block a few times while I calmed my nerves. By the time I finally talked myself into going in, it was almost too late."

"What about his family? Did you talk with any of them?"

"Not exactly. Oh, I would have known Marina anywhere. She's a grown-up version of the little girl I met when she was eight, with her delicate features and platinum hair. I didn't see Michael at the viewing, but when I saw him and Jared's grandson Jason at the funeral the next day, I was stunned at how much they look like Jared."

"What about Vicki?"

"My God! She was the real surprise. Funny, but even though I've never seen her, I had a kind of mental picture of what she should look like. There were two women in the front chairs. One was Genna, Jared's sister-in-law. She made life bearable in the Yardley house by caring for the children and helping Jared with the chores. I gave her a fleeting glance, but it was Vicki who captured my attention. Honestly, I tried not to stare at her, but she wasn't the way I imagined her, not even close. I don't know what I expected ... she's short with lovely dark hair and I think I saw a brief smile that seemed forced."

"You didn't see her like that?"

"No, I'm embarrassed, but in my mind, I saw a tall, slender, very sophisticated woman. In person, she seemed very shy and uncomfortable, though maybe it was just shock. It was the children who greeted everyone. Vicki didn't stand with them, didn't seem to be looking at Jared either."

"I'm surprised. Well, maybe it was too painful for her."

"I suppose that could be the case, but I'd certainly have been right next to him."

"You said Jared asked you to do something special for him. Did you?"

It's hard for me to talk about this because I know I'll cry. That's when I lost it, I'm ashamed to say ... doing what Jared asked. You see, when we were together, I always loved to run my index finger from his forehead around his eyes, his nose and his mouth down to his chin. His face was so beautiful. He loved my touching him like that as much as I did."

"And that's what he asked you to do at his viewing? Oh, how could you find the strength? And what would his family think?"

"I only know that's what he asked. And I honestly intended to do it, his family be damned. Frankly, I didn't care what anyone thought. But, but when I touched his forehead..."

I have to take a deep breath and concentrate on getting out the words. "When I finally touched his forehead, it felt like a rock. It was cold and hard and artificial feeling, like it wasn't even a real person's face. There was no warmth; his lips were a thin, colorless slash across his face and his eyebrows were perfectly symmetrical. He used to raise his right eyebrow when he was surprised or amused; I probably never mentioned that. I don't know if I ever saw those brows still. Anyway, I only touched him once and I couldn't do it again."

"That must have been terrible."

"Oh, it was. That's what made me cry; I was doing fairly well until then, but feeling that unresponsiveness was like a cold splash of reality I hadn't counted on. I don't know how I got out of there."

"Did anyone speak to you?"

"Only Marina. I wanted to leave so badly all I could think to say was that her father was an old friend. It certainly wasn't a lie, but it didn't scratch the surface of our relationship. I just mumbled the words and took off."

"Did you go back the next day?"

"Uh-huh. I was there in the morning before they closed the casket. All I could do was concentrate on his face from the back of the room, knowing it was the last time I'd ever see him and it was a struggle to keep my composure. Seeing Dan Kearney there helped a bit. He was Jared's best friend for so many years. When he was away for a year, Jared took care of his house and that's where we spent our last months together every chance we had. It was good to see Dan; at least someone in the room knew what Jared meant to me. But we didn't say more than a few words before the family left for the cemetery. I caught Marina looking at me as she passed by and for a second, I was afraid she'd come over and ask me who I was and why I was there. But she kept on walking and I knew Dan would never give me away if she cornered him later."

"I probably shouldn't ask about the cemetery," Abby says. "That must have been the toughest of all."

"No, honestly, the cemetery was better. At least there I had some time alone. I waited until everyone left and then I put the rose off to the side of all the other flowers. I've always believed the body in the coffin is only a shell of the person and the spirit is still alive, so I knew Jared wasn't in that box and I walked away as they lowered it into the ground."

When I look at Abby, she's got tears in her eyes. I grasp her hand and stand.

"It's okay, honey, honest. Jared was with me when I left, still tucked in that corner of my heart he's occupied from the day we met. Nothing can change that."

"I don't suppose you went to the house afterward."

"No, there would have been too many questions I couldn't answer. Jared didn't ask me to be there to meet his family. He wanted me to say goodbye to him. Once I'd done that, there was no reason to stay. So I left and came home."

We walk toward the sliding glass door, look out and see Brian waving his arms and swooping around the beach like a human seagull.

"I believe Jared is with me whenever I need him. I talk to him a lot; I tell him my plans for each day. You'd be surprised the number of times a name, a snatch of melody or a tall, lean man walking down the street reminds me of him."

"Do you still have any of his letters? You said he wrote to you all the time."

I motion toward the den with my head. "In there. Boxes of them, from the very first in October of 'sixty-one until the last one thirty-six years later. I even printed out the e-mails he sent after that so I could read them often. They comfort me when I'm missing him most.

"Don't laugh ... but of course I know you won't. You're a fan of John Edward, too, aren't you? I know I'm getting messages from Jared from the Other Side. It's good that I know to look for them, otherwise I might pass them off as so much coincidence."

"Hah! You always tell Steven and me there's no such thing as coincidence. So what kinds of messages are you talking about?"

I shrug. "Jared constantly lets me know he's in tune with my life. I hear a favorite song of ours in the supermarket as I start shopping or one's playing when I turn on the car radio on my way to the Center. A man I don't know whistles "Misty" as I pass him on the street. I find red and gold leaves on the hood of my car to remind me of our walks along the path that led to Jared's office, those kinds of things. Sometimes in the early hours of the morning as I'm just waking up, I can hear his voice as clearly as if he's standing right there. Do I ever see his spirit? No, but I don't expect to. I'm grateful for what I get."

Abby leans over and picks up a couple of DVDs that are on top of the player.

"Don't tell me. You bought this one just to hear the song?"

"Yes, I suppose. But no one sings 'Unchained Melody' like Jared did."

I don't dare tell her I watch *Ghost* and wish that, if Patrick Swayze could come back from the dead to watch over his lover, maybe Jared Fowler could too. She probably thinks I'm slightly daffy anyway; still, some things are better left unshared.

"And this one?" Abby turns my copy of *An Affair to Remember* over in her hands. "I don't think I've ever taken the time to watch this old thing all the way through."

"Oh, that one's my catalyst," I say with a smile tinged with embarrassment. "You should sit through it one day. Such a beautiful story! I love to watch Cary Grant when he opens the bedroom door and sees his painting of Terry McKay wearing his grandmother's mantilla. When I play it, I know I'll cry, so you see why I call it a catalyst. Sometimes I'm just having one of my 'feeling sorry for Joanna' days and only tears can make it better."

Before she can comment, Brian comes tearing into the house.

"Gran, look! That big ol' seagull is still out there on the dune. Golly, he's huge! He didn't budge when I went right over next to him."

"Maybe he's lost, honey, or maybe he just likes this beach as much as we do."

"Will you come visit soon, huh, Gran?"

"Of course I will, sweetheart. Now give me a huge hug so you and Mom can get on home."

~ * ~

When they're gone, I sit on the sofa and think over what I told Abby. Probably way too much. How can I expect anyone in my family to really understand what Jared meant to me? Steven especially needs to believe I once loved his father. I never told him in so many words that being pregnant with him was the only reason Phillip and I married. I never wanted to put that kind of guilt on my son, make him think in any way that his existence kept me from living the life I wanted. Steven was blameless, and both Phillip and I loved him from the day he was born, but we never truly loved each other. We were worlds apart and, had not his death intervened, we would have eventually gone our separate ways.

I know Abby and Steven wouldn't understand why I drive into Manhattan occasionally and take the ferry ride over to Staten Island. It's such a living-in-the-past kind of thing. But I like to stand on the deck and remember when Jared was with me, wrapping me in his arms as we watched the seagulls fly overhead and envied their freedom. We laughed at the one bird that seemed to be tagging along with our journey. He stayed above Jared's head and slowly let his wings lift and fall as we made our way across the harbor. Jared would whisper a phrase from a Benton poem, and I'd snuggle close against his chest.

On the return trip, I always look up at the Empire State Building, our Emerald Palace. It was alight in red and green when we first went to New York that Christmas and we stood on the observation deck and owned the world below us. I remember the laughter and the quick kisses in the cold winter wind.

We made love for the first time in our little room in the Statler Hilton and we rode in a taxi through Central Park. We watched the skaters at Rockefeller Center and knelt in a candle-lit St. Patrick's Cathedral. We ate dinner in our room and danced to music on the radio. We fell into bed early and made love until the wee hours. They were among the happiest moments of my life. And although they can't be relived, as much as I long to go back there again, I find myself replaying them over and over in my mind.

Many times a week, something reminds me of Jared and makes me smile. He kept me alive in his heart while he followed his conscience and stayed with his family. I wonder what they would say if they found out I'd been with him all along. But I won't ever break his confidence. I kept his secret as he knew I would, and no one will ever be the wiser.

Seven

Marina

There are other letters. Her grandson is six; her son, Steven, is an architect, and daughter-in-law Abby (*Abigail?*) is an attorney. They live in Philadelphia. She sees them often, so she must live nearby. Her house is on the water; she has a photo of Dad on her desk; she reads the Benton books often. She doesn't mention the Emerald Palace—I still don't know what that is. She asks about each of us and Dad tells her about Jason, who is more like a son than a grandson, about Sarah whose blond hair rivals mine at her age, about Mike (*they call him Michael*) who has a dance troupe that performs in theaters around the country. She knows this; she has been following his career on the internet. Their conversation is seamless. It's hard to imagine there were any intervening silences. She refers only rarely to the terrible rejection she felt when Dad decided to stop writing for fear of being found out. When she does speak of those days, she tells him how deeply his words pained as she read them.

"In the final analysis," he had written, *"I believe you and I can take the hurt better than Vicki would be able to."* She tells him how many times she was tempted to write anyway, force him to explain her to my mother, how hurt she was at his decision. It was only her love for him that kept her from mailing any of the letters she composed. I wonder what would have happened had she sent them anyway. It would certainly have been easier for her, but I shudder to think of the consequences for the relationship between my parents if my mother discovered Joanna's role in our lives.

She speaks of me with fondness. She is proud of my career in children's medicine. Knowing Ellen is pregnant pleases her. She prays Dad will be healthy for many more years to watch the new baby grow.

Dad almost always replies soon after he gets a message from her. He talks about her work at the youth center in her town and the career she left at retirement. I'm not sure what she did, but it involved a Ph.D. she earned from Temple University in Philadelphia.

I read and learn. It's like getting to know a relative one didn't know existed. I search the messages for clues to Joanna as a person. The hardest thing, I think, is to know how young she was when they met. Dad was instantly smitten, I gather, but not smitten enough to turn his back on us and make a new life with her.

I'm almost finished reading. The last message is from Dad to Joanna. She doesn't reply. I understand why and marvel at the way she keeps giving him the freedom to do what he has to do without criticism, judgment or anger.

December 20

My darling Joanna,
(I am struck again by the *darling*. Having heard Dad sing to her, I can hear his voice as he writes the word.)

Marina and Vicki took me to the doctor this morning. I am becoming progressively weaker and breathing is more and more difficult. The new medications helped for far longer than we'd had any reason to hope, but I think I'm now counting down to the end of my life. I am not afraid to die. I have had many years and each has been a gift. I will miss those I leave behind but I also believe, as you do, that one day we will all be together again in a special place where there won't be any pain, guilt or fear of recrimination.

I regret now, more than at any other time, the lost years. I regret the hurt I caused you, of course, but most of all I miss having been part of your life and including you in mine. We can't regain what I foolishly threw away but I can tell you again how sorry I am for what I did.

We've pretty much said it all, haven't we, my darling Joanna? We each carry our shining memories, the love that burned brightly, dimmed with distance, rekindled from time to time when we met and then glowed quietly until I almost snuffed it out. I should have known you would never let it extinguish completely.

A long time ago, I told you we would be part of each other for the rest of our lives. Now I know our connection will go on even when one of us does not. Feel my kiss, my hands on your face and know I will be waiting for you, hoping it is many years hence, but waiting, however long it takes.

Remember, I love you now and always.
Jared

His message is so final. Joanna would have no way of knowing if he ever received her answer to this, so it appears she doesn't run the risk of writing back and having her message read by one of us. Dad's computer is mute after that day. I recall too well the frequent trips to the hospital, the weakness that didn't allow him to sit at this desk for more than a few seconds, let alone long enough to write to Joanna.

The phone rings. I resent the intrusion and just let it ring. Finally it stops. I try to regroup my thoughts, decide what, if anything, to do next. The phone begins ringing again.

"Hello!" My voice is strident. I'm annoyed at being interrupted.

"Marina? Are you okay?"

"Oh, Andy, yes, I'm fine, I suppose. It's been such an emotional morning. I'm still recovering from everything I've found."

He doesn't reply.

"Are you still there?"

"I'm still here," he says, his tone impatient. "When are you coming home?"

"Pretty soon." I look at my watch and am startled to find I've been sitting here for almost three hours. "Have you had lunch?"

"I ate at the hospital. How much longer do you plan to stay there?"

I shrug and then realize he can't see that. "Is there any hurry for me to get back?"

Again, he hesitates before answering. "I just thought since I was home early, we might have a few hours together. You'll be going back to the clinic tomorrow and you know my crazy schedule. We hardly spend any time together anymore. I thought maybe we could have dinner out tonight, just the two of us."

"We can still do that," I answer as I scan the computer screen at the site I've pulled up while we've been talking. "Let me finish what I'm doing and I'll come right home."

"Okay, I'm not sure I want to ask, but what *are* you doing?"

"I've found the most recent correspondence between Dad and Joanna. It's heartbreaking to read. It was she at the funeral, just as I suspected. Turns out she's been a part of our lives for a very long—"

"What the hell? Marina, what the hell are you doing? More to the point, why are you doing it? I don't want to be unfeeling or unsympathetic, but your dad's gone. This mysterious part of his life needs to go with him. Please, please, please! Stop this crusade you're on and leave it alone!"

"But she's real! She's out there mourning Dad like we are. Don't you even want to know more about her, where she is, maybe even make contact with her?"

"What? Contact? Oh, don't be foolish! This isn't anything you should be thinking about. If your father had wanted us to be one big happy family, he'd have brought her here or at the very least told you about this woman while he was living. You have no right to dredge it up and try to make some kind of Disney movie out of it."

His voice is filled with anger. I start to respond when I find what I'm looking for on the screen.

"Andy, please listen, I don't want to fight with you and I don't want to talk about this anymore," I say, trying to be as reasonable as I can and end the conversation so I can finish my search. "I'll shut down here in a few minutes and be right home. We can talk more then, okay?"

"We can talk more, sure, but not about this. I mean it. This is foolishness, dangerous foolishness. You could bring a whole lot of unhappiness into the family with your probing. Drop it now while you still can."

"We'll talk when I get home," I say again, and then hang up.

I've pulled up the people search and typed in Joanna Webber in New Jersey. There she is. The only listing. She lives on Beacon Drive in some town called Brigantine. I jot down the phone number, feeling foolish all the while. Why on earth would I call her? Besides, I have her e-mail address if I should ever decide to try to make contact. Still, I tuck her number in my address book and put it back in my purse.

The Google map shows me Brigantine. It's an island, a tiny island off the coast of New Jersey right across the bay from Atlantic City. *My God!* I've been to Atlantic City several times. I was only a few miles from Joanna Webber. The irony is unmistakable.

I know I should be heading home, but I want to read Dad's last letter to her one more time before I go. I can hear the resignation in his words, the awareness that his illness has progressed too far to stop the inexorable slide to the end. I imagine Joanna reading these words as I feel the tears smarting in my own eyes as they must have in hers. I push the button and the screen goes dark.

All the way home, I listen to Dad's tape. He is singing to a woman he loved for four decades. She lives in Brigantine, New Jersey, an island in the Atlantic Ocean. I see the large sad eyes, the pretty face, her tears as she turns away. We both loved my father, and somehow I know we'll meet one day. I just know it. I pull into my driveway and square my shoulders to face Andy's anger.

Eight

Andy

"Don't you see how important this is?" Marina says, trying to get me to see her side.

I stand my ground. "I don't see it at all. Look, you're upsetting the family. Mike is stressed out over your obsession with a strange woman Dad used to know. He doesn't need anything else to worry about other than Ellen right now. She's been having some pains, some bleeding. He can't worry about you and Ellen at the same time. Give it a rest! In fact, forget about it. You're needed in the Fowler family right now. The Buckman family could use your attention as well. Where's Jason? Do you even know where your son is?"

"He's nearly a man and I'm not his keeper. But yes, I suppose I should know where he is. He was doing schoolwork and then they were going to hook up at Scott's to watch videos. Isn't he home yet?"

"Do you see him?" I tend to get really sarcastic when I'm mad. "Of course, he's not home. No note, no phone message, nothing. I guess that takes care of us going anywhere for dinner. We can't leave without Jason knowing where we are."

Marina tries to be helpful. "Let's wait until he gets home. It's not even three o'clock yet."

Then she attempts to change the subject. "Where do you want to go for dinner?"

She reaches around my waist and pulls me close. I'm stiff and unnatural at first; then I loosen up and bend down to kiss her.

"I don't know. You pick it. I want some time alone for us after all the emotional turmoil we've been through recently. Can we do that? Leave the stress behind, relax and have a drink or two?"

She knows we should. Her thoughts have been consumed with Dad and Joanna. She knows it's been distressing to me and she doesn't dare share it with Jason.

"Sure we can." She kisses me again. "As soon as Jason gets home, I'll warm up one of the casseroles for him and we can go out to dinner. I'm sure he won't mind."

~ * ~

Trying to concentrate on being a normal couple doesn't work as well as I'd like. Dinner is strained and it's no one's fault. Marina knows I don't want to hear anything more about Joanna but, despite her best efforts to put them aside, she's dying to talk about the letters and what she's learned.

So it sits there between us, a silent intruder on what should be a peaceful and intimate evening. Neither of us enjoys our meal. I know Marina wants to talk about it, but she knows how I'll react if she does.

When we get home, we watch the end of an old movie with Jason. Marina's not paying attention; we've both seen it a gazillion times anyway.

I'm in bed waiting for her when she comes out of the bathroom. Maybe if we can put this aside, concentrate on each other and make love, we can move toward putting aside this tension. I've turned the bed stand lamp down low and the TV is off. Usually, we're both way too tired for sex. We often joke we're nowhere near the average for happily married couples, whatever the average is. We're lucky if we're both in the mood and not too tired a couple of times a month. That's a far cry from the way it was in the beginning, but so are our lives. We were young, crazy about each other and excited about the careers we were starting. Making love happened anytime we wanted. We were never too tired.

I turn to Marina as she settles in bed. "I liked being out tonight, just the two of us. We should make it a point to do that more often."

She leans over and kisses me. I hold her close, ready as I always am when Marina's near. After all these years, she still turns me on. But I can feel that her mind isn't with the passion like mine is. She's probably thinking about Dad and Joanna being together like this, knowing it was happening while she was lying awake, scared, in her bed, all alone. Damn ... how could Dad have done that to his family?

Nine

Marina

"Daddy? Is that you?"

"Shhh, princess … yes, it's me. Shouldn't you be asleep by now?"

"I couldn't sleep, Daddy. I needed you to tuck me in. Where were you?"

He's smiling and his eyes are relaxed and kind. "Nowhere in particular, sweetheart. But I'm home now, so you go to sleep."

I kiss his cheek, smooth and warm. "Where's your fuzzy beard?"

It's our little joke. Daddy's beard is usually scratchy when he tucks me in at night. Tonight his face is soft.

"Daddy shaved earlier, dear. Now go to sleep and I'll see you in the morning."

~ * ~

Andy's face is smooth. He has just shaved, too, so as not to scratch my face. I try to pull myself back to this moment, this place, this man, my husband, but my mind keeps slipping away.

"Not tonight, huh?"

Andy has released my body and leans over to turn out the light. "Don't know where your mind is ... it sure isn't here with me."

"I can't let it go. It's too much of a shock to me, I guess, and I can't pretend it never happened."

He rolls over, his back to my face.

"Okay, let me know when you get back to *our* reality. Your son and I would like a little more of your time and attention, okay?"

"Why can't you understand how hard this has been for me? When do *my* feelings count? You've been talking too much to Mike and between the two of you, you've decided what I should and shouldn't do or say. I wish it were that simple."

He doesn't answer.

"Andy? Are you just going to ignore me now?"

He doesn't respond and I know there's no use pursuing it once he clams up and refuses to talk. No sense trying to sleep either. I get up, go downstairs to the kitchen, turn on the teapot to boil water and stand next to it so it won't whistle and wake Jason. The steam pours out of the spout and I take it off the burner just in time.

The hot tea is soothing. I don't even hear anyone come into the room.

"Still awake, Mom?"

Jason's tousled head peers around the doorway. He's in a robe and slippers.

"Oh, honey, I'm sorry if I woke you. You really need to get some sleep. Ready to go back to school tomorrow?"

"As ready as I can be, I guess," he says, going to the cupboard for a cup and saucer. He fills it and sits next to me. Jason's been drinking coffee and tea ever since he was a little boy—coffee with Dad, tea with me. He and I have had many a long talk over our teacups.

"I'm caught up with the work I know about. There might be some things the guys missed, but I'll talk with my teachers tomorrow and be sure I'm up to speed." He lapses into silence, staring straight ahead.

"Heavy mind tonight, honey?"

When he turns to me, he has tears in his eyes.

"I'm still having such a terrible time believing Grandpa's gone, you know? Every day, I think of something I want to tell him, head for the phone to call and then ... then it hits me he's not there."

I reach out for his hand. "Let's just roll with it. It's okay to pretend now and then and, in a nice way, it keeps him here with us."

He doesn't answer. A couple of sips later, he looks up at me.

"You've been in Grandpa's den a lot since the funeral. Are you starting to pack things up? What's Grandmom going to do with the room? I hope she isn't gonna change it too much."

"Well, you know Grandpa left me his desk, so yes, that will be moved. If Grandmom doesn't want them, I would like his leather chairs as well. And I've already picked out the books I want to keep. The rest will probably end up in the library at the university. So you're right; I have spent a lot of time there."

"What's bugging you, Mom? Besides Grandpa's dying, I mean. You're not here all the time, I mean *mentally* here. Is there something you haven't told me? Anything you'd like to talk to me about?"

I smile. My grown son, sounding exactly like Aunt Genna, the family shrink. He's always been very perceptive; it's hard to hide anything from Jason. What I know, however, can't ever be shared with him.

"Thanks, sweetheart," I say, patting his hand. "That's all right; I'll be okay. I'm having a very tough time, like you. And I'm handling it my own way, as imperfect as it may seem. But I do appreciate the offer and if I need to, I'll take you up on it."

We finish our tea, put the cups in the sink and turn out the lights. I say goodnight at his bedroom door and quietly slip back into mine. Andy is sound asleep. I lie there thinking about Dad and Joanna.

~ * ~

"How are my guys?" I ask, rushing into the house. "Sorry I'm late; I'll rustle up something for dinner right away."

No doubt Andy wants to ask me if I went in to work today, but he just kisses me on the forehead and doesn't say anything.

Jason picks up a book and turns toward the stairs. "Let me know when dinner's ready. I have studying to do."

"I stopped at Mike's on the way home," Andy says. "Ellen's feeling better, but Mike's keeping her off her feet for a couple of days. He's playing nursemaid, taking care of her and Sarah. I think he's going back to work Wednesday."

I quickly begin browning meat and open a jar of spaghetti sauce. The big pot of water is on to boil.

"Good. I'm glad to hear Ellen's doing better. Want a salad with the pasta?"

"Sure, sounds good to me. Got any more of that balsamic vinaigrette dressing?"

I take the bottle out of the refrigerator along with a plastic container of salad greens.

"You still take my breath away, Mare, y'know?"

He puts his arms around me as I stir the sauce into the meat.

I look back and plant a kiss on his nose. "Thanks, sweetie, but are you sure it isn't the garlic in this sauce?"

He swats me on the backside playfully and takes plates out of the cupboard to set the table.

"So what did you do today? Did you go in to the clinic?" he finally asks, trying to sound casual. The mood's been good; I hate to ruin it by being honest, but I so badly want to tell him what I learned.

"No, I don't think I'm ready for the clinic. My mind's not on the work yet, so I took a load of Dad's books to the library at the university and visited with his secretary for a few minutes. Agnes misses him a lot. You know, she's almost sixty-five? She's been with Dad since he first joined the staff. I think she probably knew him as well as anyone could."

I'm trying to sound matter-of-fact and casual.

"Agnes said Joanna used to call Dad at the office once in a while. Her letters were addressed to him there for almost thirty-seven years. Of course, she assumed Joanna was a relative or close family friend and I certainly wasn't about to enlighten her. Imagine! Agnes said he used to come in just to make a call or write a letter. She said the last time Joanna called was about five years ago. She'd been worried because she hadn't heard from Dad in several months. Remember, that's when he started getting sicker and we had him in the hospital so many times? I guess Dad had a network of people who knew about her ... first Dan, now Agnes."

"Network? What network? Two people on the planet knew he was in contact with this woman, and that's how he wanted it, Mare. Obviously, Agnes didn't know the whole story and Dan never intended to share what he knew with anybody, let alone Dad's kids or his wife. How much clearer does it have to get? You're rummaging around in a personal matter that doesn't have any significance. It died with Jared. If anybody might want to dig it up, it would be your mother. She's the one he was cheating on."

"I'm not so sure that's what Dad really wanted. Look, if he wanted to keep Joanna a secret, why didn't he delete all the computer messages, destroy the tape? Burn the Benton book of poems with her inscription in it? You've never read the letters, listened to his voice or seen what Joanna wrote. If you had, maybe you'd be more open to seeing things my way."

I hate it when I lose control and cry. I don't do it at the drop of a hat and never to get my own way, to get sympathy or stop an argument. When I cry, it's a major deal. It means I don't have any other way of handling my frustration or my sadness. This time, it's frustration, I'm sure. At least I think it is.

He's trying to be helpful. "I don't want to upset you, honest. I sure don't want to fight about this. I want to understand where you're coming from, your concern over what you're learning about your dad, but I worry about how this is affecting you, what it might do to your mother if she gets wind of all this. I want to be on your side, but what do you expect me to do?"

I sniffle a bit, reach for the box of tissues on the counter and dry my eyes.

"Nothing. Nothing at all."

"What do you mean, nothing?"

"If you have to ask, then you don't get it. It makes me angry and frustrated that no one seems to care about this but me and I'm not even allowed to get the answers I need without my little brother, my aunt or even my husband accusing me of meddling. Why can't any of you see this from my point of view?"

"I guess because we all agree your point of view is wrong and dangerous. Before you started poking around, we were a close family who turned to each other for support when it was needed. In spite of the loss of the head of that family, and by the way, for the record, I loved him as if he were my own father, we should be going on that way. But you've put the specter of this woman right in the middle of our family. We're tiptoeing around for fear Jason will get wind of it or your mother might hear us talking, and it's getting in everyone's way. I agree I haven't heard the whole thing, but that's just it. I don't want to! I don't want to get caught up in this with you. We have bigger fish to fry, honey. Like Ellen's new baby and Jason's college applications. Your job, for example. When are you going back to work? See what I mean? There's a lot going on that's being muddied up with this Joanna stuff and you're the only one who gives a damn about it. Doesn't that tell you anything?"

I feel myself tightening up again and I don't answer. Andy's exasperated and it shows in his voice. There's no more pretense at concern or understanding. Now it's Andy's singular brand of pure sarcasm coming through.

"Let's drop it, okay, Marina? Just drop it. You can go back to work when you're ready or quit if you want, tell Jason his grandfather had a mistress tucked away somewhere half way across the country and call Joanna and invite her to spend Christmas with us. I only want you to do whatever will make you get past this. Okay?"

I go to the kitchen door and call upstairs. "Jason! Dinner's ready."

"Aren't you gonna answer me?"

I look at him and feel my own anger taking over.

"Okay. I'll handle this alone. I won't bother you or Mike or Ellen or Aunt Genna. I certainly won't breathe a word to Mom or Jason. But don't ask me to quit, to just give it up, because I won't!"

Dinner is a silent affair. Jason tries to talk about a book he's reading, but in the end, greeted by one-word responses from Andy or me, he gives up and quickly asks to be excused.

I finish scrubbing the spaghetti pot, dry it and put it in the cabinet. Jason is in his room studying or listening to music. Andy has gone back to the hospital. It's a convenient hideout when we can't get through to each other, and being there beats hanging around in the silence.

All of a sudden, I need to be out of there too.

"Jason!" I shout from the bottom of the stairs. "I'm going over to Grandmom's for a little while. Will you be okay?"

"Sure, Mom." His voice is muffled from behind the closed door of his room. "Go ahead. Say hi to Grandpa for me, okay?"

I swallow hard. Jason and I both know Dad's soul is still there.

I drive with only my thoughts to keep me company and I couldn't even tell anyone what I'm thinking about. It's Joanna one minute, Jason the next, Andy the next and then back to Joanna. Joanna and Dad.

I have a lot of photos of Dad from when I was little. I know how strikingly handsome he was. Taking about forty years off the woman at the funeral home, I can see her youthful beauty. What a lovely couple they must have made when they went out to their Emerald Palace or wherever they were able to spend time together. I'm not naïve enough to believe their relationship was platonic, but it does take more than I can muster to imagine them in bed together. Like most kids, I have trouble picturing my parents having sex, let alone admitting that my father was in a sexual relationship with someone nearly twenty years younger than he. And yet, their letters reveal a depth of feeling that betrays a strong physical connection as well as the emotional one.

At the house, I walk around back before going inside. It's very dark until the motion lights on the dock sense my presence and come on to illuminate the yard and the back porch. I sit on the chaise lounge, put my hands behind my head and close my eyes.

When I open them, the sky is filled with stars. I remember something in one of the Benton poems Dad loved about God striking a match across the cathedral ceiling, or an image just as strong. He was so sentimental! How hard it must have been for him to make the decision to leave Joanna, to move so far away from her, to stay with us when things with him and Mom were so hostile. The feeling of guilt and regret washes over me as once again I realize he did it for us.

I let myself in the back door, turn on the kitchen lights and head for Dad's den. Halfway there, I remember to get the mail from the box at the end of the drive. I don't even look through it; just drop it on the hall table.

I can't help myself. I switch on the computer and read the messages again. What am I looking for in them? What's the compulsion?

But of course, I know. I want to be part of it, the feeling I hear in their words to each other. I want to be included in that relationship. I was *his* daughter, but from what I read in her e-mails, she loved me too. She also loved Michael, as she called him. She even sounded like she had a sort of affection for Mom.

I sit there a long time, mulling over what to do next. I can't keep coming here, reading these letters, wallowing in the pity I feel when I think of them going through all this anguish. Sooner or later, I have to go back to work and try to put this whole story away in my mind and move on. Surely I won't be disloyal to Dad's memory if I don't pursue this any further. He and Mom lived a storybook life, for all anyone knew.

I remember when we threw them a surprise anniversary party for their forty-fifth. It was a big bash at the Conrad Hilton where we'd booked the honeymoon suite for them overnight. They fussed at us for days afterward for having done all that planning and spending all that money. We thought they were having such a wonderful time as we all sat around reminiscing about the earlier years when we were kids. For once, Mom was smiling a lot and Dad even sang a few of our favorite songs.

Was she there, too? Did he go home and write to her or call to tell her about it? How, damn it, how could he have led a double life like that without one of us picking up on it?

"Damn it, Dad, how could you?" I bang my fist on the desk, sending the blotter flipping into the air, dislodging the photos of Joanna's ocean, her son. "How could you, Dad?"

I'm crying again, but this time in anger. His betrayal becomes more obvious to me with each new revelation. I want to have him back for as long as it would take for me to get in his face, rage at him, punish him for what I'm discovering. How could he have done this?

I pick up the photos and drop them in a drawer. I shut down the computer, walk out of the room and slam the door behind me. I go out the front door, slam it too and trudge across the sidewalk to the car. I feel like an eight-year-old who's caught her father in a lie.

~ * ~

"Hey, Judith, it's so good to have you back. How was the trip?"

"Good, thanks. Good, but tiring. Exhausting, actually. I couldn't wait to call you to see how things are going. What's been happening?"

"Oh, same old, same old, I guess. Mom's still in Florida with Aunt Genna, and I'm so damned mad at Dad, I haven't been able to go over to the house at all. Andy and Jason have been taking in the mail. I called a furniture moving company and arranged to have Dad's desk and chairs brought over. He left them to me along with all his books, you know."

"That's like your father."

"You're right. I cleared space on my shelves and put Dad's books there. I know how often he read them and as I pick each one up, dust it off and set it in its place, I feel his hands touching mine. Silly, huh?"

"No, not at all. He's probably very pleased you even want them."

"I hope so. Most of his things are with me or Mike or Jason. Mom hasn't touched his personal stuff at all and we haven't talked about his computer. Jason already has a newer, faster one, so he sure doesn't need it. Mike said something about Sarah needing a computer so I guess that's where it will go."

~ * ~

The desk is here and I'm still not back at work. The other doctors are making noises about how heavy the caseload is without the extra pair of hands to help out, but I know they'll manage. They did fine before I joined the staff.

I need more time to sort out my feelings about Dad and Joanna. And I'm angrier than I've ever been. How can I concentrate on anything else? I can't risk screwing up at the clinic with a sick kid. It's also taking a lot of energy to deal with the strained atmosphere here at home.

~ * ~

It's nearly a month since we buried Dad. A month of ups and downs, bouts of anger, sadness or silly giggling over the memory of something I did as a kid that brought a smile to his face.

I turn forty-nine. There is no big celebration this year. Andy, Jason and I have dinner at home. I miss Dad not being around to tease me about being an old woman, getting close to the big "five-o."

Mom is home from Florida. She doesn't ask me to help with any of Dad's personal things, his clothes, the items in his nightstand and his chest of drawers. I don't even know if she's doing anything about them herself.

The doorbell rings and I get up from the computer to answer it.

"Mom, how nice to see you ... come on in."

She leans over for a hug. She's tan and thinner. Some of the worry lines are shallower; the ones around her mouth seem softer. We go into the living room and sit.

"So tell me about your visit with Aunt Genna. You look well rested and I envy your tan."

"Thank you. It was very comforting to be back in my parents' house. Genna has pretty much left everything as it was, except for a few little changes she's made to suit her lifestyle. I slept late, ate when I wanted to and walked the beach every day for long stretches at a time."

She looks up and her eyes are clear. "I've decided to move to Florida."

I catch my breath in surprise. This comes without warning.

"You'd leave us ... Andy, Jason, Mike, Ellen, Sarah ... the new baby when it comes? What about our house?"

"I'd be able to come back often. I'll still be here when the baby arrives and I'll come up to help out whenever I'm needed. I can spend part of each summer here. Face it, Marina, I'm too old to put up with the cold winters any longer. While your father was alive, I didn't dare mention moving. You know how he felt about being nearby while Jason was growing up, then Sarah and oh, how he looked forward to the newest grandson. But all that's changed. I don't want to be alone in that big house."

This takes some time to absorb. I understand her logic; winters on the lake can be unbelievably savage. We had a very bad one a few years ago and I don't think she left the house more than once a week.

"I can't argue with you," I say finally. "It isn't like you won't come back. It's just I never thought we would live so far apart, that I would see our house belonging to a family of strangers. Have you said anything to Mike yet?"

She doesn't reply.

"I warn you, he's not going to be happy. Losing Dad has been hard on both of us and now we'll be losing you too. Get ready for an argument."

"He won't argue. I think he'll understand I need to get away from all the familiar surroundings. I know I can count on both of you to do whatever has to be done to help me make this move."

"Will you stay through the summer?"

"I think so. It will take a lot of preparation to put the house on the market and then by the time I got to Florida, it would be time to come back to help Ellen and Mike. Genna and I thought I should make the move in the fall. By then, Ellen will be strong enough to manage without me and I'll be settled in before winter arrives up here."

I see they've planned this carefully. My thoughtful aunt is now willing to live with the sister with whom she's always had so little in common, although Aunt Genna always tries to see Mom's point of view. Age must dim the memory of the dissension, the harsh words exchanged in the heat of the frequent arguments I remember.

"What about Christmas?"

"What about it? You can come to Florida. The children will love the warm weather. You and Mike used to love Florida when it was so cold up here."

~ * ~

She and Dad are fighting again. "They'll be better off without you. They're far too attached to you as it is. What happens if I decide to leave? It will be good for them to have this time without you around. It will definitely be good for me."

~ * ~

It's eerie, scary, almost. I hear her voice as clearly as I did that night after dinner when I started into the kitchen and was halted in my tracks by the sound of their argument. I was seven and too frightened to let them know I was there. This time, it sounded like she was threatening Dad that she might take us and move away for good. I crept up to my room and cried. No one ever knew what I'd heard.

~ * ~

When we get home from the trip, our house smells like the attic, musty and closed up. I run upstairs to my room. Daddy's suitcase is on the floor in his bedroom. I start back to ask him where he's going, but for some reason I'm afraid to do that.

Maybe I sense he might be coming back from somewhere ... somewhere he went while we were in Florida.

~ * ~

I can't hold the words back. "How close did you and Dad come to splitting up when we were back in Pennsylvania?"

Her eyes show surprise. "Why would you bring that up now?"

"Well, lately I've been bothered by a lot of stuff from a long time ago. Who better to answer some of the questions I'm asking? Don't you think I have a right to know?"

"To know what? How your father and I fought? How we didn't speak civilly to one another for almost three years? That was a miserable time for all of us; why would you want to make me relive it?"

"I guess because I was so young, I didn't understand what was happening around me. Mike and I both sensed the tension. We were both scared silly Dad would leave us and never come back, but we couldn't talk to you about it at all. And, even though Dad kept assuring us he wasn't going anywhere, we weren't sure you wouldn't just pack us up and take us away from him. Mike and I walked on eggs most of that time. Didn't you see that?"

"Marina, you need to understand. Those years were about the worst of my life. I coped as best I could with whatever was going on in my mind. I guess I never realized what effect the arguing was having on you kids; I didn't think about it at the time. If I had it to do over again, of course I'd do everything differently. I would have gone into counseling sooner like your father wanted me to. I would have faced the emotional problems I was having and done something about them, for my sake as well as yours."

She looks down at her hands. For a minute I think she's crying, but when she looks up again, her eyes are dry.

"You want to know more about those years? Well, I'm not sure I want to go back there and dig it all up." She stares out the window without speaking for several minutes. I know better than to interrupt her thoughts.

Then she says, "After we moved to Chicago, when nothing got better, you know your dad and I did split up for a few months. I was in therapy by then, though, and so was he. I think he needed to learn whether to make the split permanent and I needed to find out how to bring him back."

Her voice softens and the anger seems to dissipate.

"Actually, I loved your father more than he ever realized. The thought of throwing in the towel and giving him a divorce is what drove me to take whatever drastic steps were necessary to mend the rift, make him want to come back. We both worked very hard at it. All those months of counseling helped us all. I don't understand why you want to dwell on the past. Don't you have good memories of growing up?"

"Sure, I have lots of wonderful memories. Most of them are good, as a matter of fact. I do have some blurry recollections of events that happened in Yardley, though, and I guess that's what's triggering the need to fill in the blanks."

"Manning was the worst time," my mother says. "It started after Mike was born and got progressively worse. I was alone in my own little world most of the time and I didn't let anyone else in. Now I recognize it was some kind of post-partum depression, but then I didn't give it a name. After a time, your father got tired of trying to help me get through it and backed off. He got the job offer from Roosevelt at a very critical time. I think he was on the verge of leaving me. But I didn't want to give in—something in the back of my mind kept telling me that, if he actually wanted out, he would have made the move alone. That was the perfect time, if ever there was one. When he didn't, when it was clear we were all going to live in Chicago together, I did whatever I could to save our marriage. I figured that was what he wanted too or he would have bailed when he could."

I don't say anything. If I'm quiet, maybe she'll keep on talking.

She's silent for a few more minutes and then resumes.

"At first his heart wasn't in it, that was obvious. I think he was torn between needing to stay and wanting to go. Whatever his reason, he stayed. When we eventually did split up, he still kept coming over and spending time with you and Mike. He didn't seem interested in me, in picking up the threads and trying to make something out of our marriage, but then one day he called and asked if we could talk seriously about going for counseling together and giving our marriage one more try. I was so happy I could hardly answer him," she says in a quiet voice. "There wasn't anything I wanted more than to stay married to Jared. Whatever his reason for making that call, I jumped at the idea.

"We were happy, Marina, I believe we were. I think all the trouble we experienced made us stronger together. You and Mike were our whole worlds. Then when you left home, we were comfortable enough together to travel a bit, spend time shopping for things we loved for the house and support one another in our careers. We each had our own pursuits. You know how much I love reading and sewing, and Dad had his golf, his reading and his fishing. It was a good life and I miss him very, very much."

I listen to her with most of my questions still unanswered. Did she ever know about Joanna?

It's cruel to even entertain the notion of asking her. If she didn't know, why should I be the one to tell her what I've learned? If she did know, it would be like rubbing salt into an open wound. And if she ever found out what I know now, it would be devastating, especially that Joanna came to the funeral. So I stop myself from going into this any further.

She doesn't.

"All right," she begins with a heavy sigh, "you might as well know all of it. Your dad was in love with someone else back at Manning. She was much younger than he, but the affair went on for most of the last year we lived there. It was over shortly after we moved to Chicago, but I know he struggled with his feelings for her for several months. At one time, I thought he might leave us. I was surprised he didn't go to her when we separated. Very surprised. But he came back and everything worked out, so I can't dwell on the affair. He found someone who filled the needs I wasn't meeting, simple as that. Can't say I blamed him. Genna thinks he should have worked harder to convince me I needed counseling. She doesn't know how hard he tried. No, I can't blame him for the affair. I'll probably always wonder what happened and why he decided to stay with me, but then I'll always be grateful it happened that way."

Now she's finished. She stands and smooths her skirt.

"I think my moving away is a very good thing, Marina. I need to be in a place that isn't haunted by your father. Our house is too big anyway and every room seems to be waiting for him to come back home."

I put my arms around her. She doesn't resist and even lets her head rest on my shoulder. I know I'll never tell her Dad did go to Joanna but found her already married and, unable to make a life with the woman he loved, he came back and made one with us.

"You do whatever you have to do, Mom. Mike and I will support you one hundred percent. You've spent a lot of years doing for us; now it's our turn. If Florida is what you want, Florida is what you'll have."

"Thank you. I know it will be hard for you not to have the house to go back to and especially for Jason not being able to go to the lake and fish, but I have to think of what's best for me right now."

I walk her to the door. This time, she leans over and kisses me. It is so rare an occurrence, I know then that I won't do or say anything that will bring pain to my mother. She's been through enough. So have I, but I know for me it isn't over.

Ten

Jason

"Are you serious, Jase? She's gonna sell the house?"

Scott's almost as surprised as me.

"Yeah, I can't believe she's doing it. Selling Grandpa's house and moving to Florida? No way! What's she thinking of? Mom says I need to be more understanding, to put myself in Grandmom's shoes and imagine what it must be like for her to be in that house day after day without Grandpa."

We walk in from the back yard and settle on the porch steps.

"The thing is, I *do* understand. Every time I go over to check the house or take the boat out, I feel him, like he's gonna walk out of the garage and put his arm around me, his tackle box in the other hand. So yeah, I understand, but no matter, it sucks! What will I do with my boat? How will I get it to the lake when I want to go out and fish or just sit and think?"

"Man, your grandfather sure loved the outdoors, didn't he? I used to like helping you guys clear that big lot across from his house. I remember him showing us what poison ivy looked like."

"Yeah, Grandpa knew everything, didn't he? He taught me something new every time we were together, like fishing and golf. We had so much fun the day he put that little putting green in the yard."

Scott and I laugh at the memory. It was more like a hole in the ground with some very short grass leading up to it. I got the hang of golf, though ... it's a challenge between the player and the game and I planned to be very good at it one day.

"Did I ever tell you he and Grandmom went on a trip to California once and he actually played at Pebble Beach?"

"Sure. You bragged about that shirt and the golf ball with the club's logo on it he brought back."

"Grandpa always said we'd play there together some day. Now I can't imagine ever playing golf without him."

"What's gonna happen to the boat when your grandmother moves?"

"I don't know, but I want to be out on it as often as I can."

Grandpa and I had shopped for that boat together. Sometimes I miss the rickety old one he'd had since before I was born, but it leaked so bad he had to junk it. He was sure proud of the new one ... we spent a lot of time taking care of it.

We went out a couple of times a week during the school year when it was warm enough and nearly every day when spring and summer came. Usually, we cruised out to this little spot, kind of like our private lagoon, where it was quiet and practically deserted. We'd drop our lines and sit, sometimes talking, sometimes not.

I debate whether to tell Scott what happened the day after Grandpa's funeral. It's been eating at me and I can't tell my folks, but Scott and I have talked about weird things ever since we were little kids so I decide to go for it.

"Promise you won't laugh or make fun of this," I begin.

Scott looks at me with a question mark on his face. "Sure, Jase; I promise. What is it?"

"I don't dare tell my folks what happened. They'd say I've gone bonkers, but the day after Grandpa's funeral, I went to our spot on the lake. I got out there, dropped the anchor and sat. Didn't even have any fishing gear with me. I just wanted to be somewhere I could feel Grandpa, like, pretend he was there. Of course, I knew it wouldn't happen, but I wanted to close my eyes and find out when I opened them it was all a bad dream, that Grandpa wasn't gone.

"There were a lot of seagulls flying around, yeah, all the way out there on the lake! I get a charge out of seeing them, y'know, 'cause Grandpa used to talk about seagulls watching over him. Anyhow, one big guy with a black spot on his head swooped down so fast I ducked. I thought for a second he was gonna crash right into me. Instead, he ended up standing on the bow not far from me. So I settled back on the bench and closed my eyes. And then I heard him."

"Heard who?"

"Grandpa. He said, 'Hello, son,' so I opened my eyes a little and looked. There he was, sitting on the bench on the other side of the boat."

"C'mon, Jase, you're creepin' me out!"

"Honest, I couldn't believe my eyes. He said, 'You're missing some good fishing, aren't you?' I told him I didn't go out to fish and then I asked him how he got there. Before he could answer, I told him how glad I was to see him; that I thought he'd died.

"He smiled again and told me it didn't matter how he got there. He said he came because he knew how sad I was and how much I missed him. Then he said he loves me and hates seeing me without a smile."

Scott leans back and rests his arms on the step behind him. "I'm still listening. Then what? Or is that it?"

"No. I tried to stand and go across the boat but my legs wouldn't move. I reached out my arms and told him I wanted to hug him. Grandpa's smile got bigger. I asked him what I should do when there's nobody around I can talk to."

"Did he answer you?"

"Yeah. He said I could talk to him anytime, anywhere. He said he'd always hear me and guide me to where I need to be. I started to answer, but he was gone, and the seagull was all that was left, just sitting there, staring at me. Then, he flew up a little and landed right on the side of the boat. I reached out to touch him, but he took off."

Scott doesn't say anything. He probably thinks I've totally lost it. Then he shakes his head ... hard.

"I don't know, Jase. Maybe you were only dreaming. Do you believe in stuff like that? That people can come back after they're dead?"

"Yeah, I guess. Grandpa and I used to talk about it once in a while. He said when we die our spirits keep on living, so yeah, I believe he *was* there."

"What happened next?"

"Nothing. When I opened my eyes, I was alone. No Grandpa, no seagull. Just how quiet it gets on the lake with the sun going behind a gray bank of clouds. I turned the boat around and went in. What do you think? Did I imagine it? Was I dreaming?"

"Beats me. It's sure one hell of a story, though. I see why you wouldn't tell your parents. It might really freak them."

"Yep, that's how I saw it, too. Right after it happened, I started to tell Mom and Aunt Genna about the seagull on the boat, but they weren't listening and I think it was a good idea not to push it. They'd have told me I was whacked."

Scott gives me a little punch in the chest. "You are whacked, buddy. Always thought so; now I know for sure."

We walk down the sidewalk and Scott goes over to the big tree in the yard where he left his bike.

"I'm sorry, Jase. You've had a lot to deal with these last couple of months. First your granddad gets so sick, then he dies and now your grandmother's gonna sell his house. I wish there was something I could do to help."

"You did, you listened. Hey, that's more than I can say for my folks."

"C'mon, man, your parents are cool. They always listen and talk to you about everything."

"Not now, Scott. It's kinda weird these days. Of course, neither of them will say anything to me, but I feel it ... y'know like they say you feel a bad storm brewing even before it starts to cloud up? That's how it is in our house lately. Mom's been super quiet. There's no yelling or anything, but it's tense whenever Dad's home and they're together, which isn't very often at all. Either Mom's over at Grandmom's or holed up in the office with her computer and Grandpa's books. Dad's either at the hospital or with Uncle Mike. It's like they're both trying to avoid being home at the same time."

"What do you think's going on?"

"I've been trying to figure it out. I can trace it back to Grandpa's funeral, that much I know. They started arguing right afterward and then the silence set in. Whatever it is, neither one seems willing to give in even a little."

"I know how stubborn parents can be. My folks fight all the time."

"Yeah, I've heard mine argue once in a while, but nothing like this. Dad's jaw is set square as can be and Mom doesn't smile much anymore."

"Have you asked anybody about it?"

"Well, I suppose I could ask my grandmother but something tells me that's not the thing to do. She and Mom aren't the type to spill their guts to each other. Probably Grandmom doesn't even see what's going on. She's too busy sprucing up the house and having realtors come in to talk about listing it."

I hear the phone ring in the house, but nobody's picking up.

"Hey, I gotta get that. Thanks for listening, man. I'll call you later."

Scott gives me a quick high five and pedals away. I run into the hallway and pick up the phone.

"Hello?"

"Hey, Jase, it's Uncle Mike. Is your dad home?"

"I guess not. I was outside and nobody picked up so I guess I have the house to myself."

I don't add "as usual," though that's what I'd like to say.

"Well, when he gets home, tell him I called, okay? How's it going at school?"

"Not bad. A lot of work. You know how they pile it on when the year's almost over. I have a ton of papers due and exams to study for. I'll be glad when summer's here and I can spend time fishing ... well, maybe not this summer if Grandpa's house sells right away. No fishing if there's no access to the lake, huh?"

"Hey, I'm really sorry about that, kiddo," he says. "I know you understand Grandmom has to do what's best for her, but it's another loss for you, isn't it? There is some good news, though. I talked to her today and she said she's been advised not to list the house right now. Doesn't sound like it'll be closing for a few months, so you'll still have this summer. After she's gone, why not trailer the boat in your back yard? You're not that far from the lake and we can use Grandpa's wagon to haul it to the public slip whenever you want to go out. I know it's not the same as popping over to your grandfather's whenever you want, but at least this way you could keep the boat and get some use out of it. What do you say?"

"You're right, it won't be anywhere near the same, but I'll talk to Dad and see what he thinks of your idea. At least I'll try to talk to Dad."

"Something wrong?"

"Uh, I'm not sure. Have you noticed anything? Has Dad said anything to you about what's going on with him and Mom?"

Uncle Mike doesn't answer right away. "Maybe you ought to talk to them. I don't think it's something I need to get in the middle of."

"Easy for you to say. Just try getting the two of them in the same room at the same time these days. We hardly ever have dinner together and you know what a stickler Mom used to be about our family dinners. That's when we're supposed to talk, open up about anything that's on our minds."

"I don't know how to advise you. Maybe if you can't get them together to talk about what's bothering you, you should ask them separately. At least you'd get some kind of answer. But I think they're the ones who should be explaining whatever's happening. Ask them!"

"Okay, thanks. I've been wanting to but the time never seems right. Maybe I'll talk to Mom when she gets home or Dad if he comes in first. It's like a revolving door around here."

"Well, you take care, buddy, and remember to leave your dad a note to remind him to call me. Keep me up to speed on the boat situation and we'll see what we can work out, okay?"

"Thanks, Unk." I use a nickname that always makes him laugh. "Thanks for your help on the other thing, too."

"Don't mention it, kiddo. See you later."

Well, that's interesting. Uncle Mike isn't surprised about Mom and Dad. He knows what's going on, but he doesn't want to talk to me about it. Now I know I have to get answers from them. I hear the Outback pull up to the garage. I don't think it's strange that Mom loves driving it; she says it makes her feel like Grandpa's close by. I understand.

The back door slams. She's in the kitchen, leaning against the counter talking on her cell.

"Again?" I hear her say. "You won't be home again? What's going on, Andy? This is the third night in a row you've stayed at the hospital and won't be home for dinner. What am I going to tell Jason? He's probably already wondering what's going on. Can't you put this anger aside and come home so we can have a family dinner?"

I walk up a couple of steps, sit on the stairs and listen. Little kids do this when they don't want their parents to know they're around. I'm way past that; I should be able to stroll into the kitchen and confront my mother with my questions. Apparently, she knows I have them.

"No, I haven't changed my mind," she says, her voice brittle. "No, I don't know what I'm going to do. I haven't decided, but as you're so fond of reminding me, it's nobody's business but mine. You've all been very clear that I'm the only one who cares about this, so what I do shouldn't matter anyway. Right? I'm cooking dinner in about an hour and it would be nice if you showed up."

She clicks off without saying goodbye. I'm feeling shaky as I stand and go on down the steps.

She comes in from the kitchen and looks startled to find me there.

"Hi, sweetie!" Her voice is unnaturally high. "How was school?"

I can't play dumb any more.

"It was fine. Okay, I've crept around you and Dad for the last week or so and now I need to know ... what's going on?"

"Nothing, son. Just a little disagreement."

"No, it's not little. I heard you on the phone. I don't think I've ever heard you sound like that. Why is Dad so angry?"

Her face is pink and she won't look at me. I know she doesn't want to tell me anything. So I keep badgering.

"You guys don't fight; you never fight. Now you can't even be home at the same time. Why? What's goin' on?"

"It's very complicated," she says, not talking down to me because she never does that; she's just being evasive. "I don't know how to explain it without raising more questions than I can answer. Can I ask you to trust your dad and me to work it out?"

I'm not ready for that. Sure, I trust them. I don't know how serious this is, so how can I not give them time? Even adults screw up once in a while; maybe this is something I should back away from and let them handle in their own way.

"Okay. So it's probably none of my business. But having you and Dad at each other's throats might make it my business if I have to live with you like this, so fix it, whatever it is. Please?"

"How about we talk with your dad together tonight? I hope he'll try to get home for dinner, but if he doesn't, we'll wait up for him and talk it out as best as we can. I think he deserves to know how concerned you are. Agreed?"

"Sure. Besides, I have to remember to tell him to call Uncle Mike. He came up with an idea for Grandpa's boat that I want to bounce off both of you."

"Uncle Mike." She says his name with an exasperated tone in her voice. "Absolutely, don't forget to tell him."

Sounds like Uncle Mike is in on the situation between my parents. He and Dad are pretty good friends. They do stuff together and seem to enjoy each other's company. It's clear that Mom's upset Uncle Mike called. I sure wish I knew what this is all about.

~ * ~

Dad never showed for dinner, but I'm not surprised, given the tone of Mom's voice on the phone. I'm not sure I would want to come home after that either.

I'm on the way to my room when he comes in the kitchen door. Mom's in the office on the computer. I poke my head into the doorway.

"Dad's home. You coming out?"

"In a minute," she says, never looking away from the monitor. "In a minute."

I meet Dad halfway down the hall.

"Hi, pal! Sorry I didn't make it for dinner. How was school?"

"You know, you guys ask me that every day. It's study, classes, homework, band practice, same old same old."

"When's the band starting the spring competitions?"

"Already has. I missed the first two because of Grandpa. We have one in two weeks and a couple before school's out. I'll put the dates on the calendar in case you can make it. Oh, before I forget, Uncle Mike wants you to call."

He's distracted, going through the pile of mail on the table in the hall.

"Uncle Mike? Wonder what he wants," he mutters. "Where's your mother?"

"Right here." Mom's coming out of the office. "Too bad you didn't get home for dinner."

I don't hear any sarcasm or anger in her voice. Dad apparently does.

"I told you I wouldn't be home," he says, his tone defensive. "Don't know why you were surprised."

"Never mind. Jason and I had a talk earlier and I suggested we bring it up again when you got home so we could both address his concerns, right Jason?"

"Right. I guess I'm willing to accept Mom's explanation, but I need to hear from you that it's on track."

We walk into the living room and sit, Dad and me on the sofa, Mom on the chair next to it.

"What's up, sport?" Dad looks like he honestly doesn't have a clue. Sometimes I think he underestimates my ability to zoom in on things that are supposed to be too 'grown up' for me to know about. This is one of those times.

"Come on, Dad, you know what's up. You and Mom have been at it since Grandpa's funeral. Mom says whatever's happening is between the two of you and you'll work it out. If that's the case, I'm okay with giving you time, but I'm not okay with the way we're living right now."

I look from one to the other. My mother is looking at Dad like it's his turn to say something.

"Mom's right. This is our problem and I promise we'll do our best to resolve it quickly. I'm sorry it's affecting you."

"Well, it is. I hate seeing you like this. Promise you'll do whatever needs to be done to fix this?"

"Sure, son," Dad says. He gets up. "We'll do our best."

And then Mom goes back into the office and Dad goes upstairs. This is how they intend to settle whatever it is? At times like this, I wish Grandpa would come back like he did before. He would get right to the bottom of whatever is wrong and help sort everything out. I find myself wondering if this has something to do with Grandpa. Mom and Dad started this deep freeze right after the funeral. What the hell could be going on?

Eleven

Marina

I've been reading about Brigantine. It sounds like such a serene, lovely place. The island got its name from a kind of ocean-going vessel from the sixteenth century. I'm fascinated to learn there is a lighthouse, a wildlife sanctuary and a place where stranded sea mammals are brought for emergency medical care and rehabilitation. I envy the hours Joanna must spend being at home so close to the sea. I wonder if my father ever visited her, ever sat near the dunes with her and walked the beach. I know they met occasionally during the long years apart but I don't know where, when or how often.

Reluctantly, I shut down the computer. It's late; tomorrow is another day. I need to call the clinic and explain to Hank why I can't come back yet, although Joanna and Dad move further back in my conscious mind with each passing day. I say that and then laugh at myself, realizing how far from the truth it is. Who am I trying to fool? What was I just doing now? Thinking about Joanna, trying to squeeze into her world, pushing myself closer and closer to her.

I turn out the lights in the kitchen and go upstairs. There is no light under Jason's door. Hopefully, he's taken his worries and put them aside so he can sleep.

"Going to the clinic tomorrow?" Andy is toweling his hair dry as he turns out the bathroom light.

"No, not yet."

"Why not?"

"I still have a lot on my mind. First of all, I think we need to resolve things between us. I was very upset to hear Jason today. He must have been carrying those questions around for days, not saying anything to us."

Andy gets into bed, the lamp on the nightstand still lit.

"Agreed. I guess we get ourselves so tied up in knots over stuff we think is important we don't notice how much it affects him."

"Right now, I'm caught up in something I want to know more about, that's all. I feel more strongly every day that I need to contact Joanna and find out what she has to say about her relationship with Dad."

He sighs, turns out the light and rolls over, his back to me. "Sounds like we're back to square one. I rest my case." His voice is flat and he doesn't turn to kiss me goodnight.

I can't sleep, so I go downstairs and sit at the desk, trying to organize my thoughts. It's becoming increasingly obvious to me I won't let this go until I've actually met Joanna. For all I know, she might even be unwilling to meet me and that'd be the end of it. But I won't know until I try.

Tomorrow morning, Judith will be home from the latest fashion shoot. I'll call her; she'll listen to what's going on and advise me, calmly and without anger, like she's always done with every crisis I've handed her.

~ * ~

It's a gorgeous spring day. There's a warm wind off Lake Michigan. The almanac says we're in for a scorcher of a summer, but it was wrong with a prediction of a bad winter, so I don't put much trust in the forecast. Anyhow, right now the weather is perfect.

Judith isn't home when I call at mid-morning, so I take my time running errands, stopping at the supermarket and the bank, filling the wagon's gas tank. It doesn't get the mileage my Buick does, but for now I don't care. It's been a few days since I've listened to Dad's tape, so I slip it into the player.

He's not even part way into the first song when I push the eject button. Not today. I can't do this today. Don't know why, but hearing Dad's voice plummets me into a total funk, adding to my miserable mood.

I'm almost home. I pick up my cell to call Judith again; the need to tell her about Joanna is getting stronger, but I just get her voice mail.

I turn the corner toward home, planning what to say to Judith. I see Mom's car in the drive. She's waiting as I park and get out of the Outback.

"Did you go to the clinic today, Marina?" My mother's tone is disinterested like the question is a mere formality.

"No, I'm not quite ready yet."

"I had two realtors at the house today and decided to list with Donna from ReMax. She's had a lot of experience selling lakefront property and was very impressed with the house and the lots. She suggested I wait until mid-summer to list. She says if it sells quickly, as she thinks it will, I can delay settlement until just before I'm ready to move to Harbor Bluffs."

She has a wry smile on her face. "You know, when you were very little and Gram and Papa moved down there, I always told people they lived near Tampa but I never said where. It seemed like such a silly name for a town, like something out of a romance novel. Anyhow, I'd better get used to it, hadn't I?"

"I think it's a lovely name for a lovely town," I tell her as we walk into the house. "You and Aunt Genna will enjoy cavorting on the beach, hanging around with all the old folks, playing bingo..."

"Marina Buckman! Don't you even joke about old people! I'm one of them, you know ... a lot older than your aunt."

"Good God, Mom, I was only kidding! Are we a little thin-skinned today?"

"Sorry, I guess I'm getting the jitters about actually going through with the sale. I keep thinking how much Jared loved the house and I worry I'm not doing the right thing."

"Of course Dad loved the house, but he's not here to pay the taxes, keep the property up and take care of all the high maintenance you'll be facing if you stay. Anyway, Dad was getting to the point where he hated the winters as much as you do. I know it'll be tough giving it up and then coming back here to visit and finding someone else living there, but it's the right thing for you and you know it!"

"I suppose I do. Every now and then I get a little pang of doubt, that's all."

She snickers. "Besides, what would I do every day in the winter when I couldn't even get out of the garage without either Andy or Mike shoveling the drive first? I don't look forward to that nightmare at all."

"Then see? Go ahead with your plans and ignore all those doubts."

"Thank you, dear. That's the reassurance I needed. I'm on my way to the museum to see a few of my friends. Oh, how is Jason? Please tell him it looks like he might have most of the summer to use the lake. I'm sure he'll like that."

"Jason's fine. He has two band competitions this month so he stays at school a lot to practice. He's also looking at college catalogues trying to decide where to apply next fall. He's trying for early decision somewhere with a good music program. I could be wrong, but I think he'll stick with music. He doesn't talk a lot about what he wants to do with his future."

"He still has plenty of time for that. Do you and Andy have any special plans for the weekend?"

"No, we don't. Andy will probably be on call and I have tons to do here at home."

"You two shouldn't work so much. You need time for each other. You know Jason can stay with me anytime you want to take a little time for yourselves."

"Thanks, not now, but maybe we'll take you up on that later on."

I walk her back out to her car, hoping I didn't sound too preoccupied. With a final wave, she's out of sight and I can get to the phone. I hope Judith will be home this time.

~ * ~

"That's what friends are for, honey," Judith says when I tell her how grateful I am she dropped everything to come over to talk "Actually, I'm glad for the excuse to be out of the apartment and away from the telephone. Sometimes I think I should be cloned. The agency keeps growing and I need to be everywhere at once. Okay, now, I want to know everything. How's everyone doing? Most of all, how are you? Have you been holding up? Are you back at the clinic full time?"

We talk as we walk down the hall to the office. Jason is in school and Andy's at work, but I want the privacy anyway. And I want to be in this room for other reasons as well.

We settle in Dad's soft leather chairs.

Her dark eyes are fastened on me. "Well? What else has been happening?"

"I've found more ... what we talked about ... Dad's other life, the other woman? I don't know if I'm handling it right or if I should be handling it at all. I'm too close to this to make good decisions, I'm afraid, and that's why I need to talk with you."

I stand and pace across the room and back. Going behind the desk, I open a file on the computer and turn the monitor around so she can see it.

"I found these. Not long after we talked, I was at Dad's sorting through his books and I looked on his computer. They tell the whole story with a few little bits and pieces missing. I've been almost obsessed with this. I want to reach out to Joanna but I'm not sure if I should. That's why I called. Who, if not my best friend, is better suited to listen and advise?"

I point to the monitor. "Dad wrote this letter to Joanna back in December. I need you to read it before we go any further."

Resting her chin in her hand, Judith scans the screen. Only a slight widening of her eyes shows any emotion. She gets to the bottom and then scrolls back to the top and reads it again.

"My God," she says so quietly it's all I can do to hear her. "How did you find this?"

"I helped Dad learn the computer, remember? I taught him some of the programs like Outlook and Word. We set up his e-mail together. It was just a crazy hunch that made me check his folders. But wait ... this is only the beginning."

I open another file and sit back as Judith digests the rest of the letters.

"And now I think you should listen to this," I say when she's finished. I swivel in my chair and slip the cassette into my tape player on the shelf.

Judith's hand flies to her mouth at the first sound of Dad's voice and then she sits back in her chair, closes her eyes and listens silently.

When the first set finishes, I turn it off.

"You say she was at the funeral? The woman your father wrote to, that you think he was singing to?"

"Uh-huh. She came late, but then she was at the service in the morning and at the cemetery. I was curious at the time and wanted to talk with her at the house but she never showed up.

What I've learned has come mainly from the letters you read and little flashes of memory I dredged up from when I was a child, before we moved here. Before I met you," I add with a smile. "Things weren't always rosy back in Pennsylvania. I heard and saw things that at the time were very frightening to the kid I was. Now they fit into context. That's when Joanna and Dad were together and, no matter what happened after that, they stayed in touch for almost forty years."

Judith shakes her head, whether in disbelief or amazement, I'm not sure.

"How upsetting all this must be for you. I can't imagine how you've coped with finding out about something your father clearly wanted to remain a secret."

"But did he? That's what I don't get! If he didn't want Joanna's existence to be discovered, why didn't he just destroy this tape? Erase the messages? Burn the books of poetry? Oh, I haven't told you about them yet, but we'll get to that. Why would he have kept the tape in his car where he had to know someone would find it? It's clear he knew he didn't have much time. Why didn't he get rid of everything if he wanted Joanna to remain hidden?"

"I can't answer that. No one can, I guess. Why do *you* think he left the clues? I'm sure you have a theory and I'm willing to bet that's at the root of your distress. What do you think your dad wanted to happen?"

"God, I've wracked my brain for that answer! It's been on my mind since the first sight of Joanna, I guess. I've got the feeling that, in some weird way, Dad wanted us to find her, to know about their relationship. Why would he have asked her to come out here when he died? For heaven's sake, he even told Jason he didn't want a funeral, but he knew Mom would insist on one, so he asked Joanna to be here. Didn't he think we'd ask who she was? Want to know about the photos and the poetry?

Dad used to laugh at my love of solving puzzles. Surely he knew I'd keep at this like a dog with a bone until I figured it out."

"Who else knows?" Judith is staring at the tape deck like she expects Dad's silky voice to resume its song.

"Just Aunt Genna, Andy, Mike and I guess Ellen … Mike's so angry I'm sure he's told Ellen the whole story, at least the way he sees it anyway. I certainly haven't brought any of this up with Mom or Jason."

"Mike's angry? I guess I can understand that. It's only natural for him to be upset with your dad for having kept such a secret for so long. Maybe when he's had time—"

I interrupt her with a hand in the air.

"Wait, he's not angry at Dad. He's angry with *me* for dredging up all of this, for what he sees as putting stress on the family. Like I said, everybody who knows about this is insisting I drop the whole thing and go on as though Joanna doesn't exist."

"And you? What do you want to do?"

I take a deep breath and exhale slowly. "I want to know her. I want to do what I think Dad wanted me to do … find a place in my heart for her. But I'm totally alone in that. And obviously what I want to do is driving a wedge between me and my brother *and* my husband. I need another opinion, my friend. What would you do in my place?"

She purses her lips and stares up at the ceiling.

"You know better than to ask that. I'm not in your place; no one is. What you need to ask yourself is why you're so driven to dig into this and whether any good can come of it. I think that's the bottom line. If you contact Joanna and develop some kind of relationship with her, what effects will that have on your other relationships, the ones with your mother, your son and the other people in your life?"

"If I could only make them understand!" My fist pounds the desk, startling Judith and even surprising me with the force of it.

Judith's eyes narrow. "Understand what? That you think there's someone out there who shared your father in a way you never did? Someone he loved, perhaps, in a way he never loved anyone else? Including you? Come on, Marina! This is a thing between you and your father. You must see that. You were Daddy's little girl and it bugs you that he might have been in bed with Joanna while you were alone in your room back in Yardley scared to death he wasn't coming back. You want to know what I think? I think you need to take a closer look at your own feelings about Joanna and your father before you decide whether contacting her is the wise thing to do. Are you sure your feelings toward her are so sweet, so accepting? She was 'the other woman,' your father's mistress. Maybe your dad's leaving all the clues didn't have as much to do with your getting to know Joanna as it did with your understanding a little of what his life was like back in those days. Maybe he wanted you to see he wasn't so perfect and maybe he hoped for your understanding and forgiveness. But contacting Joanna? You'd better think hard about that. Marina? Did you hear anything I said?"

"Uh, sure. I heard you. But there's one more thing. One thing I haven't told you."

I open the desk drawer and pull out the photos of Steven.

"It's about him."

Judith turns the photo over and reads the name on the back. "Who's Steven?"

"He's Joanna's son. She sent Dad these pictures God-only-knows-when. I found them in his desk drawer. My aunt Genna said he looks just like I did at his age. What do you think? Did I look like that when we were kids?"

She holds the picture and looks from it to me and back again.

"Uh-huh, quite a bit. I'm not sure where you're going with this, but I bet I can guess. Do you think Steven is your dad's child?"

"I don't know what to think. This is probably so far out I haven't even mentioned my suspicions to Andy or Aunt Genna. But that's one of the main reasons I'm having such a hard time letting go of this whole Joanna thing. What if Joanna and Dad had a child together? What if I have a brother I don't even know?"

She hands the photo back to me.

"Of course, that would complicate everything," she says. "But knowing your father as I did, I can't imagine he could have denied the existence of his own child. Look how he loved you and Mike. He would have loved any child of his just as much. No way could he turn his back on his own son. Uh-uh. No way. I think you should just rule out that possibility entirely."

"I'm glad to hear you say that. I think so, too. It seems to me that having a child with Joanna would have blown the whole affair wide open. Dad would have wanted to give the boy his name, have a hand in raising him. And yet, the resemblance is so strong."

"You said Joanna was married when your dad went looking for her. Do you know anything about her husband?"

"No. Joanna never mentions him in any of the e-mails. I know she and Dad wrote to each other during those four decades and I'm sure Dad knew about him, but—"

"Well, maybe that's your answer. Maybe her husband was blond and Steven took after him. Maybe, just maybe, Joanna couldn't leave her husband because of their son. Ever think of that?"

I let out a long breath. "No, I didn't. Wow, what a cruel twist of fate that would have been, huh? Dad left Joanna because of us and Joanna stayed with her husband because of Steven? Oh, my."

Judith shrugs. "No saying for certain. No way you can know unless you do meet Joanna one day and ask. But I'll stick with what I said ... no way your dad could ever turn away from a child of his. So, putting Steven aside, what other justification can you find for looking Joanna up?"

"Oh, damn it … none, I guess, besides my own need to get to know her, talk about Dad with her. I was hoping you'd go for the idea and encourage me. But you're right. If I force my mother to face the fact that Dad hid Joanna away all these years, it'll probably destroy my relationship with her. I can't do that."

"So where does that leave you?"

"I have to think about it. I have to think about the people I'd hurt if I pursue this. I'm not sure how it will go from here. I wish I could make it all go away … my eyes and open them to find all the e-mails, the songs, the poems … all of it, gone for good. I feel awful knowing I've probably spent all this energy and created so much dissension in my family for nothing."

"You know, my friend, it does seem you're the only one who cares about your father's past. Maybe you do need to back off."

I feel like I want to cry. Deep inside, I know I won't go any further and I feel like I'm giving up something hugely important. I wanted to know Joanna; I wanted to get close with her, understand what she and Dad had together. Realistically, I know that can't happen and yet I'm sad that it won't. I dab at my eyes and look at Judith.

"I know you're right. I know I should back off. Nothing's worth the risk of dredging up something that can only hurt Mom all over again. I'll try, Judith, honest I will, but it doesn't mean I have to like it."

Part Two

Twelve

November 2002

The look on Jason's face said it all. In one hand he held the envelope with its jagged edge showing how he'd ripped it open. In the other, he brandished a letter over his head, waving it as he came into the room.

"Dad, I'm accepted! They want me! Is this sweet or what?"

Andy jumped out of his chair and wrapped Jason in a hug. "That's terrific! Congratulations. I'm proud of you. When your mom gets home, we'll celebrate. Maybe dinner out?"

Jason stepped back and gave his father an intent look. He didn't see any hint that Andy was anything but pleased with the news. *At least Dad's okay with my choice*, he thought.

Andy took the letter and scanned the contents. It wasn't any different than the standard college early acceptance. He knew how much Jason wanted this, so he kept the smile on his face, hoping Marina would follow suit when she got the news.

"So what's the next step?"

"Nothing, except keep my grades up for the rest of the year and wait to hear from them sometime in the spring. I'm in. No more 'where to go to college' worries. What a relief!"

"Come on, buddy, you must have known you didn't have to worry; your grades have been super all through school. This is simply the reward you get for all your hard work."

Jason's face sobered. "But how do you think Mom's gonna feel about my going to Manning State? I can't help thinking she'd rather I picked another school. Why, for Pete's sake, would she feel that way? After all, Grandpa taught there. You'd think that would be enough to make her happy. I know he had a whole career at Roosevelt, but when he talked about the place he was the happiest, it was always Manning. Besides, the music program is one of the best in the country and you two won't have to pay a penny. Grandpa's trust will cover all four years unless there's a huge change in tuition, so why isn't Mom happy? Is it because I'll be so far from home?"

"No, I don't think it's the distance so much. Sure, Mom and I would rather you'd stay here and go to Roosevelt, Northwestern or the University of Illinois, but going away is part of what college is all about. It'll be good for you to be on your own, spread your wings a little and see another side of life in a different place. Besides, you'll be home at semester breaks and the holidays, so no, it's not the distance."

"Then I don't get it. You know how hard it was to convince her to let me apply. She kept saying I could do a lot better than Manning. I don't know why she even finally agreed."

"Because she wants what you want. She loves you, and once she saw how determined you were to make Manning your first choice, she dropped her objections and that was that."

"Anyhow, I'm glad we can stop wondering and I can finish my senior year knowing where I go from here."

"And that would be?" Marina asked from the doorway. "Is there a piece of news I missed?"

She looked from Andy to Jason. "Well?"

"I got in, Mom! The letter just came … here, read it. Early acceptance. I'm so psyched!"

She scanned the letter and looked over the paper at Andy who stood behind Jason watching her reaction.

"Well, congratulations, sweetheart," she said reaching out to draw Jason into a hug. "I know how much you wanted this and I couldn't be happier for you."

Andy saw the touch of sadness in her eyes, but nothing in her voice gave her away.

"Let's celebrate! What do you think, Andy?"

"Exactly what I just said to Jason. Thought we'd all go out to dinner. How about it?"

Jason turned toward the stairs. "Give me a few minutes to make some phone calls. Can we go in about a half hour? I want to let Scott and a couple other guys know."

"What about Uncle Mike? Can we tell him?" Marina asked as Jason bounded up the steps.

"Sure! He told me I'd get in without a hitch, so I know he'll be happy for me. I'll be down in a sec."

Marina sagged as she turned to Andy and walked into his open arms.

"How did I do? Do you think I convinced him I'm happy with his choice?"

"Uh-huh, you did fine. Before you came home, he was asking if I knew why you weren't real keen on Manning. He's a pretty sharp kid; he caught on to your reluctance from the start. He thought maybe it was the distance, but we agreed it would be okay since he'd be home for breaks and holidays. I don't know if he'll bring it up again, but I'm proud of you for changing your mind and giving him the chance to do what he wants so badly."

"I know. I don't have any concrete reason for objecting to Manning. It's just that there were so many memories tangled up with that place and then everything I learned after Dad died … I guess I wasn't ready to have Jason pick that university, of all places. It was selfish of me, and my reaction when he first told me was uncalled for. I want what's best for Jason like you do, hon. If studying music at Manning will make him happy, then it's settled. Why don't you call Mike and Ellen and let me change and freshen up a little before we go out."

Andy watched her climb the stairs, her step a bit heavy. *Good for her*, he thought. The last months hadn't been easy. For a while, he had been worried there might be serious trouble boiling up between them. Marina was so engrossed in the relationship between her father and the woman Jared had known when she was a child. And to think she actually wanted to contact Joanna whatever-her-name-was and take the risk of disrupting the whole family. Whatever had happened to change her mind, to make her step back and think twice about everything had been a blessing. He suspected Judith might have played a role in the change of heart, but mainly he was simply grateful it was all over. Marina hadn't talked about her father and this other woman for months. She'd gone back to work at the clinic, helped Mike and Ellen when Adam was born and even taken a few days' vacation to spend time with her mother as Vicki's move to Florida got closer.

Vicki had not been able to sort through Jared's things but never said anything. Everyone assumed it had been done. Marina finally got up the nerve to ask and found that his closet, chest of drawers and even his briefcase hadn't been touched, so she took the chore upon herself.

Andy remembered how hard sorting through her father's clothes and personal items had been. Many nights he knew

Marina lay awake, sometimes leaving their bed to spend hours in the den, her face white with fatigue the next morning. She was obviously agonizing over the task of disposing of her father's things as well as dealing with what she knew about his past. But gradually each day got a little better.

She seemed lighter, less weighed down with her father's secrets. Once the house on the lake was empty and Vicki was safely settled in Florida, Marina was less preoccupied, more in tune with him and Jason. *I don't know what went on in her head*, he thought, *but whatever it was, it's sure good to have her back.* Life had finally returned to normal. They were even making love regularly again.

~ * ~

Marina stared at her image in the mirror. The strained expression had finally faded. *I guess I look okay.*

Whole days went by without thoughts of her father and Joanna intruding on her tranquility, but only she knew the struggle it had taken to reach that point.

I didn't really have a choice, did I? Marina asked the face in the mirror. And her effort had succeeded. She hadn't put the disk containing those messages back into her computer once; she stopped listening to her dad singing to Joanna. A couple times she slipped and read the Benton poems, but even that, too, finally ended.

For it all, she was rewarded by her husband's attentiveness, his pleasure at her "coming to her senses," as he put it. Mike even took her aside after Adam's christening to thank her for abandoning her interest in Joanna. *Dad's probably smiling down at all of us today*, he had said.

Now here we are, so happily celebrating Jason's good news, sharing it with everyone in the family, patting him on the back and being glad for him. Yet soon he'll be right there, right where it all happened and I'll have to pretend I know nothing.

She smiled at her image ruefully and wondered how Joanna would feel about Jared's grandson being at Manning State. *It won't matter*, she muttered to herself. *I'm not going to think about this anymore. Joanna will never know.*

Thirteen

August 2003

Andy pulled into a parking slot in front of the rest stop on the Pennsylvania Turnpike at a few minutes after noon. Marina was dozing, the map askew on her lap. Jason's eyes were closed, too, but whether he was sleeping was hard to tell. He was wearing headphones as he had been for most of the ride, so Andy reached around and tapped him on the knee.

"Jason! We're stopping for lunch, buddy. You sleeping?"

"No, just listening," the boy replied without opening his eyes. "Where are we?"

"Almost to the Valley Forge exit. We've got forty-five minutes to go, maybe less, and I was kinda hoping you'd take over for a while after lunch. These interstates are so boring and I'm tired of driving."

Flipping off the headphones, Jason grinned at his father. "Boring to the driver, maybe, but I've had great music to keep me company. I guess it bored Mom to sleep, huh?"

He playfully reached over and tweaked his mother on the ear. "Earth to Mom! Jason to Mom! Come in, please!"

"I wasn't sleeping," Marina said indignantly. "I was dozing a bit. Where are we?"

"Not sleeping, huh? Dad just said where we are. Guess you didn't hear him 'cause you were in such a deep doze?"

Andy pushed open his door, stood outside and stretched as he looked around.

"This is pretty country, guys. Didn't realize how hot it is out here, though. Let's get lunch over with so we can keep moving. I'd like to get to Manning as soon as we can."

~ * ~

Traffic was increasingly heavier the closer they got to Philadelphia. At Valley Forge, they were stuck in a line of cars that inched its way along. Jason sat, impatiently drumming his fingers on the steering wheel. In a few minutes, though, he was able to pick up a little speed and soon found the roadway clearing. Andy closed his eyes; Marina resumed her reading. Jason let his thoughts wander to what he would find when he arrived at Manning.

As much as he'd hated leaving his friends, graduation had been as perfect as possible without Grandpa. Grandmom and Aunt Genna had come up from Florida and applauded wildly each time his name was announced for yet another award. Every time he looked out at their faces, Jason imagined his grandfather sitting there as he'd believed he would be. As he knew he *was*.

Classes at Manning were slated to begin the last week of August, with freshman orientation the week before. The package he had received from the college was fat with forms to be filled out and returned, packets of information about living and boarding arrangements, rules and regulations ending with a long list of required reading for the summer. Not that he minded. Next to fishing and music, reading was his favorite pastime, so he carefully ran through the titles, making as many as two trips a week to the library and lying awake long after midnight wading through the often-complex novels.

He had already been in touch with his suitemate, a guy from Newark, Delaware. Todd's parents had also been baffled by his choice of Manning when he lived only blocks from the University of Delaware. Todd wasn't certain of a major yet, although he was leaning toward psychology. From their phone conversations, Jason knew they would get along well. Todd was a jazz junkie, too; that was good enough for him.

At the exit, Jason reached for the ticket he'd tucked into the visor. Andy woke as Jason fumbled for his wallet.

"I've got it, Jason."

Taking the money from his father, Jason paid the toll and once again moved into heavy traffic.

"Guess this is the best we're gonna do," Andy remarked, craning his neck to look in front of them and then at the long row of cars in back. "This is almost like State Street in Chicago, for God's sake! No sense trying to hurry. No one's going anywhere very fast."

"I wish we had time to see Philadelphia," Marina grumbled. "It's just a few miles away and I've heard how pretty the skyline is. Oh well, we'll see it tomorrow on our way to the airport. How far is it to the university?"

"About twenty minutes, I think. I hope we aren't crawling like this the whole way."

The further north they traveled, the more traffic dropped off, leaving them space to travel faster as they passed into a more rural area.

"How are you holding up, Jason?" Marina asked.

Without looking back at her, Jason grinned. "Terrific! Dad was right; it's really pretty here. Lots of rolling green, even some good-sized farms. I'm surprised. I guess I thought Manning would be like an extension of Philly, crowded and all concrete."

"The pictures weren't like that at all, honey," Marina reminded him. "And from what we saw on the internet, the campus has a lot of open space, even a couple of lakes."

She pointed at a sign in front of them. "I guess we'll see it for ourselves pretty soon. It's only eight miles."

Not long before they neared the downtown area, a green highway sign directed traffic to the right for Manning University four miles north. There were homes on both sides of the roadway, two narrow lanes shaded by old oaks that met in the middle of the street. The houses sat back from the road, most with deep front porches sporting American flags that rippled gently in the hot summer breeze.

"How can there be a university here?" Jason asked.

Marina laughed. "We're about to find out ... hey! Get over to your right! Looks like the entrance to the campus is dead ahead."

Jason turned into the gated road that wound slowly past a small lake to his left and a combination of Georgian and modern brick buildings on the right. One side street was closed for construction with heavy equipment and dusty vehicles parked along the curb.

At the first crossroad, Jason pulled onto the shoulder and stopped. He looked up a narrow street to an expanse of green lawn with an imposing building at the far end, a clock tower on the top.

"That's Albertson Hall, the place I'll go to register for classes," he said excitedly. "I recognize it from the website."

Eager to show off his knowledge of the campus, he continued, pointing. "Next to Albertson is Kenton Hall. Just think. That's where Grandpa's office was, and right across the quad is the library."

Marina laughed soundlessly. *Just think, indeed.* What did Jason think she'd been doing the whole trip out? Of course, he'd have no way of knowing how she dreaded this moment. Maybe Andy had an inkling, but not even he could appreciate how difficult being here was.

~ * ~

Marina's apprehension had begun with the arrival of Jason's admissions package. The brochures showed the campus in all its spring finery ... the dogwoods along the lakes, the green lawns and old Georgian buildings. Of course, the campus was much larger than it had been when her father was there, but the name Kenton Hall jumped out at her, the only familiar building on the map.

It isn't fair, she'd thought, her eyes closed, lips compressed. After all the hard work to erase Joanna from her mind, soon she'd be at the very place where Joanna and her father had met and begun their affair.

Judith had listened as Marina railed on about the irony of Jason's choice. Then in her quiet, sensible way, she pointed out, "You haven't any choice, you know. To give Jason a hard time about the college he picked because of the unpleasant history behind the place wouldn't make any sense. Jason certainly doesn't know anything about his grandfather's younger years. All he knows is what your dad talked about, how much he loved Manning. Why wouldn't Jason be delighted to be there? You have to let him go."

As usual, Judith had been right on the money. As his senior year hummed along, filled with the excitement of his new driver's license, Christmas in Florida with the family, the prom, friends, parties and finally graduation, Jason's anticipation of attending Manning State mounted. Marina and Andy watched him begin to take on a more mature attitude, become the college student he so wanted to be.

Marina looked out the window to the left, her eyes squinting through the brilliance of the sunshine bouncing off the lake. *And now we're here.* Slowly, she turned the other way. Jason had parked the car on the side of a roadway lined with brick buildings. At the top of the drive on the right stood Kenton with its wide, graceful steps leading up to massive wooden double doors.

~ * ~

"C'mon, Mike! I'll race you. Bet I can climb up faster than you!" Their father stood on the sidewalk below, not paying much attention, his gaze fixed across the quad beyond Albertson toward the woods.

"Daddy! Watch! I'm gonna beat Mike up the steps! Daddy, watch!"

Halfheartedly, her father turned toward them. "Marina, Michael, stop! You're all dressed up. Come on now ... we'll go to the snack bar and get a soda before the play."

He held out his hands, reaching for theirs. "We can skip together, can't we?"

Giggling, they frolicked their way across the quad. At the head of the little path through the woods, they broke into single file.

"This is like the woods Hansel and Gretel went through, isn't it, Daddy? But as long as you're with us, nothing will ever hurt us, right?"

~ * ~

"Mom? Have you seen enough of this part of campus? Can we go on to my dorm? Mom?"

Marina's eyes cleared as she focused on her son behind the wheel. Oh, this was going to be so much harder than she'd feared.

~ * ~

Getting Jason settled in his tiny fourth-floor room in Jackson Tower wasn't as difficult as they'd expected. A heavy trunk filled with clothes and bedding had been sent ahead, so they took the rest on the elevator on the small furniture dolly they'd stowed in the back of the Subaru. A couple of boxes of books, a small television set and Jason's precious CD player and stereo system made another trip. Finally, Andy and Jason carried the computer and monitor into the room. Marina had finished making up the bed and was hanging clothes in the closet.

The room was pretty much as they'd expected, with a door leading into the bathroom Jason would share with Todd, who hadn't arrived yet. Marina sat on the bed and watched as Andy and Jason assembled the sound system and hooked up the computer. *It's a bit Spartan*, she thought, looking at the barren white concrete walls. She knew, though, that in a few days Jason would have posters hung and photos arranged on his desk, the room as comfortable as the one at home had always been. *He's a bit of a nester*, she thought. *Not a bad trait in a man.*

Jason was gleeful, practically bouncing with excitement. "I know it's hot, but would you mind if we walked around campus a little? I want to get the feel of it and I want you to know where things are so you'll know what I'm talking about when I call or write about them. Okay?"

Marina opened the bathroom door. "Let me take a second, honey. You and Dad go on ahead and I'll meet you in the lobby."

Inside, she locked the door to the adjoining room and leaned heavily on the sink. The walk would undoubtedly bring back more memories. Places she'd long forgotten, or thought she had. Questions that skittered around in her mind like blowing pieces of dust. Where did they meet, where did Joanna live, how could their togetherness have gone undetected in this tightly arranged place? There were barely a few yards between academic and residence halls. She knew the original campus consisted of only a handful of buildings nestled among those that had been built in the last forty years. Mentally, she tried to remove the newer ones and picture the campus as she remembered it. She imagined her father making his way from Kenton to the student center. If he'd been with someone frequently, everyone on campus would surely have known. She wondered how far into the future such a scandal might have been projected. Thankfully, her son's last name wasn't Fowler. Shrugging off the thought, she squared her shoulders and unlocked the door, going out into the room Jason would occupy for the coming year.

As the elevator slowly descended to the ground floor, she thought no matter what Jason had waiting for him here at Manning, he was strong and smart enough to handle it. She only prayed nothing would happen that would tarnish that sacred image he held of his grandfather.

~ * ~

Beyond the confines of Kenton Hall, the quad and the small patch of woods, nothing else triggered memories. It was indeed a beautiful campus, the walk unhurried and punctuated by Jason's narrative as he quoted from the information he'd received in the mail or from pages he'd visited on the internet.

"I sure could use something cold to drink," Andy interrupted at one point as Jason led them in still another direction toward a tight cluster of two-story buildings.

Jason pointed. "The student center is right across the street. We can take a break there."

The building wasn't at all familiar to Marina.

~ * ~

They'd begun skipping again as they came out of the woods and crossed the street to the place where Daddy said they could get their sodas. The sidewalk slanted up to a small door that Daddy reached across Mike's head to open. The room wasn't big, but it was crowded with students and very noisy. Daddy was talking to the people and she tried to pay attention but she wanted to get her drink and go back to the theater to see the costumes.

~ * ~

Inside, she was convinced this was not the same place.

"Is this the original student center?" she asked Jason.

"No, I don't think so. It said on the website the original was torn down in the seventies and this larger one built. That's about the time the college changed over to a university and enrollment really increased a lot. Why? Do you remember any of this place, Mom? Did Grandpa ever bring you and Uncle Mike here?"

"It's hard to remember back that far, Jason."

Marina looked around the room and shook her head. "There was only one time I recall clearly and that's why I asked about the student center. Dad brought us to campus to see a musical and we came here, or to whatever building used to be here, for a drink before the play. I vaguely remember Kenton Hall and the quad, but nothing else."

She hoped Jason didn't pick up on the little lie.

"You were probably too young, huh?"

"Uncle Mike was about five, I guess, and I wasn't quite eight. We left Manning the following summer so, yes, it's been a very long time."

~ * ~

After dinner at a nearby restaurant, Andy and Marina left Jason so he could spend the evening with his new suitemate. They'd reserved a room at a small bed and breakfast not far from the university and gratefully sank onto the bed, dangling their feet off the side.

Andy exhaled deeply. "I'm exhausted! I can't remember when I've walked that much."

Marina was almost too tired to answer. "Me too. I could close my eyes and fall asleep right now, clothes and all."

Andy rolled to one side, his eyes fixed on her face. "You were very brave today. I was proud of you. Was it as hard as you thought it would be?"

She felt tears starting but knew she couldn't show them, even to Andy.

"Harder. Oh Andy, it brought it all up again! Every bit of it. Dad and Joanna, Dad and Mike and me, the feeling of safety I always had with Dad and then the knowledge there was someone in this world, this place, who was so important to him. He must have risked everything for that affair. I guess I hadn't remembered how small Manning was, how few places there would have been to hide. Now I can just imagine … everyone must have known. You don't suppose Jason will ever get wind of it, do you?"

"Nah, not after all these years. People forget; people leave for other places; people die, like Dad. I doubt there's anyone left who remembers him. He was only here five years, remember, not an entire career and that was a long, long time ago. No way Jason will ever stumble on anything that would clue him in."

Fourteen

Even though it had been almost two years since the horrific terrorist attacks that were spawned in the air, Marina was still uneasy about flying. Knowing Jason would worry if he knew how she felt, she didn't mention it as she and Andy got into the taxi in front of Jason's dorm.

"Have fun, honey!" she'd called as they pulled away. The decision to leave the Outback with him hadn't been a snap one. They'd worried that having a car on campus might be a distraction. But once he assured them he'd use it only on weekends, they relented.

Philadelphia hadn't been disappointing. With a late afternoon flight time, she and Andy had been able to take a brief tour of the downtown historical sites. They stopped at Independence Hall and waited in a long line to clear security for the chance to see the Liberty Bell up close. The Delaware River breeze on Penn's Landing was refreshing, so they walked over to where a very good jazz band from Rutgers University was performing. They agreed the Philadelphia riverfront didn't measure up to Navy Pier in Chicago, but it made for a fun change of scene.

In the taxi on the way to the airport, with Joanna on her mind, Marina asked the driver where they were in relation to the Temple University campus. He told her they would have to go several miles to the northern part of town to get there. *Just as well*, she thought.

~ * ~

She was totally unprepared for what she felt when she walked into the house. It was so quiet. No music blared from the second floor. Jason's room looked barren and cold, posters off the wall, knick-knacks and photos missing from the dresser. No computer, no stereo. She sank onto the bed and caught her breath. Andy found her after he'd roamed the first floor calling her name.

"You okay? Miss him already, huh?"

She didn't trust herself to answer without crying.

Andy looked around the room. "Yeah, me, too. I guess this is what all parents go through when the baby bird leaves the nest. Wonder how long it takes to get used to the quiet?"

Marina looked up and gave him a slight smile. "I bet *he's* not homesick. He's probably having a ball with all his new friends and looking forward to the start of classes. I think we were wise to let him go so far away. Even if it is Manning with all its ghosts, he'll be totally on his own and whatever he does with his life will be his own choosing. Sure does make for a big adjustment here, though."

~ * ~

Actually, Jason *was* homesick at first. His days were filled with new experiences, new people, new places, but at night, after everyone had closed the doors to their rooms, he lay awake, wondering how things were going at home, wishing he could tell his mom and dad about everything that was going on.

Gradually, that feeling diminished. In its place, Jason often found himself up well into the night drinking black coffee while finishing an assignment or compiling necessary research for a required paper. *Amazing how fast these professors threw us right into it*, he thought. *I guess if we're good enough to get in here, we're good enough to hit the ground running. No easing into anything, that's for sure.*

Surprisingly, while he enjoyed his introductory courses in music, Jason found himself delving even more deeply into composition and reading. A freshman year language arts course was required, taught by a likeable young instructor, a graduate assistant who pushed his students to write. Getting A's proved easy for Jason. At the end of the first three weeks, he knew he was polishing his writing skills already, thanks to the careful critiques of his instructor and his determination to be an effective communicator.

Being where his grandfather had been, looking across the quad at the window of what had once been Jared Fowler's office, walking along the same polished halls to and from some of his music classes, Jason felt he was never alone, that his grandfather walked beside him, encouraging him, smiling with him at each new discovery.

~ * ~

Jason was immersed in the catalogs at the library, savoring the silence and the comfort of the old building with its upstairs classrooms and musty corners. One of his new composition assignments was to write about someone who'd greatly influenced his life.

He had chosen to write about his grandfather. Despite his love for Marina and Andy, no one had touched him the way Jared Fowler had. It was a given from the start that he'd dedicate this writing assignment to his idol.

He and Todd had checked each other's topics and talked about what they planned to write.

"I want to go deeper into Grandpa's life," Jason said one night as they sat in Todd's room listening to a Winton Marsalis CD. "He was a Navy pilot in World War Two and after he got his bachelor's degree, he went straight on to his Ph.D. Then he came here to teach and direct. The college was pretty small then, so probably everyone knew him. I'm sure if I look through the old newspapers, I'll find something. No way *The Target* didn't print some news stories about him."

So here he was in the library, slowly scanning the microfiche, starting with issues from the late fifties. He knew his grandfather had come to Manning in '57, so he started there. Almost immediately, he found an item announcing Fowler's arrival.

The article talked about his war service, his doctoral thesis subject (*stage fright? No kidding!*), the degrees he had earned. It said Dr. Fowler would be in an office in Kenton Hall and was already assembling a cast for the first play he would be directing. Manning State was fortunate to have him on the faculty, the article concluded, as it wished him well.

In '58, there were rave reviews of the two plays his grandfather had directed. Jason made quick notes as he scrolled down the pages. He jotted down favorable comments about Fowler's work as well as his penchant for spending time with his students. It was a trait, the paper said, that was rapidly making him one of the most popular faculty members on campus.

Each year, play after play, Fowler was frequently featured on *The Target's* pages. The article in the November sixteenth, 1960 edition praised his direction of the complex play *Under Milk Wood*, a dark study of life in a small town done entirely by voices of cast members dressed in black. While he made a mental note to check out the play when he had a chance, Jason kept on reading.

The May seventeenth, 1962 edition announced Fowler's departure. The following week, Jason was surprised to find a small box on the third page asking, *"Which wife is Dr. Fowler taking with him?"* Wondering what he'd missed, Jason scrolled back to the previous issue and again read the story about his grandfather's new job at Roosevelt University. He had to read it twice more before he saw the reason for the follow-up comment. *"A wife and two children will accompany him,"* the article said. Jason chuckled. Obviously, the editors were satirically admonishing themselves for the mistake they'd made the previous week. *They must have meant* his *wife*, Jason thought, smiling quietly at the fun the newspaper writers poked at themselves and imagining how his grandfather must have enjoyed the play on words.

The last mention of Fowler came in the edition following his final musical, *Oklahoma*. Although the review was flattering, fewer comments were made about the play than of the farewell cast party he had thrown for his students afterwards. Jason smiled as he read about the warm send-off everyone had enjoyed. *It was so like Grandpa to show his appreciation that way.*

A photo accompanied the article. There he was, Jared Fowler, tall and handsome, surrounded by students. He was looking at the young woman next to him and holding her hand. The rest of the students were looking at her, too. No one was smiling; in fact, they all looked sober and uncomfortable. The caption didn't give him any clues to what he thought he saw.

Departing Theater Director and Associate Professor of Drama, Dr. Jared Fowler, is shown with Joanna Ransome ('63), the play's production supervisor, at the biggest cast party ever held on the Manning campus. Calling his years at Manning, and particularly this one, "the most precious of my life," Dr. Fowler expressed his appreciation to the cast and his students for their support and caring.

Jason studied the photo for a long time. He looked at the face of his grandfather, his mind contriving explanations for what might have been going on as the photo was snapped. *Which wife is Dr. Fowler taking with him? Nah, I'm imagining things,* he told himself as he instructed the microfilm machine to print out the page.

He left the library, a folder containing the photo in his hand. Back in his room, he took it out and stood it against the computer monitor. Jared Fowler's face, the expression in his eyes, made Jason think there was a special connection to the girl. *Couldn't be,* he thought. His grandfather was married. *Mom and Uncle Mike were little kids; they moved right after that. No way there was anything going on.*

But try as he might, he couldn't get the images and the words out of his mind. Jason felt a profound unease, like he'd intruded somewhere he neither intended nor wanted to go.

Fifteen

The photo went back into its folder in Jason's desk drawer. He worked diligently on the paper and thought the final product was pretty good. So, too, did the instructor, who promptly asked Jason to read parts of it for the class.

"Imagine, folks, Jason here is treading on the path of the great director, Dr. Jared Fowler!" said the instructor, gesturing theatrically. He smiled. "Thanks, Jason. I enjoyed reading about your granddad. You know, you ought to walk around campus a little during Alumni Weekend. There might be some of his former students here. They probably could tell you even more about him."

"Thanks," Jason agreed tentatively. "That's a good idea."

~ * ~

"What do you think, Todd? What do you make of all this?"

Jason had finally decided to share what he had learned. Over dinner a few days later, he talked to Todd about his misgivings.

Todd listened patiently to the story about the newspaper article, the follow-up question and the caption for the photo. When they got back to the dorm, Jason showed him the picture.

"Well? What do you make of it?" he repeated.

Todd shook his head. "I don't know what to tell you, J."

He stared at the picture for a few minutes. "You sure look a lot like him. Just the hair color's different, but especially the eyes. Shit, it must be weird to know you look so much like somebody else."

Jason scrutinized the photo again.

"Yeah, you can really see the resemblance here. Actually, I've always been kind of proud that I look so much like him. But what do you think about this girl and the 'which wife' thing?"

"Don't know what to think. But hell, that was ages ago! What difference does any of it make now?"

Jason replaced the photo in the folder. "I guess that's what I wanted somebody to tell me. My grandparents had been married for over fifty years when Grandpa died. Don't know what I was thinking ... 'which wife!' How stupid!"

"But what the T.A. said, now that's not a bad idea. Why don't you check out the list of alumni next weekend and see if anyone's back from the years he was here. Who knows? You might even run across one of his drama students who made it to the big time."

~ * ~

Joanna pulled her car into the driveway in front of the small bed and breakfast in Yardley on the Friday of Alumni Weekend. *I don't know why I'm doing this*, she thought. She sat there for a few minutes, fighting the urge to back out and go home, down the country roads that would take her to the ocean, to her solitude, back to the book that was finished but for the final proofreading.

A commitment is a commitment, she reminded herself, slowly opening the door and pulling her overnight case from the back seat.

The letter had arrived a good two months ago. The new director of the counseling psychology center had been doing some reading and discovered the work by Dr. Doris Wayne, Manning State's first counseling psychologist, who had conducted a well-known research study during her first year at the college.

"I was thrilled to discover that you had worked with Dr. Wayne on this project," the letter said, *"and I am writing to invite you to speak to a group of graduate students about the study. We would like to know how the topic was selected, more of Dr. Wayne's background than we can find in biographical accounts and anything else you think might be of interest. I hope you will consent to share with us."*

She had agreed to make the trip. She had met Doris in her freshman year, developed an almost sisterly relationship with her, worked long hours with her on the now-famous research and stayed in Doris' life right up to her death in 1992. *Only for Doris,* she thought. *There wouldn't be anyone else who could lure me back to Manning.* But of course, there was. She knew someone else might also be responsible for her return.

After all, it was October. She would be back on campus at nearly the same time of the year she and Jared had first met, the time Doris introduced them and explained their research to him. While Doris talked, Joanna had studied his face. He had caught her at it, too, and embarrassed her when he asked about her part in the experiment. She knew she had blushed and grown flustered when she tried to answer his simple questions. It was then he had first looked at her with those compelling eyes and spoken her name with a voice that still echoed in her mind, rapped tenderly at her heart.

I'll feel him with me, she mused silently. *We'll be together on campus again. I guess that's why I agreed to come.*

~ * ~

"What do you say, Todd? After dinner, want to go into town for a movie?"

The two were walking across campus from Jackson to the dining hall. Todd didn't have a car, so he and the other guys often piled into Jason's for their trips into Manning for a movie or hanging at the mall checking out the girls.

In the dining hall lobby, Todd stopped to say hi to some of his friends from one of the other dorms. Jason looked around, noted a new standup bulletin board in the aisle next to the door. His glance passed over and then turned back to the poster on the easel.

"Hey, I'll be right back," he said to Todd, who was too engrossed in his conversation to notice.

Jason walked over to the display and stopped about two feet away from it.

Alumni Weekend
Graduate Psychology Students
and anyone interested in the
theories of Carl Rogers are cordially invited
to a lecture/discussion with Manning alumna
Dr. Joanna Ransome Webber
Where: Student Center Conference Room
When: Saturday from 1 to 3 p.m.

Dr. Webber's face stared out at him from a large, color photo. Something about the name clicked in his mind. Dr. Joanna Ransome Webber. Then he remembered—the old newspaper clipping with his grandfather! Had to be the same person. How many Joanna Ransomes could there be? Especially alumna?

Turning, he gestured to Todd who was breaking away from the crowd.

He inclined his head toward the board. "Come look at this. Can you believe it?"

Todd read the announcement and looked at the picture. "So? Since when are you interested in psychology?"

"Look, doofus, look at the name of the speaker. Joanna Ransome? Ring a bell? My grandfather and—"

"Oh, wow! Joanna Ransome! Do you think it's the same person?"

"Of course. There can't be more than one Joanna Ransome who was here then. Remember you said I should try to find somebody who knew my grandfather, even studied with him? How much better can this be?"

"Right. It's is as good as it gets. Maybe you can talk with her before she does her thing. She might even give you some time after it's over. If she and your granddad worked together, I'll bet she'd be happy to meet you."

"I'll give it a try," Jason said as they went down the hall. "Something tells me she's going to be a real link to him. Imagine! Forty-odd years after he taught here, I'm gonna get to talk to someone who actually knew him."

"What about that photo? Still have questions?"

"Yeah, I guess, but I don't think I want to get into that. And when I meet Dr. Webber, I sure don't want to start off on the wrong foot by saying or asking something I might regret. They worked closely together, y'know. He was saying his goodbyes at that cast party. Why wouldn't everyone look a little serious?"

"Well," Todd said, "if you still have any doubts, you'd have the chance to clear them all up when you talk with her. You might even unearth a mystery connection," he narrowed his eyes, waved his hands in the air and imitated the theme from *The Twilight Zone*. "Doo-doo-doo-doo, doo-doo-doo-doo!"

"You're crazy, man, you know that?" Jason was laughing as they walked toward his car.

~ * ~

Back in his room after the movie, Jason waited until the lights went out under the door to Todd's room. He opened the drawer and took out the folder. Standing the photo against the computer, he stared at his grandfather and Joanna.

What was going on, Grandpa? Was she just somebody you worked with on the play? Did you hold everyone else's hand at that party? And why was that year so precious?

Leaving the photo on the desk, he turned out his light and got into bed. Maybe meeting Dr. Webber wasn't a very bright idea after all. What would he say to her? *Hi, I'm Jared Fowler's grandson.* Then what? C'mon, he was more socially adept than that. Making small talk with strangers was something he did easily. Besides, he and Dr. Webber were already connected. She just didn't know it yet and he wasn't exactly sure how.

~ * ~

Joanna slept in later than usual, took a leisurely shower and put on a dark blue suit with a sleeveless silk blouse. Every time she wore a blue silk blouse, she thought of the one Jared always loved. She had worn it often when they were together and even today it hung on a satin hanger in the back of her closet, at least a couple of sizes too small and faded from disuse. Each season she managed to have a blue silk blouse in her wardrobe, just for Jared.

Brunch was extravagant, tables laden with pastries, hotcakes, casseroles, toast and eggs. Joanna groaned at the sight of so much temptation.

Reminding herself gently that the scales had begun to creep up a bit, she put some scrambled eggs on her plate and added a mound of fresh California strawberries. A cup of fragrant hazelnut coffee completed the meal, during which she good-naturedly resisted the urging of her hostess to sample more of the food that was artfully arranged on the buffet.

Looking at her watch, Joanna realized it was still far too early to show up on campus for the, what should she call it … appearance? Lecture? She settled on "program." In reality, she hadn't done much to prepare, only thrown together a couple of pages to hand out. She hoped the students would have enough questions about Doris's work to fill the two hours allotted.

So what to do to kill time? She smiled goodbye to the hostess. As she walked toward the door, "Misty" began playing softly overhead.

Of course, that was her answer … she could spend some time with Jared, walk through the woods, perhaps sit on Kenton Hall's steps. It had been a few years since she had done that. Jared would be happy to know she was back.

~ * ~

Jason spent most of his Saturday morning working on the piece he was perfecting for his upcoming audition for the university's jazz band. Underclassmen were welcome to try out for the three empty slots and he intended to be good enough to snag one. The practice rooms in Kenton Hall were nearly deserted as they were on most Saturday mornings, when early practice was the last thing on most students' minds.

At about noon, he carefully wiped the drumsticks and stowed them in their case, returned the drum to its storage closet and put the sheet music back in the drawer that had his name on the identification plate.

He started slowly up the stairs, his mind on the coming meeting with Dr. Webber. He'd have time for lunch as he waited to intercept her before she went into the conference room. Maybe he'd find Todd or one of the other guys in the dining hall.

Jason rounded the corner toward the huge foyer with its polished floor and marble walls and looked toward the door of the office that had been his grandfather's. *What had it looked like inside?* Probably neat and orderly, like everything else in Dr.

Jared Fowler's world, a place where he could sit with students and work out their problems.

There was a woman standing outside the office door. She was petite and trim, neatly outfitted in a dark blue suit and simple navy pumps. Her hair touched her shoulders; her hands hung at her sides. What intrigued him was that she didn't move, just stood very still.

Deciding not to bother her, he began to walk toward the outside double doors. As he reached them, he looked behind and saw she had remained motionless.

Turning back, he said, "Excuse me, may I help you with something?"

It was Joanna Ransome. He recognized her as soon as she turned. He was totally unprepared for her reaction, though. The color drained from her face as her eyes widened and he heard a sharp intake of breath.

"Oh, my God," she muttered, meeting his eyes. "Oh, my God."

Sixteen

Joanna didn't know why she'd chosen Kenton as her first stop on campus. Maybe it was because the public parking lot was located right behind the building and maybe because the temptation to revisit the home of Jared's office was too great. She left the car and walked toward the steps. There was so much new construction taking place, many more new buildings since she'd been there in '95. She had written to Jared about the way the college had changed, lamenting the loss of the intimacy and warmth of the tiny campus they had loved.

She hadn't intended to go in. No one was around to ask her purpose, though, so she went up the steps, opened one of the double doors and walked into the lobby. It was dark and still. Directly ahead were the doors to the auditorium where she'd received her degree, thanks to a teeming downpour that had ruined their outdoor graduation plans. She opened a door and peeked inside at the rows of newly-reupholstered seats and the stage where Jared's plays had been performed. Closing the door quietly, she turned back to the foyer. On the left was the door to Jared's office. He'd kissed her there for the first time and, closing her eyes, she could still see the mementos of his theater career framed on the wall and smell the fragrance of tobacco and Old Spice.

She walked toward the door and stopped. If she listened carefully, she would hear Jared's voice welcoming her as he did every time she stopped in between classes. The rumbling bass echoed through the emptiness now, and hearing it made Joanna smile.

When a male voice interrupted her reverie, she turned, ready to politely greet whomever had intruded.

The handsome face in front of her swam slightly as she fought to keep control.

How could he be here? How could someone look so much like Jared? Am I hallucinating? The thoughts flew through her mind in an instant as she felt the young man's hand reach out to steady her.

"Are you all right?"

She managed a weak nod. *This can't be! Right here outside Jared's office, this apparition standing right in front of me, this younger version of Jared...*

Then she could see him clearly. Instantly, she was back in the funeral home in Illinois, watching Jared's family file slowly out of the room after the service. This must be Jason, she remembered then ... Jared's grandson, the grieving young man she'd ached for as she saw his tears, heard his choked sobs. *And now he's here?*

Stepping back to release his hand from her arm, Joanna fumbled with her purse and took out a packet of tissues. Removing one, she dabbed her eyes, took a deep breath and looked up.

She managed a weak smile. "I'm so sorry. I didn't mean to alarm you. It's just that I was certain I was alone. I'm fine, truly I am."

"I'm glad," Jason replied. "I'm sorry I startled you, Dr. Webber. Welcome back to Manning."

Joanna took a step backward. "How do you know who I am?"

"Easy. Your picture is on a large bulletin board in the foyer of the dining hall. I've been waiting to talk to you ever since I saw it."

"My program is on a research project I helped complete many, many years ago. Are you a psychology student?"

Jason shook his head, the light hair falling over his eyes.

"No, actually I'm a music major, which explains what I'm doing here. The jazz band tryouts are next week and I'm hoping to qualify, so I was downstairs practicing. It wasn't your program that caught my attention, Dr. Webber, it was you. I recognized your name from an article in *The Target* about my grandfather. Oh, I'm sorry, I didn't even introduce myself ... my name is Jason Buckman. My grandfather, Jared Fowler, worked here for about five years and I believe you knew him well. You were in a photo the paper ran that was taken the night of Grandpa's last cast party. When I saw you were coming to campus to speak, I decided to find you and see if we could talk about your memories of him."

Without waiting for her answer, he went on. "He talked often about this place. He loved Manning, which is one of the reasons I decided to enroll here. We were very close. He died about a year and a half ago and I still miss our talks about the old days. I thought maybe you had some particular memories of him you'd be willing to share."

Particular memories? Oh Jason, you can't imagine the memories I have of your grandfather. But I truly don't think you want to know. How to handle this? What to tell this earnest teenager with the face of the man I loved?

She needed some time … time to absorb the shock of seeing Jared's grandson standing right outside his door. Glancing at her watch, she said, "Of course I'd be pleased to talk with you. Right now, I need to be at the program and I think it will probably last about two hours. Where would you like to meet?"

"How about the snack bar in the student center? On second thought, it can get awfully noisy in there. Maybe the lounge in my dorm would be better. I'm in Jackson Tower, right behind the student center. It would mean a lot to me."

~ * ~

It was fortunate that Joanna was able to easily discuss the project she had worked on with Doris. She thought she was probably getting the gist of all the questions and she hoped her answers were coherent. Her mind wasn't on the topic at hand; she was thinking ahead to what she would say to Jason, how she would paint the picture of her relationship with his grandfather. She had mixed feelings about the chat. On one hand, she relished the chance to spend some time with this replica of Jared. On the other, she knew how carefully she would have to tread the fine line between describing a popular professor who was idolized by his students and someone she loved very deeply.

Is this why you brought me here today, Jared? Did you want me to meet your grandson, the boy you loved so much? What do I tell him? How can I speak to him about you in neutral terms, darling Jared, the student discussing a favorite professor? How can you ask me to do this? We never intended for your family to be brought into our world and now Jason is here, in our place, asking me about our time together. I don't know if I can do it.

~ * ~

It was almost three. Jason closed the book he'd been reading, stood and walked toward the door of his room. His eyes rested on the folder on the desk. He had been debating ever since he had run into Dr. Webber about taking the photo with him and asking her to tell him about that night. Now he made up his mind in an instant. If he didn't ask, he would always wonder. What better time than when she was right here, the only person who could fill in the blanks.

Why had she been she so stunned when she saw him? She'd said she was startled. *If you ask me,* he thought, *it was more than that...she was blown away!* He supposed Todd was right; the resemblance to Grandpa was uncanny. Maybe that's what threw her, sort of like seeing a ghost. But why no reaction to the news that he'd died? She didn't say, "I'm so sorry to hear about his death." It was like she already knew.

Joanna wasn't waiting in the lounge. No one was in the room at all, so Jason sat, folder on his lap, and waited. After a few minutes, it occurred to him she might have been held up at the program longer than she had expected. He could save her the walk and simply meet her there.

The distance was short. As always, Jason enjoyed walking through the golden and red leaves that were matted along the sidewalks like pieces of bright lace against the hem of a long gown. He particularly loved the small stretch of woods between the center and the library, the path he took to most of his classes in the new music building next to Kenton. He enjoyed the quiet sense of peace he found on this campus and with each day he understood even more why his grandfather had loved it.

There was no one standing outside the door to the conference room. Peering inside, he saw only empty chairs, a sheet of paper or two on the dais in front. He glanced around the foyer and down the hallway for some sign of her. It was a few minutes after three. Perhaps she'd stopped in the snack bar for a cup of coffee, so after a few minutes he walked in and looked around. Only a few tables were occupied; Joanna was not there either. Returning to the foyer, he sat again, tapping his fingers on the folder in his hand. Where could she be?

When a half hour had passed and she still hadn't appeared, Jason slowly made his way back to his dorm. In his mail slot there was a note from the residence assistant.

Jason:

You had a call from Dr. Joanna Webber. She said to tell you she was called away unexpectedly and wouldn't be able to meet with you. She said she was sorry and hoped you didn't wait too long. She didn't leave a number.

Al.

Disappointed, and feeling very angry, Jason went back to his room, dropped the folder on his desk and stood staring out the window. What could have been that important? Why did she leave without rescheduling a meeting?

Seventeen

"Damn it!" Jason shouted, slamming his books down on the desk. "She didn't show up! I was really looking forward to talking to her!"

Todd looked at him with surprise. "Hey, what gives? Man, I've never seen you this mad. Aren't you overreacting? She had some place to go, so?"

"So, she promised me she'd be there. She seemed fine about getting together. Hey, if it was true she had to go so suddenly, why didn't she at least leave me a phone number? It's almost like she decided to blow me off."

The phone on Jason's desk jangled loudly. Todd stood and went through the doorway of their common bathroom. Looking back, he said, "Go ahead, answer that. I'm gonna do a little reading and after you calm down, we can go out for something to eat."

"Yeah," Jason replied as he picked up the receiver.

"Jason? Hi, it's Mom. Haven't heard from you in a few days so I thought I'd try catching you in. Am I lucky or what?"

"Yep, I'm here." His voice was flat, dispirited.

"Is anything wrong, honey? You don't sound like yourself."

"No ... yeah, something, but it's not important."

"Well, how are things going out there? Any word on the date of your audition for the jazz band?"

"Not yet. They're supposed to post the dates on the board on Monday. I'll call you when I know."

"You sound totally down. Are you sure there's not something bothering you?"

"Well, I was hoping to talk to you about it after my meeting today, but I got stood up, so you might as well know. Don't know if it'll ever happen anyhow."

"Jason, you're being vague."

"I don't think I told you, but we had an assignment to write about someone influential in our lives and I wrote about Grandpa's life. Well, while I was doing some research in the library, I found some old newspaper clippings. In one of them, there was a picture of him taken with some of his students at a cast party his last year here. Turns out, one of the people in the picture was actually a guest speaker on campus this weekend, an alumni forum, or something like that. Anyway, I ran into her in Kenton and asked if we could get together to talk about Grandpa. She sounded okay with it, even like she'd be glad to get together. But she never showed up. And then I got a message saying she was sorry, she'd been called away and that was that. No explanation at all. Can't figure it out."

Marina had been listening with chagrin and a growing sense of dread. *Oh, no, Jason's going back to the old days, just as I feared. This girl in the photo ... please don't let it be Joanna,* she prayed silently. There were so many students that worked with Jared; *please let it be any one of the others.*

When he finished and stopped for breath, Marina said, "I'm sorry about that, honey. Who was the student?"

"Some famous psychologist named Dr. Joanna Webber. She was Joanna Ransome when she had her picture taken with Grandpa."

Slowly exhaling, trying to sound normal, Marina asked, "Did she leave you a phone number or any way to reach her?"

"Nope. Man, I am so disappointed! From what I read, I think she probably knew Grandpa well and I was counting on talking about him."

"I'm sorry too," Marina lied. "Oh well, you tried your best. She's probably a very busy person and it was so long ago, perhaps she didn't want to take the time."

On the other end of the phone, Jason let out a long breath.

"I suppose that could be it," he said, his tone doubtful. "Still, that was so rude. She never even left her phone number."

"Look, I'm certain there's a simple explanation. Some people are so preoccupied with their own lives they don't think about how their behavior affects others. She probably didn't realize how important this was to you," Marina reasoned. "You wrote a tribute to your grandfather and he'd be very proud of you. Why not leave it at that? Now, I'll be anxious to hear that the audition has gone well. Your dad and I can hardly wait to come out for your first band concert."

"Well, I hope there will be one," Jason said, his voice brightening. "I wish you could hear the piece I'm working on for the audition. Pretty good, if I do say so myself."

"I'm sure it is, hon. Keep up the good work and I'll check with you again in a few days. Everyone sends their love."

"Thanks, give mine back. Talk to you soon."

He hung up and sat at the desk. He looked at the photo again—Joanna Ransome holding his grandfather's hand. *I don't buy her I-was-just-a-student crap for a second. I saw the expression on her face in Kenton. Think that far back? She didn't have to dig very far back for that look she gave me. Grandpa isn't ancient history to her. She just doesn't want to tell me why and that's why she didn't show up.*

~ * ~

The back door closed as Marina switched off the phone.

"Marina? You home?" Andy's voice got louder as he came closer to the den. "Hi, babe! How was your day?"

Marina turned to look at him. "It was fine until about three minutes ago. I just got off the phone with Jason."

"Is something wrong? Is he sick?"

She shook her head and put the phone down in the charger. "No, he's not sick. But something is bothering him, my worst nightmare come true."

Andy sat down across from her. "What is it?"

Her face was grim. "It's Joanna Ransome. Name ring a bell? Well, coincidentally, Joanna turned up in person at Manning and Jason came this close to talking with her about Dad." She put her two fingers within an inch of each other.

"He went looking for her when he found out she would be on campus for Alumni Weekend. Apparently, he'd come across some old clippings when he was doing a paper about Dad and they were pictured together. He met her, of all places, in Kenton Hall and arranged to see her after some program she was involved in so they could talk about Dad. When the time came, though, she never showed up. So now Jason's upset because he thinks she has something to hide."

"Is that what he said?"

"In so many words. I tried to slough it off by saying Joanna was probably very busy, but I don't think he bought my explanation. Now I'm not certain he won't try to contact her again and that really worries me."

"Did she leave him a number? An address?"

"No, neither. That upset him ... she didn't at least leave her number. And you know Jason, how tenacious he can be when he wants to get at the root of something. I'm concerned he'll poke around campus until he finds a way to track her down. Then what? What if they actually get together and he pumps her for information about Dad?"

"I don't have an answer to that one. Boy, how I wish we didn't know any of this. No, no, I won't go back and revisit the hours we spent arguing over your digging into Dad's past. That's all behind us and I do understand now why you needed to know. But the fact remains we *do* know. I guess we wait and hope Jason drops this and moves on."

Marina sat silently for several minutes. When she spoke, her voice had a hint of defiance in it, as if anticipating an argument.

"I've been thinking. Maybe it's better for Jason to hear the whole story so he'll see the wisdom of leaving it alone. No ... no..." she raised her hand in protest as Andy tried to interject. "No, you know Jason's old enough to understand situations like Dad and Joanna. He's a bright guy. He reads, he watches TV, goes to movies. People have affairs and some manage to work through them without the total destruction of their families. Dad did that. Surely Jason could eventually learn to see this affair that way."

"I wasn't going to argue with you," Andy said. "I'm not against Jason's knowing about what happened. It's just that I'm looking a step ahead. Suppose he finds out Joanna and your father were in contact right up to Dad's death. How do you think he'll feel about your father then? That's what I wouldn't want to see happen. Hell, I'm surprised he hasn't put two and two together and remembered seeing Joanna at the funeral home or the cemetery. Let's hope he wasn't paying attention."

"Agreed. And all the more reason why we should talk with Jason before he figures everything out on his own or finds Joanna somehow and coaxes the details out of her. Look, he's going to know Monday when his audition for the jazz band will be scheduled. They told him they'd give him a decision right away. That means sometime before the end of next week, he'll have news for us, either good or bad. Why don't we go out there and spend a couple days with him? We could fly out Friday and come back Sunday. Either way, we need to be the ones to talk to Jason about his grandfather. What do you think?"

"I agree that's a logical thing to do, maybe the best we *can* do. I don't want Jason hurt. If he hears from anyone else about the campus gossip back then, he'll be crushed and angry. Maybe we can present the circumstances in a more acceptable light, help him understand what happened. But Mare, if he has a chance to talk to Joanna before we can get there, do you think she would be bitter enough to bad-mouth Dad to Jason? You're the one who's read her e-mails. Do you think she's vindictive?"

"Exactly the opposite. I never detected any anger toward Dad in anything she said. In fact, I remember her saying she wished at times she could have felt angry. Maybe that would have helped ease the pain of missing him so much."

She looked up, relieved. "No, honey, I honestly think Joanna would be gentle and discreet with Jason. But he doesn't need to hear anything from anyone but us. Let's hope he's so busy with the audition and his classes he doesn't have time to do any more detective work."

~ * ~

It had been easier than he'd expected. The Alumni Office in Albertson Hall was a small room barely big enough to hold a couple of file cabinets and a desk with a computer on top. The young woman looked up as he approached.

Her voice was husky and low, pleasantly professional. "May I help you?"

"Yes, I hope you can. On Saturday, the psych department held a seminar in the conference room at the student center. It was on a topic I've been researching and I would like to have been able to speak with the presenter. By the time I found out about the program, it was over and she'd left campus. I know she's an alumna from the class of 'sixty-three. Is there any way you can help me contact her?"

The shining auburn hair swished gracefully as she shook her head no.

"I can't give out the address or phone number of a member of the alumni association. I'm sorry. You're welcome to write her a letter that I can mail to her so she can contact *you* if she wants to. But if the psych people invited her here, wouldn't they know how to find her? Maybe somebody there could tell you."

"I guess I'll have to try that. Maybe they can direct me to Dr. Webber."

"Dr. Joanna Webber?"

"Yes, Joanna Webber. Do you know her?"

The young woman smiled broadly. "Not personally, but I sat in on that program even though I'm only a freshman, and she was wonderful. I enjoyed listening to her stories of the work she did with Dr. Wayne in the early sixties. After the program, she came in for a few seconds to update her e-mail address for our files. Oh, now that I know who you're talking about, there's no problem at all. Dr. Webber made it a point to say she'd be happy to hear from any of the Manning students who wanted to contact her. I assume you're one of us?"

"Yes, I'm Jason Buckman," he said as he put out his hand to shake hers. Her grip was firm, her long fingers grasping his for a moment before she released it to riffle through a file on her desk.

"Nice to meet you. I'm Amy Lassen. This job is part of my work/study scholarship. It lets me set my own hours pretty much so I can study and still have some kind of a life. Yes, here it is. I knew I'd put it in a folder so I wouldn't forget to make the change on our website."

Taking a Post-it note from the pad on her desk, Amy wrote the address and handed it to Jason.

"Here you are. I'm sorry I can't do more than that, but it's a way for you to contact her. Did you read the study she did with Dr. Wayne?"

"Not exactly," Jason confessed, blushing. "I wasn't being quite upfront with you. I'm not exactly researching her work. I wanted to talk to her because my grandfather was a professor here when Dr. Webber was a student. They worked together his last year when he directed *Oklahoma!* and I wanted to talk with her about him. You know, little things she might remember that would give me a different picture of my grandfather. We were so close and I'd like to know more about him from his younger days."

"Wow! Imagine that! Small world. It seems she was pretty well known on campus then, too. One of the people at the seminar said something about Dr. Webber making quite a name for herself back in those days. I hadn't thought Dr. Wayne's project was so well known, but I guess I was wrong."

"The psych people sure thought it was interesting," Jason countered. "They dug far enough back to find out she'd worked on it."

"Yeah, Dr. Webber told us how she and Dr. Wayne spent hours transcribing tapes of interviews with student subjects who volunteered to help with the research. She got us laughing when she talked about how it was often really hard to decipher Dr. Wayne's Southern accent. Her imitation was hilarious! Here," she said, taking a sheaf of papers from the desk. "Take this with you. I'll need it back; it's a handout the department had for the workshop. It explains the research project and her part in it. Maybe that'll help you when you finally get to talk to her."

"Thanks, that's very nice of you. I'll read through this tonight and get it back to you in the morning."

"You're very welcome. I'm right here from ten to noon tomorrow. I hope you can stop by."

Cute gal, he thought as he stepped toward the door and then turned back.

"I'll be here around noon. Maybe we could have some lunch?"

"Great, see you then." Amy watched him leave. *God, he's hot*, she thought. *Lunch? Well, that's a start.*

~ * ~

Dear Dr. Webber (Jason's e-mail began)*:*

I was disappointed we didn't get to meet as planned. I hope you weren't ill and that you simply needed to get back to your office quicker than you'd expected.

I still would like to talk to you. You are the only person I've found who actually knew my grandfather here at Manning. I know he was popular from the news items I've read, but the articles don't go beyond the usual flattering stuff about his ability as a director and love of his work. I already know that. I'd like to get a more personal glimpse into him when he was younger, the things he liked, the places he went, the way he related to everyone he worked with and taught. Details only someone like you can provide.

It would be no problem for me to meet you, wherever you are. My schedule is flexible and I have a car on campus. Let me know. Thanks,

Jason Buckman

~ * ~

Joanna sat at her desk, thinking about the trip to Manning, reliving the sudden rush of grief she'd felt as she walked across campus onto the path through the woods. She'd gotten over her shock at encountering Jason and she was looking forward to greeting the tree she and Jared had spoken to each time they passed the little pine.

She remembered the first time she'd heard him do it, his deep voice soft and gentle. *Hello, tree.* It had been very tiny when he first noticed it and he made it a practice to say hello whenever he passed by. She'd played along, told the tree how pretty it was and found out later how endearing Jared had found that fleeting moment.

On her last visit a few years ago, she'd found the tree had grown far above her, a proud fir that didn't seem to recognize her from the past. Now, she looked in vain for it. Standing on the path, she looked left and right and then, getting her bearings, she realized it was gone, cut down to widen the path for the students who still used the shortcut to the library. Her disappointment was so great, it was like a precious piece of her and Jared had been ripped from the place they loved.

After that she knew it would be impossible to talk to Jason about his grandfather without the sadness giving her away. So she simply left, her excuse flimsy and hollow.

Her e-mail chime sounded, pulling her back to the present. She opened the message. Jason hadn't given up; he'd found her. She read and then slowly reread the message. It hadn't worked, her vain attempt at keeping Jason from asking her about the years she knew his grandfather. She should have known he would keep trying to talk with her. She had probably made a mistake by not confronting the issue right then and dealing with Jason's questions. Now she was left with another decision, plus coming up with a satisfactory explanation as to why she hadn't shown up.

If she simply didn't answer, what was the likelihood he would give up? He might, but there would always be questions in his mind. Perhaps he had heard echoes of a piece of the gossip that had floated around campus then, however unlikely that would be, given the span of time since she and Jared Fowler had been the subjects of much speculation. But what if he had? What if her appearance at Manning triggered someone's memory? How could she be responsible for Jason's hearing about her and his grandfather through the wrong channels, to be left with snippets of the truth that by then would be distorted into something ugly or malicious? No, that couldn't happen. She needed to be the one to tell him in as artful a way as she could manage about the wonderful man his grandfather had been. She could easily come up with harmless tidbits any student on campus might have known. There would be no need to reveal anything that might point to a more serious relationship.

Easier said than done, she chided herself. Merely talking about Jared might give away the depth of her feeling for him. She never was much of an actress. Jared used to tease and tell her she'd better stay away from the poker table because she wore her emotions on her face for everyone to read. What would he want her to do now? Above all, Jared wouldn't want his grandson hurt. He wouldn't want Jason to come through this with a negative opinion of anything he'd done or about the man he was.

She smiled slightly. *The image again, huh? Even in death you're fighting to keep that image for your family, the one that nearly ended our relationship for good. Well, Jared dear, once again I'll protect you. I'll see your grandson and talk with him about you. I won't say or do anything to tarnish his memories of you, his hero.*

Clicking on "Reply," Joanna wrote:

Dear Jason:

I am truly sorry I had to leave so abruptly and you were disappointed we didn't get to talk. It may be some time before I can get back to Manning, but you would be welcome to visit me whenever it's convenient for you. Your grandfather was a remarkable man and I'd be happy to share what I remember of him with you. Let me know if you decide to come to Brigantine and I'll send a map. It should take you about an hour and a half to two hours to get here. The weather is still occasionally warm

enough to sit on the beach, so plan to make your trip worthwhile by staying for the day if you can. I look forward to seeing you.
Cordially, Joanna Webber

She clicked on Send and walked out of the den into the great room. Sitting heavily on a chair, she looked out to the ocean. The clouds were heavy and gray, the wind pummeling the dune grass down to meet the sand. She let her mind wander, giving in to one of the rare bouts of self-pity she allowed herself.

In the end, Jared certainly had the best of everything. He lived a charmed life—fabulous career, loving family, beautiful home—and in his background, veiled and kept tucked out of sight, there was this "other woman" who loved him enough to let him enjoy all of that without demands or recrimination. *And me, the other woman? I have no one to blame but myself for still being alone. Certainly I could have found someone else, remarried. I didn't because I didn't want to; it was that simple. Vicki had him for over fifty years ... how lucky she was! I had pieces, tiny slivers of his time and yet ... and yet they were enough to bind me to him forever.*

No, no, no ... no more tears. It had been ages since she'd cried, really cried over what might have been. She'd cried at Jared's funeral; just seeing him had opened the floodgates. But this was different. Tears shed now were feeling-sorry-for-herself tears. She tried not to go there. Nothing could be gained by focusing on the what-ifs.

Besides, there couldn't be anything in her demeanor with Jared's grandson that would give her away. She'd have to make a list of safe things to tell him. She could recall the kind of music his grandfather liked, describe the office with its displays of playbills and theater posters. She could even find a way to talk about graduation day in 1962 when Jared walked in the grand march wearing his grad school colors, but she'd have to be sure the photo she snapped that day was safely out of sight. Too bad. She would have liked to share the one picture of his grandfather she was sure Jason had never seen. She knew she could talk about things that would be okay; she could manage to keep it impersonal and yet satisfy the young man's yearning for a peek into his grandfather's life as a young professor.

I can do this, she mused. *And in reliving the past to a small degree, I can bring Jared back for his grandson ... and for me, even for a little while.*

Eighteen

Jason's tone was filled with sheer excitement. "Mom! Fabulous news ... I made the band."

"Oh, I'm so happy for you! But when was the audition? Why didn't you let us know you were scheduled?"

"I didn't want to take the chance you'd get your hopes up, and then if I didn't make the band, you'd be disappointed. This way, the news turned out to be good. Is Dad home?"

"He's due any minute. Wait till he hears this! He's going to be so proud. How many freshmen made the cut?"

"Only me. The other guy on percussion and the girl on sax are sophomores."

"Gosh, I wish I could have been there to hear you play."

"Well, you'll almost get that wish. They taped the auditions and I'll be getting a complimentary copy next week. I'll send the CD home so you and Dad can hear it."

"We'll do you one better, honey. Dad and I have a surprise of our own. We're coming to see you. In fact, if Dad is able to clear his calendar, we thought about planning to spend the weekend of the seventeenth with you. Is that okay?"

"Gee, it *would* have been great, but there's more news. Do you remember Dr. Webber? Well, I managed to get her e-mail address and wrote to see if she'd still consider meeting me. She answered with an apology plus an invitation to go see her in New Jersey. She lives on an island off the southern coast, somewhere down by Atlantic City. She's sending me a map, but I've already found it on the 'net and it looks like a really cool place. Anyway, I e-mailed her back and we set up a visit for that Saturday. But I guess I could change the plan if this is the only time you and Dad can come."

"Your dad and I had our hearts set on seeing you as soon as possible. Could you reschedule Dr. Webber?"

"I guess so. Is anything wrong? You sound kind of serious."

"No, honey, nothing's wrong. Dad and I miss you, that's all. We need some time away and we thought how much we would enjoy flying out to spend a weekend before winter sets in. And now that you've made the band, we definitely have a reason to celebrate."

"Sure. No problem. I'll e-mail Dr. Webber and explain. I'm sure she'll understand and we can change the date. Let me know when you're coming. I'll meet you at the airport and we can either hang out around Philly or come back here. I'll leave it up to you and Dad."

Marina clicked off when they'd finished their conversation and immediately connected to Andy's cell.

"Andy?"

"Hi, Mare! What's up?

"I just spoke with Jason ... in the nick of time, it seems. The good news is he made the band and he's thrilled. But he's also contacted Joanna and made plans to see her the same weekend we'd planned to go to Manning. He's agreed to change his plans, thank heavens! So at least we'll be able to talk with him before she does."

Andy gave a low whistle. "Good timing."

"Yes, it was. Guess she had second thoughts and decided she wanted to talk with him after all."

"Don't be so sure it was Joanna's doing, babe. You said it yourself—Jason can be persistent. Knowing him, he probably tracked her down and didn't leave her much choice."

"Could be. But at least we'll see him first and prepare him for whatever he might learn from Joanna. I'm sure after we've talked to him, he'll be even more anxious to meet her, but at least he'll have had time to think about what he wants to say."

"That'll be our job. It'll be up to us to protect Dad's image in Jason's eyes. I only hope Joanna feels the same way."

~ * ~

Dr. Webber:

I just talked to my mother and found out she and Dad are planning a trip to Manning the same weekend we were supposed to get together. I couldn't very well ask them to postpone the visit. It's hard for them to get time off together. I apologize, but it looks like I'm going to have to reschedule. Would you let me know if this Saturday would work for you instead? If not, we can postpone for another week or two, whatever is best for you. I'm sorry. Let me know.

Jason

~ * ~

Don't do it, Joanna, she told herself. She thought seeing Jason this weekend might not be a good idea. He should have the time with his parents first. *What if Jason told them he was going to see me? What if one of them mentions it to Vicki? Surely Vicki would remember my name, even after all this time. Maybe she wouldn't know me as Joanna Webber, but how many Joannas could have worked with her husband at Manning?* Silently, she berated herself for accepting that invitation, going back to campus at all and worse yet, agreeing to see Jason. *How did I get into this mess?*

~ * ~

Jason turned back to the small stack of papers on his desk, determined to try once again to understand the project Dr. Webber and Dr. Wayne had done.

He read through the synopsis of Dr. Wayne's project, but wasn't exactly sure what she'd been trying to prove. It had something to do with the notion that people who are very neurotic don't see the real world like those whose mental states are more stable. Neurotics distort reality, Dr. Wayne had proved, so it conforms with their own ideas of how their worlds should be. The concept sounded very interesting and he hoped Amy would talk to him some more about Carl Rogers, the psychologist credited with defining the theory. Dr. Wayne had used mirrors and specially made glasses that changed the way the test subjects looked. When they checked themselves out in the mirrors and described what they saw, Joanna had been the one who recorded their responses and later transcribed the tapes for analysis. The handout explained that the students had taken psychological tests before the glasses thing, and those who were really disturbed looked through any pair of glasses and reported that their images weren't changed at all, no matter how distorted they really were. *I guess she figured the nuttier people are, the less realistically they deal with life*, he thought. Nothing new about that. He wondered if his grandfather had known Dr. Wayne, too, and quickly decided he must have. *Manning only had about fourteen hundred students and a couple hundred faculty then*, he mused. *Everybody probably knew everybody on campus.*

Gathering the papers together, he re-stapled them and reached for the phone.

"Amy? Hi, this is Jason Buckman. How are you?"

"Fine. A little stressed out, you know, with work and this paper I'm doing, but otherwise I'm okay. You?"

"Pretty good. I wanted to tell you I made the jazz band and make sure we're still on for lunch tomorrow."

"Congratulations! I'd heard there was only one freshman accepted this year. I'm so glad it was you. And yes, tomorrow is fine. By the way, did you get a chance to read Dr. Wayne's material?"

"Yeah, I read it. But I guess I'm a little on the thick side. I think I got the gist of what she did, but I'm not sure I completely understood the idea behind her experiment. Maybe you can explain it to me in simple words of two syllables or less."

He heard her giggle. "C'mon, I think you're a lot smarter than you're letting on. I bet you understand just fine. Actually, the theory is pretty fascinating. We can talk about it at lunch."

"Oh, yeah, I almost forgot to tell you. I e-mailed Dr. Webber and she's agreed to talk with me. She even invited me to her place at the shore. Brigantine, it's called. Do you know where it is?"

"Sure, I know exactly where Brigantine is. When are you going?"

"It's not nailed down yet. We set a date for the eighteenth, but my folks called and said they wanted to visit me before the weather got too cold so I wrote Dr. Webber back and asked if we might change our plan to this Saturday instead. She hasn't answered yet, so I'm not sure exactly when I'm going. What time tomorrow?"

"I have a ten o'clock in Holford Hall and then I'm done for the day. How about meeting in the student center around noon?"

"Sure, then we can go off campus for a sandwich or something. I only have one class tomorrow and I'd like to get away for an hour or so."

Amy had been on his mind a lot since they'd met. He was intrigued by her soft-spoken, gentle manner. He had dated a few girls during his senior year in high school and a couple since he'd been at Manning, but most of them turned out not to be his type. Airheads, some of them. But Amy ... he had the feeling she was different from the rest, not only intelligent but also a good listener and fun to be with. He turned back to his computer still thinking of her. Yeah, he'd like to get to know her a lot better.

Hmmm ... still nothing from Dr. Webber. He dashed off a quick e-mail to his mother to give her an update.

~ * ~

Hey, Mom! You and Dad can come on out as planned. I've asked Dr. Webber to change our meeting to this weekend instead. Haven't heard from her yet, but if she agrees, I'll get up early Saturday morning and drive down. It takes a couple hours. I'll let you know for sure if I'm going so you won't be looking for me. Hope you and Dad are having fun in the house all by yourselves (ha, ha, only kidding).

Love, Jason

~ * ~

Marina was about to turn the computer off for the night. Her day at the clinic had been extremely difficult. A strange malady had descended on a neighborhood elementary school and the medical staff had been inundated with children complaining of rashes on their arms and legs. The county health service had been called and they'd sent for an infectious disease specialist to see if they could get to the root of the problem. But as the day wore on, the children who had been brought in first were being sent home as the rashes subsided, and new cases were arriving. Most of the children had been discharged by seven o'clock, but by the time she'd finished her reports and driven home, it was nearly nine and she was exhausted. She didn't envy the school staffers who would be up most of the night and working well into the weekend to thoroughly clean the school and try to find out what had caused the mysterious skin blotches.

There had been the usual witty e-mail from Aunt Genna, going on about a shopping spree she and Vicki had taken to a group of outlet stores near Tampa. Vicki seldom wrote. She was content with an occasional phone call, knowing Genna kept everyone up North informed about their comings and goings.

As she was about to log off, another message came through, this one from Jason. Her eyes raced across the screen, reading about his tentative plans to go to Brigantine Saturday to meet Joanna.

She looked into space and sighed. Now what? The phone made her jump.

"What?" she said without thinking as she picked up the receiver. "Hello?"

"That's a helluva greeting!" Andy's voice was warm as he teased her gently. "What?"

"I'm sorry, it was just reflex. I was finishing up an e-mail from Jason and was so upset it was like I was in another world when the phone rang. But I'm so glad it's you!"

"Now what?"

"Funny you should say that. That's exactly what I was asking myself when you called. Now what? Jason wrote to tell us he's possibly meeting Joanna this weekend instead of next because of our visit. He's written to her suggesting the change but he hasn't heard from her one way or the other. I say again, now what?"

"Damn! And we thought we'd bought ourselves some time. Well, looks like we've been outfoxed. Our son has a mind of his own, that's for sure, and he's bound and determined to talk with Joanna as soon as he can. All I can say is, I hope she can deal with whatever he wants to know and present her relationship with Dad as casually as possible. Any other suggestions?"

"Uh, you're gonna think I'm off the wall, hon, but here goes. What if I call Joanna, tell her what we know and discuss what she's going to tell Jason, maybe even ask that she not see him until we've been there?"

Sirens were growing more strident in the background as a group of ambulances drew closer to the hospital. Andy saw the ER chief motioning to him.

"Oh shit, we've got something big coming in and they need me in triage. I don't know what to say about your idea. I guess nothing we do is going to make things better or worse, so why not? If you think you can talk to Joanna without scaring the bejesus out of her or upsetting yourself, go ahead. Hon, I'm sorry, I have to go. Looks like I'm gonna be late getting home tonight unless the next shift turns up on time and I'm not needed too long. 'Bye. I'll call when I can."

Marina slowly put down the phone, her brow furrowed. The situation would be comical if it weren't so damn serious. A little over a year ago, she'd been itching to meet Joanna. She'd knuckled under to everyone's insistence that she back off and forget about contacting the "other woman" in Dad's past lest Jason find out about his grandfather's secret life. *Now it seems we've come full circle, huh? Like it or not, I'm going to talk with Joanna, if only to enlist her help with Jason.*

She had kept the address and phone number in her book in the desk. Carefully, she thumbed through to the "W" page.

Resting her head back on the chair, she closed her eyes. She had butterflies in her stomach and her hands were actually shaking a bit. Talking about encountering Joanna had been one thing; being seconds away from doing it was another. What would she say? How could she broach the subject? What would Joanna say when she heard how much Marina knew?

Before she could get cold feet, Marina quickly dialed the number. It rang twice.

"Hello?" The voice was low and slightly husky. *Your father was an old friend.* Marina remembered hearing that voice.

"Is this Dr. Joanna Webber?"

"Yes, it is."

"This is Marina Buckman, Jared Fowler's daughter."

The silence at the other end was finally punctuated by a low clearing of the throat.

"Why, Marina. I'm surprised to hear from you. I suppose Jason's told you we met on Saturday. He's a fine young man. You must be very proud of him."

"Yes, I know you've met him, Dr. Webber..."

"Call me Joanna, please."

"Thank you," Marina replied. "I heard you met Jason and he's asked to visit you to talk about Dad and the memories you have of him. He wants to come to your home this weekend."

"Yes, I haven't had a chance to answer his e-mail, but you're right. Is there a problem with that?"

"I don't know, is there? Frankly, I'm a little worried about how that meeting will go. You see, ever since Dad's funeral, I've been discovering things that have given me a pretty clear understanding of who you were to my father and—"

"What have you found?"

Marina's voice rose slightly. "For starters, I know you and Dad were having an affair when I was only seven years old. I also know you and he were together while my brother, my mother and I were in Florida a couple of times and there was a possibility at one point that Dad would divorce my mother so he could be with you."

Nothing but silence on the other end.

"To take it a bit further, I also know you and Dad stayed in touch for the next forty years, give or take a year. You were at the funeral and you came because Dad asked you to be there. How am I doing so far? Did I miss anything?"

Marina heard a deep sigh at the other end of the line.

"No, dear. Unless you want to include the part about how much I loved your father and how sorry I am you've had this heaped on you all at once. You weren't supposed to know any of it and frankly I'm baffled as to how you found out."

"That's another mystery. If Dad were so set on no one in his family ever knowing about the affair, why did he leave so many clues? It was so obvious!"

"Clues? What kind of clues?"

"To begin with, he put all your e-mails in a folder on his hard drive. He left photos of the ocean view from your house and several of your son in his desk drawer. I also found the book of poetry with your inscription inside. But I suppose the most upsetting to me was the tape. I stumbled on it by accident the first time I drove his car. Why wouldn't he have destroyed something so personal?"

The tape ... Joanna's voice was unsteady and meek. "I honestly don't know. I'm very sorry you had to find out that way. It must have been a shock. But believe me, nothing your father and I felt for each other interfered with his devotion to you and Michael. I know how deeply he loved you both. He never wanted to hurt either of you and did everything to protect you from the truth."

"Well, he didn't do a very good job of it, did he? He left a bunch of crumbs scattered through the forest that were easy to follow. And now Jason's involved in this whole mess and I'm trying to find a way to protect him."

"You're afraid I'll say something to Jason that would be demeaning to your father? Oh, Marina," she almost whispered the last two words. "Oh, no. Please believe me, I could *never* do that."

Marina felt the anger subside, like a calming hand resting on her shoulder. She hadn't intended to come across this harshly. Once she got past her initial anger over the affair, she had felt only sympathy for Joanna. But as soon as she heard Joanna's voice, the hurt little eight-year-old surfaced, some of her old fear and resentment bubbling out all over again.

"I'm sorry, I didn't mean to come on that strong. I guess we'll have to trust you. My husband and I wanted to talk to Jason before he met you. We thought perhaps it was time to tell him what we knew and have him hear about you and Dad from us. But he's a very persistent kid. He keeps pushing until his curiosity is satisfied. I suspect he already knows there's more to this than meets the eye."

"In that case, maybe it *would* be better if you and Andy saw him first," Joanna suggested. Marina winced slightly at the familiarity Joanna had with the names of her family. "Would you like me to e-mail back to him and say this weekend isn't convenient? I can easily put him off for a few weeks."

"Please. I know you won't say or do anything to hurt Jason, but in the long run I think he'll be better off if we tell him. Then when he does see you, he'll be able to ask the kinds of questions that will let you speak freely about Dad, but your answers won't be as likely to upset him."

"Fine, I'll e-mail him tonight and ask him to hold off for a week or two. And by then, what will be will be. I've always believed there are no such things as coincidences. The fact that you 'happened' to learn about our relationship, the fact Jason 'happened' to choose Manning and then the way he 'happened' to see that old newspaper clipping. If I didn't know any better, I'd say there was a master hand at work."

Nineteen

Jason got the e-mail from Joanna and called Amy's cell phone. "Hi, Amy. It's me. I heard from Dr. Webber. It seems she had plans to spend Saturday with her family in Philly and she won't get home until Sunday morning, so we decided to put off our visit until the week after Mom and Dad are here."

"Jason, I know it's late and we're getting together for lunch tomorrow, but could you meet me for a few minutes now?"

"Of course. It's not *that* late. Something wrong?"

"Uh, no ... no, I just need to talk to you. I'm leaving the library, on my way out the front door as a matter of fact. Can you shoot over to the student center?"

"Sure. Meet you there in a couple minutes. Is everything okay?"

"Absolutely! See you in a sec."

~ * ~

"Amy? You look pretty serious. What gives?"

They had ordered Cokes and were sitting at a small table in the back of the room.

"I don't know if I'm doing the right thing, but I heard something tonight I thought you ought to know. Before I say anything, though, I want to be sure you won't get mad. Believe me, I'm only telling you because you're likely to hear it from someone else and I'd rather we talked first. Okay?"

Jason put his elbows on the table and leaned forward, his dark eyes intent on Amy's face.

"Look, Amy, we're only starting to get to know each other, but I have a feeling we're gonna be good friends. Friends don't hurt friends, right? So you can tell me anything. Out with it, please. What's going on?"

"Okay, remember I told you somebody said Dr. Webber had made quite a name for herself when she was here?"

"Yeah. And?"

"Well, I took it to mean she'd been some kind of celebrity because she worked with Dr. Wayne and helped set up the counseling program. That would be enough to make her a standout, wouldn't it?"

"Sure. Go on," Jason prodded.

"Tonight at dinner, I mentioned you'd been in touch with Dr. Webber and were possibly going to visit her to talk about your grandfather. One of the girls, a junior on my floor, made a snide comment about Dr. Webber, insinuating that she was picking up with you where she left off with your grandfather. I thought for sure she was joking."

"Huh? Run that by me again?"

"No lie. She actually implied Dr. Webber and your grandfather were more than student and professor, and she might be looking to hook up with you the same way, I guess because you look so much like him. So I put her on the spot and asked whatever gave her that idea. She told me her grandmother was on staff here in the early sixties, a geography professor, I think, and she remembers everyone on campus knowing Dr. Fowler and Joanna Webber were a couple. She *was* Joanna Ransome then, right?"

"Yes, she was," Jason managed in a strained voice.

"She said they were together all the time until your grandfather moved out to the Midwest somewhere. Look, I gave her a hard time at first, but then I decided not to push it. She doesn't know you and she doesn't have any reason to make this up. But I wanted to be sure before I said anything to you. Should I have kept quiet?"

Jason stared into his Coke glass unblinking. "Y'know, the first time I saw that picture in *The Target* archives, the one from the cast party with my grandfather and Joanna Ransome in it—the very first time! I looked at Grandpa's face and I wondered what was *really* going on. The first time! I guess I was right. Damn! And if I could see there was something special between them from just one photograph, imagine what the people who were there were seeing. I guess Grandpa was really the talk of the campus and it seems now his notoriety didn't have a friggin' thing to do with his teaching."

"I'm sorry, Jason. If I didn't like you so much, I wouldn't care how or when you found out about this. But I know you're reaching out to Dr. Webber and I thought you ought to know what I heard before you talk with her. I didn't want you blindsided."

Jason stood. "I need to get back to the dorm," he said flatly. "I have a lot of stuff to take care of."

He turned toward the door, then back again. "Uh, thanks, Amy. I'll see you tomorrow."

Amy watched Jason's tall figure, his head bent and his shoulders slightly hunched over, as he walked out the door. The thought crossed her mind she might have blown any chance she had of hitting it off with Jason by repeating what she'd heard, but she thought she'd done the right thing, no matter what. Amy could only imagine what he was thinking, how this echo from the past might affect his feelings toward his grandfather. *Tough,* she thought. *Why can't people mind their own damn business?*

~ * ~

Outside the student center, Jason stopped on the steps, shoved his hands into his pockets and looked around. He had been so excited about being there. He had walked around campus like he owned the place, proud of being related to Dr. Jared Fowler. He had even flaunted his grandfather's achievements before the entire comp class. Did any of them know? Had the gossip surfaced by then?

What were the odds, he wondered, *that someone would dig this business up and throw it right in my face? Spread it around campus like a wagonload of shit? How far had it gone?*

He'd begun to walk ... down the steps, across the street, into the little woods by the library. It was very dark and getting cold. He walked up the sidewalk to Kenton Hall, stood staring at the window of his grandfather's office and then sat heavily on the top step.

I wanted to love this place like Grandpa did. I wanted to sit by the lake in spring and smell the dogwood blossoms he told me about. I wanted to finish school here, graduate and know Grandpa was watching me take that diploma. I really wanted to love this place. Now what do I do?

Suddenly, he felt a cold grip on his heart. His mother, his uncle and his grandmother! What if they found out his grandfather hadn't been the man they thought he was? How would they react? He sat on the step with his arms tucked under his jacket, studying the blinking stars in the cold October sky. He wondered how it could be so warm all day and then feel like winter when the sun set.

He stumbled down the steps and turned toward his dorm. He needed time to sort things out, figure out how he was going to be able to tell his parents everything he'd heard. God, his mother would be so hurt and disappointed! What if she refused to believe what he told her? Even after he showed her the picture and maybe even had Amy repeat what she'd heard? *No. Mom and Dad know there'd be no way I'd put Grandpa down unless there was a damn good reason.* He looked at the lantern burning low on the brass chain above the Kenton doorway, casting shadows against the night.

Grandpa, how could you do this to us? How could you?

~ * ~

Todd poked his head around the corner of the bathroom door at the sound of Jason's key in the lock.

"Hey, Jason, where you been? Isn't it a little late?"

"I've already got one mother; I don't need another one," Jason snapped, dropping his jacket on the bed.

Todd put both hands up in front of his face. "Whoa, where the hell did that come from? I was just asking, man!"

"I'm not in the mood for company. I need some time alone."

Todd's expression turned serious. "What's up? You were fine an hour ago. What happened?"

"I don't want to talk about it now, okay? Leave me alone. I've got a lot on my mind."

Todd stepped backward into the bathroom and slowly closed the door behind him. *Whatever it was that upset Jason is sure big,* he thought. He'd better give his friend some time to sort stuff out. Probably girl trouble. Maybe he and Amy hadn't hit it off as well as he had hoped. He would wait until Jason was ready to tell him about whatever was bugging him.

~ * ~

The ocean air was crisp and salty. Joanna closed the sliding glass door at the front of the great room and pulled the drapes closed. Most times, she didn't bother; no one ever walked in front of her window, only the sea birds. She absently drifted around the room turning out lights, fluffing cushions on the pastel blue sectional, patting pillows and standing them up in the corners of the sofa and straightening pictures on the wall. In the den, the computer screen still glowed on the desk. She had written to Jason and begged off for this weekend, inventing a trip to see Steven and Abby. She knew Marina and Andy needed to talk with Jason first. After that, she would be able to fill in whatever he wanted to know. That is, if he still wanted to talk after he knew about her and Jared.

It was overwhelming. She had been a secret for so long, safe with Jared where no one in his family knew about them, with only her shoeboxes filled with letters and printed out e-mails attesting to their bond. Mostly, secure in the knowledge she had held a place in his heart right up to the end, she carried on, living contentedly, enjoying her family, her work and her writing.

Tonight, though, she was in the mood to spend time with the past. These moments were thankfully rare, since she had gotten to a place where the present was comfortable and fulfilling. But seeing Jared's grandson and getting the phone call from his daughter ... all the memories had come back, reminding her of the years they'd had with him, the things she knew only from his letters or calls.

This wasn't going to be easy, even knowing Vicki hadn't found out and there was no anger in Marina. Joanna felt like someone was flicking ice water at her heart, an unsettling feeling that told her all wasn't as sanguine as it appeared.

Pushing the cassette into the player, she sat back in her chair, closed her eyes and sank into Jared's voice. He was standing at the bar in the Downtown Club, a small microphone in his hand, Jim Brodborough at the piano behind him. His eyes were on her and his voice was like cascading silk. His love wrapped around her and she felt the strength of his caring. It was so good to be back there again.

Still, that inexplicable shadow hovered menacingly over her, disturbing her tranquility. She tried in vain to shake off the foreboding, but it wouldn't go away. *Jared ... why now, why?*

Twenty

At midnight, Todd finished the last chapter of his book, turned off the light and crawled into bed. It was quiet on the other side of the door but he could see a streak of brightness coming through. He thought perhaps Jason had fallen asleep studying and forgotten to turn off the lamp on his desk. He got up and tapped on his door gently.

"J.? You awake?"

The chair scraped on the linoleum as Jason stood. "Yeah," he said, pulling open the door. "I'm still awake."

Todd gazed at his friend, at the knitted eyebrows, the rumpled hair and morose expression. "Geez, man, you look awful! What's up?"

Jason turned back toward his desk. The picture of his grandfather and Joanna was propped up against the monitor.

Todd sat on the bed, the covers still neatly arranged. It was obvious Jason hadn't even attempted sleep. "C'mon, J., I know something's really bugging you. Do you need to get it off your chest?"

Jason still didn't answer. He stood staring at the picture and then suddenly snatched it from the desk, crumpled it tightly in his fist and hurled it against the wall.

He stood clenching and unclenching his fingers. Todd knew then that the problem with Jason was bigger than any girl thing.

"Jason, do you want me to call Kramer?"

The residence assistant's name was Allen Kranmer, but at first sight the boys on the floor had dubbed him "Kramer" after the gangly, awkward member of the *Seinfeld* cast. It was his job to deal with any troubles the students might have and everyone agreed he was capable, understanding and always willing to listen.

"Well? Should I call him?" Todd repeated.

"My grandfather sure was an important guy at Manning," Jason said, ignoring Todd's question. "He was *so* well liked, *such* an excellent director and the *ultimate* professional. Oh, and did anyone mention he was screwing one of his students? Oops, how did that get left out of his impressive bio? Just a minor oversight, I guess, something Grandpa conveniently decided to duck when he left here and started over in Chicago. Of course, by then he'd left a trail—other professors, probably hundreds of students— they all knew. Unfortunately, people have long memories and damned if one hasn't come back to haunt me. Now the whole mess is all being dredged up again."

Todd listened quietly, hurting for the pain in his friend's voice. He still wasn't clear about all that had happened, but he got the idea. Someone must have explained the photo to Jason and what they said contradicted everything he believed. He could see Jason was battling with his own ideals.

"I don't know enough about the situation to make much of anything. And in spite of what you've been told, I think you're overreacting. A lot of men have affairs. The important thing is, if there really was an affair, it happened a long time ago."

Jason interrupted, his tone ugly. "I don't buy that for one fuckin' second. I know all I need to know. Apparently, while he was putting on the front of being such an upstanding director and friend to all his students, he was banging Joanna Ransome, a junior, practically out in the open. And Mom and Uncle Mike were home with Grandmom, totally in the dark. How often did he leave them alone? Hell, my mother was only seven years old! Apparently, Grandpa was such a good actor he fooled all three of them into believing whatever alibi he concocted for all the time he wasn't home. Fuckin' clever of him!"

"Calm down. Where did you hear all this crap anyway?"

"Not that it matters, but Amy told me. Seems one of the girls in her dorm has a grandmother who was on the faculty with Grandpa and she remembers the gossip. When Dr. Webber came to speak last weekend, this girl mentioned it to her grandmother and got an earful. I guess everyone's buzzing about them by now, knowing I'm his grandson. Anyway, Amy was worried I'd get wind of the gossip so she thought she'd give me a heads up."

He exhaled loudly. "Hey, I'm really sorry I'm unloading on you ... I'm just so totally pissed off!"

"I'll say it again. The whole thing sounds like cheap gossip to me. Look, remember that exercise we did in comp class, the one about communication from one person to another?"

"You mean the one where someone told a story and then each person repeated it? Yeah, I remember."

"Well then, you remember that by the time the story got to the last person it was totally different. C'mon, dude, you weren't here in the sixties when this supposedly happened. Neither were any of the people who are talking about your grandfather. And so what if somebody's grandmother was here, who's to say her memory's so sharp?"

He chuckled. "Who knows? Maybe she was after your grandfather herself and was jealous of his friendship with a young pretty student. She's probably some petty old lady who's found a way to smear his name, knowing he can't fight back. Sorry, I don't mean to make light of something you're taking so seriously, but there could be a logical explanation for this so-called affair between your grandfather and Dr. Webber. Why freak out? Why not sit down with her and talk? Tell her what you've heard and get answers straight from the horse's mouth? You're already believing the worst, so what have you got to lose?"

"And what if she doesn't deny it? God, now I'm afraid to talk to her. What if the gossip turns out to be true?"

"Then deal with it, man. You can't possibly deal with something until you know for sure what *it* is. If there was an affair, there's probably a lot more to the story than the one somebody's grandmother is spreading around. Dr. Webber may not be able to tell your grandfather's side of everything, but she's the only person who can answer for herself."

~ * ~

Jason pondered that option for the next several days. He and Amy had dinner together Saturday night in a little Italian place on the highway about five miles south of campus. He'd made up his mind he was going to forget about his grandfather and try to enjoy himself, get to know Amy better. They had even laughed a lot and he found himself warming to her gentle humor. He loved the way she cocked her head and smiled at him when he was talking. She wasn't shy, but she wasn't overbearing either. Their conversation was relaxed and unhurried. When Jason reached for the check, he glanced at his watch. He realized they'd been sitting there for nearly two hours.

"That was fun, Jason," she said as he held open the door on her side of the Outback. "And the food was great! I'm even all set for lunch tomorrow," she said, indicating the Styrofoam container on her lap. "Nuke this baby for a couple seconds and I can enjoy lasagna all over again."

"Hey, notice I didn't leave any to take home?" Jason asked, smiling. "You're right; this is a good place to eat. We'll have to come back again."

He rested his slender hands on the wheel. "Thanks for a good time. I'm sorry I haven't called you for a few days. I had so much to sort out, so many questions running around in my head, not to mention a few pop quizzes and overdue practice with the band."

Amy reached across the seat and gave him a gentle hug. "No problem. I hope you've figured out how to deal with the thing with your grandfather. Have you talked with anyone about it? Other than Todd, I mean."

"No. Not yet. Todd thinks I should go to Brigantine and ask Dr. Webber about what I suspect. He's probably right. I'm so confused about what's the best thing to do. This goes so far beyond me and Dr. Webber, Amy. This is my mother, my uncle and especially my grandmother. How do I go on as if everything's normal after I've heard this vicious gossip?"

"You find a way to make it okay. And the only way you can do that is to get a grip. For all you know, the story's a big lie. How well did this grandmother know your grandfather anyway? Why would you be so quick to believe there was an affair between him and Joanna Webber?"

"You didn't see the picture. And I can't show it to you now because I pretty much destroyed it. You could actually see the expressions in their eyes, and he was holding her hand, too. I felt what my grandfather was feeling just looking at him. Yeah, there was an affair all right. I'd like to know how it happened and why Grandpa was willing to risk his career by being so public about the relationship. And I still haven't figured out what, if anything, to say to Mom and Dad on Friday. Do I tell them? Or do I wait until I talk with Dr. Webber?"

~ * ~

Todd had gone home to Delaware and the suite was dark when Jason got back. He couldn't get his mind off Amy. She was a terrific girl in every way. They'd made a date to meet on Tuesday after their last class and he was already looking forward to seeing her again. If only he could shut out the nagging thoughts about his grandfather and Joanna Webber.

He looked at his watch … the crystal gleaming in the light from his desk lamp. He didn't remember, of course, but his mother had told him how his grandfather taught him to tell time. When he was a little boy, he had loved climbing into his grandpa's lap and listening to the gentle pulse of the second hand as it marched around the dial. Grandpa's watch was on his wrist now.

He sat on the bed, staring into the past. He searched every corner of his memory, trying to find a time he didn't believe his grandfather was perfect. When he was eight, he and Grandpa practiced baseball in the back yard. Even when he batted at thin air, Grandpa never spoke harshly, never criticized, never reacted with anything other than patience and love.

He remembered the first time Grandpa came to see him march in the high school band. The bass drum was nearly as big as he was. Jared had adjusted the straps on his shoulders, given him an encouraging pat and said, "Get out there, son, and strut your stuff!"

He remembered Grandpa telling him about taking Uncle Mike to baseball games and coaching his Little League team. He worked long hours in the theater, but his stories made it seem like when he wasn't working, he was always home. *There could never have been room for anyone else in Grandpa's life.*

Did he ever say anything, anything at all that made Jason wonder? Oh, there were times on the boat when Jason would watch when his grandfather didn't know he was looking and he'd see the shadowed darkness in his eyes. Grandpa would sit in the bow and let him fish, sometimes gently trailing his hand in the lake, his head back, eyes closed to the sun.

~ * ~

"What were you thinking about just then, Grandpa?"

"Oh, life, Jason; I was thinking about life."

"What about life?"

"How it takes you where it wants you to go; how there's a grand plan for each of us and sometimes we don't end up doing what we thought we might."

"Is there something you're not doing, Grandpa?"

No answer. His eyes are still closed; there's a slight smile on his face.

"Grandpa?"

He still doesn't open his eyes.

"Nope. Right now, all that matters is this lake, the fish and you, my boy. I'm exactly where I should be."

Jason laid down, his arms behind his head on the pillow. He had to know.

~ * ~

It was early when he awoke; the clock on the desk read seven a.m. At least he'd had a few hours' sleep, but his clothes were wrinkled and he had a bad taste in his mouth. Stale coffee.

He felt somewhat better after a brisk shower. Later, he wondered exactly when he had made the decision, but at the moment, he didn't stop to take the time to debate with himself. Shoving his wallet into his back pocket, flinging his jacket over his shoulder and grabbing his keys, Jason closed the door to his room, walked quickly to the parking lot, got into the Outback and drove out the campus gates.

He drove south to Yardley, crossed the Delaware River and headed for the shore. He'd forgotten to bring the map that was on his desk, but he vaguely remembered the best route. Glancing at the gas gauge, he saw he could easily make it there without filling the tank.

After about an hour, Jason pulled into the parking lot of a large convenience store. He bought a bottle of Evian and a New Jersey highway map. From there on, he would need some kind of direction. He sat in the car and studied the map. Finding his present location, he traced the rest of the route to Brigantine and realized he was very close. It wasn't even ten o'clock. If Dr. Webber was due home sometime this morning, he thought he might beat her there. So what? He could always sit outside of her house and wait.

After riding past the towering casinos that filled the marina area and crossing the Brigantine Bridge, he pulled over to the curb and studied his surroundings. Most of the buildings were bright white, descending down into sand of the same color. Some of the businesses had small patches of green grass growing in front, but mostly the landscape was composed of sand, stones or gravel. *Either they're too busy to mow or it's too hot here in summer for lawns to grow*, he thought.

From overhead, he heard the incessant squawking of birds. *That could get annoying*, he mused, rolling down the window and craning his neck to look upward. What was making all that racket? Seagulls, of course. The sound reminded him of being on the boat with Grandpa and the eerie experience he had the day after the funeral. He thought about another conversation they'd had when he was about ten.

~ * ~

"Tell me again about the seagulls, Grandpa, when you were on one of those boats in New York."

"It was a ferry, son. It took people and cars across the harbor from Manhattan to a place called Staten Island. There were always lots of seagulls in the harbor. Some people don't like them; they don't sound very pretty, do they? But I love seagulls. I love how free they are, the way they swoop down and then shoot up into the air so high. Some of the happiest times of my life were spent riding that ferry! And you know?

There was one seagull that seemed to stay right over my head, like he was watching over me to be sure I got safely to the other side. Every time I saw him, I would think of a couple of words from an old poem I knew a long time ago, something about flotsam and jetsam and buoys and gulls. Wish I could remember the whole thing ... I think it would make you laugh. Maybe someday a seagull will find you and make sure you get where you need to be."

~ * ~

Jason shrugged off the feeling of melancholy that swept over him. He needed to get to the truth, but now what? He had impulsively made this trip without knowing how to find Dr. Webber once he arrived. He thought of calling one of the guys on his floor to have them check his desk and see if they could find the address, but he realized he'd not only locked his door but he'd neglected to pick up his phone on the way out. *Duh, not very bright, Buckman,* he muttered.

Looking around for a gas station or somewhere he could find a phone book, he thought how foolish he had been. Suppose she wasn't home. Suppose her phone number wasn't listed. He thought again of the map on his desk. He couldn't remember a street number or even a street name. What did pop into his mind was "Starling," the name of the condo where she lived. At least he knew that name. Maybe it wouldn't be too hard to find.

He waited while a seagull with a black spot on its head waddled slowly in front of the car, turning to study the human intruder with solemn, large eyes. Then he pulled away from the curb toward a Texaco station at the end of the block.

Twenty-one

Joanna let herself in the front door and set the bags of groceries on the counter in the kitchen. It didn't take long to unpack and stow her purchases in the pantry.

Walking into the great room, she pulled open the drapes and looked out at the beach. The morning sun was beginning its inexorable trek across the sky, not quite at midpoint yet but sending rays of brilliance bouncing off the waves. There were a few whitecaps, she noticed, but the sky was far too clear for a storm. Maybe there was one brewing somewhere, though. She slid open the doors and stepped outside.

Looking at the dunes in front of her, she spotted her friendly seagull sitting atop the sandy mound. The bird was larger than the others with a fleck of black on his head that made him stand out from the rest. Seemed every time she went out to the beach, he was sitting on his dune staring back at her. She gave him a little wave and watched as he lifted his wings and flew off toward town.

She went back inside to the den, flicked on the computer and released the plantation shutters to let in the light. Patiently, she waited for the old computer to boot up.

There was the usual spam and a note from Beth. Thanks to e-mail, she and her former college roommate kept in touch almost daily. For years they had written or called sporadically, mainly on birthdays and at the holidays. Now, the day didn't seem complete unless she got at least a quick hello from Beth. She quickly typed a response, sent it off and turned away from the computer. Brian loved to e-mail, so she often stayed online and came back to the computer several times during the day. Still, since Jared's death, the thrill she had experienced every time the messages came up was gone. There would never be another one from him. Thinking of Jared, his grandson popped into her mind.

She knew the time would come that she would have to meet Jason. Well, she was ready. She believed she would be able to handle anything he threw at her. After Marina and Andy told Jason what they knew, his questions about Jared might be uncomfortable, maybe even hostile, but Joanna was prepared. After next weekend, she could expect to hear from him, of that she was certain. No matter how carefully his parents presented the tale of her and his grandfather, Jason would probably have more questions than ever. Joanna hoped he would want to know the good things ... places they went, things Jared talked about, what she knew about the Fowler family's lives.

Despite the bright sunshine, the air was cool. Deciding against changing into shorts, Joanna put on sandals but stayed in slacks, draped a sweatshirt over her shoulders and went out the back door. She took a sand chair from the patio and walked through the cut in the dunes out to the water's edge. While the sun was high, she could enjoy the ocean for at least a little while. Nothing pressing to be done. She had the whole afternoon to herself.

~ * ~

The guy at the station knew exactly where Starling was. Not only that, he knew Joanna Webber. She was a year-'rounder, he said; *everybody* knew Joanna. Jason swung out of the station onto Brigantine Boulevard. After a few blocks, he turned toward the ocean and found himself at a dead end with Joanna's building in front of him. He parked the car and walked up the sandy walkway to the door, up the steps and into the foyer. There were only eight units, two on each side of the four-story building. The tiny directory by the elevator said Webber, 101. This was it, a heavy oak door decorated with a sprig of eucalyptus tied around a piece of dried driftwood with a pale blue ribbon. He took a deep breath, exhaled slowly and pressed the doorbell. He heard the chime ring faintly inside. When there was no sound of anyone approaching, he rang again. Still no response.

Serves you right, you dork! he grumbled under his breath. *Two hours on the road and she isn't even home.* He knew he should have called before bolting out of his room. At best, he should have called before he got too far away from Manning. He could have saved himself the drive.

Dejected, he went back outside and walked slowly toward his car. Looking back, he saw a car or two parked in the spaces of the open garage beneath the building, the dunes jutting almost right up against the edge of the concrete floor. A sea wall about three feet high ran part way across the front. Overhead, the seagulls squawked at one another, swooping down and then up again.

One lone gull with a fleck of black on its head sat on a piece of decorative piling in front of the building, looking up at Jason. As he turned to the Outback, the bird let out a shrill and demanding cry. Jason watched the gull jump awkwardly to the ground and patter toward the underground garage.

Putting his keys back in his pocket, he followed the gull up the walk through the passageway in the seawall. Seeing the "Do Not Walk on Dunes" sign, he moved a few feet onto the wooden walk leading to the beach. The sunshine reflected off the water and made him squint. The waves crashed in loud cascades as they broke a few feet from the shore and then rolled gently into the sand. Shading his eyes with his hand, he looked at the vast ocean, mentally comparing it to the calmness of the lake on which he and his grandfather had spent so much time together. This was so very different, he decided, so wild and natural.

Then he realized he wasn't alone. Directly in front of him, with the gull a few feet away, a woman sat in a small chair facing the water. She didn't turn. Obviously, over the sound of the surf she hadn't heard him approach. He studied the back of her head, the graying honey hair and small shoulders. It *had* to be Joanna. And as he stood debating whether to announce himself, she turned and saw him.

She removed her sunglasses and stared at the young man standing a few feet away on the beach with his hands in his pockets. He was tall, with narrow hips and long, muscular legs. His sandy hair was blowing in his face and the fingers he put up to push it back were shapely and slender. Again, that same strange feeling swept through her as it had the first time she had seen him. The resemblance was amazing.

"Jason?"

She gripped the arms of the low-slung chair and stood. "This is certainly a surprise."

He stared at her dumbly ... she looked small and vulnerable, not at all like the crisply professional woman he'd seen on campus.

"I need to talk to you," he said. "It can't wait."

In one swift motion, perfected from many years of practice, Joanna snapped the chair closed, lifted it and shook the loose sand from the legs. She tucked it under her arm and turned toward the house.

"Come in, of course. I'm pleased to see you."

On the patio, she put the chair back with the others and took off her sandals. Jason politely tapped his feet against the door ledge before stepping through the open glass doors.

He stood awkwardly in the center of the great room, his eyes sweeping around, taking in the cool seashore pastels, the artwork on the walls. A framed photograph of a young boy, hair almost white, eyes blue and deep set, stood on one end table.

"Please, sit down. Make yourself comfortable. Would you like something to drink?"

"Thank you, no. I won't be staying long."

Jason watched her as she sat gracefully, crossing her ankles, leaning back against the cushions.

"You said you needed to talk with me and it was a matter of some urgency. What is it?"

Now that he was there, sitting right across from her, Jason's resolve to vent his anger, to lash out at her, seemed to have subsided. She had large eyes, open and frank, and her voice was soft and very gentle. It would be difficult to be harsh with this woman. And yet...

He raised his eyes and met hers. His first words cracked. "I've heard some gossip on campus I can't ignore. My gut tells me it isn't just talk, but you're the only person who can separate fact from fiction."

He paused, his voice stronger.

"All the way down here, I tried to think of what I would say when I saw you. Now the only thing that comes to mind is one question: Exactly what was my grandfather to you?"

Joanna studied her hands. She didn't respond immediately. When she looked up, Jason saw the sadness in her eyes.

Her voice was hardly above a whisper. "What did you hear?"

He stood, paced across the room and turned to face her.

"Well, to put it bluntly, I hear it was pretty much common knowledge around campus that you and Grandpa were having an affair. Apparently, it was the year he moved to Chicago. My mother was just a little girl then. I'm having a hard time dealing with the possibility that her father was spending time with you when he should have been home taking care of his family. So I have to ask ... did you? Did you have an affair with my grandfather?"

"I don't know how to answer you. I don't want to cloud the image of your grandfather, but I can't lie either."

"Is that a yes or a no?"

"It's a yes, I suppose, if you simply want to put a label on our relationship. Yes, I know there were people who looked at it as merely an affair. But we didn't. We were—"

Jason interrupted. His voice had changed, hardened. "Let me see ... from what I understand, Dr. Jared Fowler was married with two kids, but in the meantime he was sleeping around with you on the side, humiliating his family by not hiding that fact around campus. And you didn't consider it an affair? What the hell *did* you consider it?"

Joanna's voice was calm, quiet and even. "I understand your anger, Jason, but I can't let this conversation continue this way. I loved your grandfather very much and I know how much he struggled with his conscience to avoid hurting his family. We both deserve more than your sarcasm. We can either talk about what you've heard with mutual respect or we can end the discussion now."

Jason stopped pacing and stared. *Who the hell does she think she is?* This was the person whose name was infamous on Manning State's campus so long ago that no one should have remembered it, and yet the scandal had been so great her reputation lived on even now. And she had the gall to scold *him*?

"Respect? Who are you kidding? You certainly weren't respecting my family when you were sleeping with my grandfather. Neither was he, so don't talk to me about respect. Forget it. I'm outta here."

He turned and strode toward the sliding glass door, then turned back to face her.

"I shouldn't have bothered to come."

Joanna stood, a sadly patient look on her face as she watched him step across the threshold onto the concrete floor of the parking garage.

His voice was bitter and his words clipped. "I hoped all along you'd deny it. All the way down here, I thought maybe you'd laugh it off and assure me you and Grandpa were just good friends. In my heart I guess I knew better. The gossip's all true, isn't it? God, how could you? How could both of you? But I guess the last laugh was on you, wasn't it? He left you and moved away. He stayed with his family and forgot you ever existed. You got what you deserved. I only hope and pray my mother and grandmother never find out. They'll never hear about this from me, that's for sure, and don't worry, you won't ever see me again."

Before she could reply, Jason turned toward the street, sprinted up the walk and into the wagon. She watched the car make a neat K-turn and speed away toward the boulevard.

She lowered her head, closed the door, walked into the den and picked up the photograph on her desk.

He's very young, my darling. Impulsive, judgmental and very young. I could never have made him understand how we felt about each other. Perhaps his mother can ease his pain and restore his respect for you. I'm only sorry he didn't give me the chance.

Twenty-two

Marina put the phone down. Still no answer. She had tried both Jason's room and his cell. He always had the voice mail activated, so she had left a message each time. *This is so unlike Jason,* she thought. She had called at about ten to say hello and to see if there was anything particular he might want them to bring from home. Despite the news she and Andy would give him, she was so looking forward to seeing him again. It was taking longer than she expected to become accustomed to life without her energetic son bouncing around the house.

Checking her watch, she dialed another number.

"Dr. Andy Buckman, please ... thank you."

"Andy? I'm so sorry to bother you at work, but I'm worried about Jason."

"Why? What's wrong?"

"I tried to call him this morning just to say hi and chat a bit. He wasn't in, so I assumed he was with his friends or at the library or out with his new girlfriend, Amy Whoever. I called twice right after lunch. Still no answer. It's nearly three and he still isn't there. I'm worried, Andy!"

"About what? It's Sunday. He and the gang might have driven into Philly. You know how much they like hanging around on South Street. If it's really bothering you, call him on his cell. But be prepared … he's gonna give you hell for being too much of a worrywart."

"That's just it. I *did* try his cell. No answer there, only voice mail and I've left him several messages."

"Okay, maybe he simply forgot to check it. Wait till later tonight and try again. He's a big boy; you can't know where he is every minute of the day like you did when he was twelve."

"That doesn't mean I don't still want to try," she admitted. "Okay. We can give him a call after dinner and hopefully both get to talk with him. What time will you be home?"

"Believe it or not, I was about ready to finish my last report and sign out. It's been kind of quiet here this afternoon and I'm glad for the chance to be home early."

"Good. I'll see you when you get here. Be careful on the highway. Love you!"

Hanging up, she wandered into the den. There was a cold wind blowing off Lake Michigan. She was thankful her mother was safely tucked away in the warmth of Harbor Bluffs, enjoying the warm weather. The move had been a wise one. *In more ways than we could have foreseen*, she mused.

When the phone rang, she clicked it on, blurting out, "Well, finally, there you are! Where have you been?"

"Marina? This is Joanna Webber. I'm sorry; it sounds like you were expecting someone else."

"Oh, Joanna. Yes, I was. I've been trying to call Jason all day, but I guess he's out with his friends."

"No, he's not. That's why I'm calling. Jason was just here."

"There? At your place? Whatever for? I thought we'd agreed you'd put him off for a week or two until we could talk with him."

"We did. But Jason didn't know about our plan. And then something happened that made him drive all the way down here without any notice."

"What? What happened?"

"Seems someone picked up a piece of gossip about your father and me and passed it along to Jason."

"Oh no! Oh, damn! Who would have dug up something like that after so many years?"

"He didn't say. He didn't say much, in fact. I was on the beach; I looked up and found him standing there. We went into the house, sat down and he asked me point blank whether it was true his grandfather and I had an affair when we were younger. I told him I didn't want to hurt his image of Jared but I couldn't lie either. He raised his voice and spoke disrespectfully of his grandfather, so I asked him to either show some respect or end the conversation. He said a few other things and then stalked off."

"Where did he go?"

"I don't know. I thought it best not to stop him. He's hurting very badly and—"

"You didn't try to stop him? To reason with him?"

"No, I didn't. In his current frame of mind, reasoning would have had no effect whatsoever except to make him angrier. I thought it best to let him go, sort out his feelings and then discuss them with you and Andy. He was very worried about what might happen if you or your mother were to find out. He said he would never tell you and he was furious with me, so anything I would have said would have only made matters worse."

"Oh no, what do I do now? I'm a thousand miles away and Jason's out there all alone, God-knows-where, driving around disillusioned and angry. For God's sake! After all our careful planning..."

"I'm sorry, Marina, that's all I can say. He's young and he doesn't have the maturity or life experience to understand how things happen sometimes."

"I wish I could find him and talk to him. Obviously, I can't get there very fast ... damn it anyway! Oh, I wish I knew what to do."

"How about his residence assistant? Did Jason ever mention him?"

"Once he jokingly told us the guy's name sounded like Kramer and he looked like the guy on *Seinfeld*, but he never said anything about how qualified he was."

"I'm sure he's qualified or the university wouldn't have hired him. Jason should talk to him. You might want to suggest it."

"I may do that, but right now I'm so furious! You and Dad a lifetime ago and now you and Dad again, but this time my son's in the middle. How could you let this happen? I'll call you later after I finally reach him. Goodbye."

Joanna put the phone down in slow motion. This was the kind of anger she had always expected if anyone in Jared's world found out about them. While they were together, their love affair had been idyllic ... supportive friends, her parents angry but not taking steps to expose their relationship, and no one clouding their feelings with guilt. Or so they thought.

Funny, she and Jared had talked about that the last time they met in 1993 in Manhattan, the day she had given him a copy of the tape she'd had made for him. As they reminisced, they realized it had never occurred to them as they traversed the campus, smiling lovers' smiles, talking to trees, that anyone would see anything but their joy. In retrospect, they acknowledged there must have been gossip, but at the time they saw nothing but their feelings for each other.

Joanna remembered words from one of Jared's letters: *The winter brings warm memories of walking across the campus to the student center for coffee. I used to wonder what people were saying as we sat there together. Wonder, not worry.*

Ah, love could be so blind. They were so naïve then! They never suspected someone would store what they knew and use it so destructively. *Why would anyone want to taint our love affair with malicious gossip? And at Jared's grandson's expense. People can be so cruel*, she thought bitterly.

Waiting would be agonizing. It might be a few hours before she heard from Marina. *If she ever contacts me again*, Joanna thought. *I didn't ask to be dragged into their world, but now that I'm there, I'm sorry it's going like this.* Meeting Jared's family should have been a thing of happy remembrances. She sat and looked at Jared's photo. *What next, my love? I think you're responsible for what's happened and, if I'm right, you owe it to all of us to fix what's gone wrong.*

Twenty-three

Jason's mind was racing wildly, his thoughts tumbling over one another, his anger pumping adrenaline, making his heart beat rapidly. Once over the Brigantine Bridge, he retraced his route. Glancing at the gas gauge, he realized he had better find a station or he would never make it back to Manning. A Mobil sign rose above the fast-food restaurants behind him, so he swung into a parking lot, made a U-turn and went back.

With a full tank, he waited at the curb for traffic to pass. On a railroad tie decorating the flowerbed next to the entrance, he watched a graceful seagull posing in the mid-afternoon sun. As he pulled into his lane, the bird spread its wings and flew off. In his rear view mirror, Jason could see the gull, its wings gently flapping, gliding behind him. Later, when he got back onto the two-lane road and began the last leg of the trip to the university, the seagull flew alongside the Outback for a few minutes and then turned away.

It sure looks like the same one, he thought. *But then don't they all look alike? What is a seagull doing this far from the ocean?* He shrugged off the thought. There was no time for introspection or anything but concentrating on his driving and his anger. He could hardly wait to get back to his room where he could gather his thoughts.

Finally, he was back in the parking lot. He sat in the car for several minutes, pondering his options. He could hang in at Manning, move on and ignore the gossip. Sooner or later, everyone would forget about his grandfather and Joanna. He could shrug it off, acknowledge that his grandfather had been a jerk and ride it out that way. Or he could pack it in, transfer to Roosevelt or somewhere else and get out of this place, away from old memories and gossip.

He yanked the keys out of the ignition, got out and slammed the door. A few feet from the car, he aimed the remote over his shoulder and clicked, the brief beep and flash of headlights showing he'd locked the car.

There was a time when spending a couple hours practicing in Kenton's musty basement rooms or shooting the breeze with Todd and the guys would have been something to look forward to. Now, his heart wasn't in his music or his friends.

He took both steps to the dorm at once. As he reached out for the door, Allen Kranmer pulled it open from the other side, nearly throwing Jason off balance.

"Yo, Jason! What's up?"

"Nothin', just getting back in."

"So I see. Out with Amy?"

"How did you know about her? What, do you have your spies planted all over campus or something?"

Allen laughed. "No spies. Just my own eyes and ears. I've seen you two together and heard some of the guys mention you'd taken her out."

"Do you know her?"

"Not personally, but her RA and I have gone out a couple times and she thinks a lot of Amy. I value Jessica's opinion. Jess has a pretty good feel for people."

"Well, I'm glad you approve, but it doesn't matter anyway. I don't think I'm gonna be around here a whole lot longer."

"What? I hope I didn't hear what I thought I heard. You leaving Manning or moving out of Jackson?"

Jason brushed past him into the foyer. "Manning. I'm thinking of transferring."

"What for? Didn't you just make the jazz band? Why would you be thinking of leaving?"

"It's a long story. I don't want to go into it now. It's been an ugly, nasty day and I'm exhausted. We'll talk some other time, okay?"

Allen looked at Jason with a wide, friendly smile and kind eyes.

"Listen, the university put me in this dorm to help you guys. I don't put my nose into anyone's business unless I'm invited, but I can't do anything for you if I don't know what's going on. I'd hate to see you make the wrong choice for the wrong reasons, so why don't we sit and talk about it?"

"Not now, okay? I want to get some rest. I'll stop down sometime tomorrow, I promise. Who knows? It might do me some good to get something off my chest."

Reluctantly, Allen slapped him lightly on the back.

"Okay, man, tomorrow. You really do look like you need some sleep. Give me a call. I'll be here until about two."

Jason went into the hall and onto the stairs, hoping to avoid any encounters. He slipped into his room and locked the door. There was no sound from the other side, so he assumed Todd hadn't gotten back.

He picked up the cell phone he had left on the desk. There were several messages. One was from Amy and four were from his mother. Again, he felt the coldness in his stomach. How would he be able to talk to her with the anger seething in his gut? He had never been able to hide anything from her, least of all something this powerful. She would sense something was wrong and never let up until he spilled it all.

The phone on his desk shrilled. Talking to people couldn't be avoided, he knew that. Pretending he wasn't there wouldn't work either; if it were his mother, she'd only worry about his persistent absence. He picked up the receiver.

"Hello?"

"Jason! Thank heavens you're there!"

"I'm here, Mom. Where else would I be?"

"There, of course, it's just that I've been trying to reach you and was worried something might be wrong. I'm trying to learn to let go, honey, but this empty-nest thing isn't easy. My mother hen instinct still wants to check up on your every move. How are you?"

Jason took a deep breath. "I'm great. Working hard on a paper and trying to keep my head above water. That's where I was all afternoon—the library, trying to get some research done. Sorry if you worried, but you need to stop. I'm doing fine."

Marina's heart sank. *He's lying to me because he doesn't want me to know about Joanna. If he tells me where he was, he'll have to tell me what he heard about Dad.*

Knowing she had to go along or end up going into the whole sordid mess over the phone, she forced a light tone.

"Good for you, kiddo. When's the paper due?"

"Next Monday. But I don't want to spend the weekend while you and Dad are here worrying about the deadline. I want to hand it in before Friday. You are still coming, aren't you?"

"Oh, yes, honey, we are. I wanted you to know we'll be coming in to Philly International at ten-twenty on Friday morning and our flight home is Sunday at five-fifty in the evening. Does the Friday time work for you or should we take a limo to Manning?"

Jason thought about the long ride from the airport to Manning, knowing he'd have a hard time making small talk. It probably would be easier to meet them on campus where he could find the right words to tell them what he had discovered.

"I have a class that was rescheduled for ten," he said, regretting the lie. "I could cut, but it's kind of important, so I guess the limo's a good idea. Do you mind?"

"Not at all, hon. So unless something changes between now and then, we'll see you around lunchtime. Dad sends his love."

"Thanks, tell him I said hi and I'll see you both on Friday."

~ * ~

"Okay, Jason, what's up?"

Allen sat back in the chair in his small room, crossed his legs and leaned forward. Jason sat across from him, uneasily wringing his hands.

"I don't know where to start."

"Anywhere. We can always go back if you think of something you forgot. Why not start at the beginning?"

"The beginning? I guess that would be when my grandfather died about a year and a half ago. He and I were very close … the only difference between us was our ages. I spent as much time with him as I possibly could. I guess you could say he was like a second father to me. He was a teacher, a mentor and most of all, my best friend. I was pretty shook up when he died."

When Allen didn't comment, Jason continued.

"My grandfather taught at Manning State when he was in his thirties. He was in the drama department and directed all the campus plays. All my life I heard about Manning and how much he loved this college. I couldn't wait to get here myself. I knew I'd love the campus like he had. And at first, that's exactly what happened. That is, until Friday night."

The look on the counselor's face encouraged Jason to continue.

"Amy and I were on the phone and she said she needed to see me. We went out for a Coke and she told me about some old campus gossip about my grandfather and one of his students. Rumor had it the two of them were a hot item on campus his last year here. Seems everybody knew they were having an affair."

"How can you be certain it's true? You know gossips don't usually have reliable sources."

"Yesterday, I went to see the woman he was supposedly involved with. I confronted her with the rumor and she admitted it happened."

"Did she explain?"

"No. Even if she had tried, I didn't hang around to listen. The first thing she did was jump on my case about my tone of voice and she refused to talk to me unless I was more—what did she say—respectful? Hell, I didn't feel respectful. I still don't. I left and came back here. That's when you ran into me."

"So all you know is there was an affair. How long ago was this, Jason?"

"In 'sixty-one or two. She was a junior when they met and he was about thirty-six, I guess."

"And you're the only one in your family who knows about this?"

"Yeah. And that's part of my problem. My mother and dad are coming here on Friday and I'm gonna have to tell them. I don't know how. But if I make up some reason not to stay at Manning and I transfer out, there won't be a chance they'll hear the story and the whole thing will just die out."

"I see. You figure you can spare your mom the shock of finding out her father was less than perfect by sacrificing a promising career at Manning? How do you think that'll work for you?"

"God, you sound like a shrink. I can *make* it work, I think. There are other colleges with good music programs. At least somewhere else, I won't be living with gossip and stories about something my grandfather did years ago, something that's become a campus legend."

"You think it's such really big news?"

"With some people, sure. At least the ones that live in Amy's dorm."

"Jason, this is a very big school. It's at least ten times the size it was when your grandfather was here. Most of the students have a lot more to do than hunt down gossip. Obviously, whoever told Amy about the affair just enjoyed raking up some dirt, but I have a feeling the thrill won't go far or last long. Is it worth leaving a place you like without giving the rumor mill a chance to shut down?"

Jason sat back in his chair, lowered his head into his hands and thought. What would he tell his parents about why he wanted to transfer? They knew how much he liked Manning. His mother in particular would dig and dig until she got to the real reason and he would have to tell her anyhow.

Resting his elbows on his knees, Jason looked up at Allen.

"It probably wouldn't work. Sooner or later, I'd end up telling my folks everything I know anyhow. You're right, it does seem stupid to leave Manning when the truth is gonna come out anyway. You've been a big help, Al. Thanks."

"Don't mention it. I like you and I'm hoping you'll enjoy a great four years here. You have a lot to offer. And besides..." He grinned. "Who would Amy date if you left? I hear she's sorta stuck on you."

"Who said that?"

"That's on the down-low. I never reveal my sources. But I hear she likes you, so if I were you, I'd quit worrying about some ghost from the past and concentrate on positive stuff, like the band and Amy."

They stood and walked toward the door. As Allen opened it, he said, "Get some rest, man. This thing's been eating at you, I can tell. And when you feel up to it, you might want to reconnect with that woman you saw yesterday. You really should give her a chance to give you her side of the story."

~ * ~

When Jason talked to Amy the next day, he didn't tell her about his visit with Joanna Webber. Not that he didn't trust her to keep it to herself. He wasn't ready to discuss what had happened at the beach house or about his reaction to Joanna's admission. He and Amy had lunch together on Wednesday and kept the talk light.

~ * ~

At the airport, Marina and Andy waited impatiently for their bags, watching other passengers heft suitcases off the carousel and go toward the exit. Finally, Andy spotted his pullman and a couple of pieces later, Marina's came out of the chute.

They had decided at the last minute to rent a car. It made sense to have their own transportation so they wouldn't be stranded if Jason needed to be elsewhere for part of the time they were there. They found the rental car pickup area outside baggage claim and sat on a bench waiting for the next shuttle.

Looking at the small bag Marina clutched tightly, Andy raised an eyebrow.

"Are you sure you want to show all that stuff to Jason?"

"Uh-huh. I think it's best if he gets it all. He'll have a hard enough time accepting this relationship between Joanna and Dad. When he reads the poems and the e-mails and sees the pictures, I think Jason will be sensitive and compassionate enough to grasp the depth of Dad's feeling for Joanna and hers for him. Without a deeper understanding, I'm afraid he'll continue making something sordid out of their relationship. Look what a difference it's made for you. Finally getting into their heads, reading the e-mails and hearing the tape made you change your mind in a hurry."

~ * ~

Jason sat in his room, mentally tracing their route. He knew it wouldn't be much longer before they would get there and he would have to tell them about his grandfather and the campus gossip.

How could you put us through this, Grandpa? he asked silently. *Why couldn't you have been the perfect person I always thought you were?* He sat thinking about his grandfather, a heavy sadness replacing the anger in his heart.

Twenty-four

When the phone rang, he jumped, looked at his watch and realized his parents had arrived.

Marina rushed over to hug him as Jason walked into the lounge. Behind her he saw his father with a broad smile on his face, waiting his turn.

"You look wonderful, son. I guess you're eating enough and getting enough sleep. Those late hours don't seem to be hurting you any."

"I'm doing great, Dad. Mom, how was your flight?"

"As good as any flight can be with two hours of security checks and the butterflies in my stomach whenever we take off or land. I never particularly liked flying, but now it's worse than ever."

"Did they feed you on the plane or did you stop for lunch on the way up?"

"Are you kidding? Peanuts don't make a meal," Andy answered. "We dropped our bags at the bed and breakfast and came straight here. I'm starved. What do you say we find a nice quiet place to eat?"

"I know just the spot. Amy and I have been there a couple of times and we both like it. Food's good and it's never too noisy."

"Amy? She's the girl you've mentioned in your e-mails. What's her last name again?"

"Lassen. She's a psych major and a terrific girl. I hope you get a chance to meet her while you're here."

"We'd like that very much." Marina looked at Andy and winked. This was the first time her son had even mentioned a girl more than once or twice.

They caught up on family happenings at the restaurant. How fast Adam was growing, how Sarah was doing in fourth grade, how Uncle Mike and Aunt Ellen were putting an addition on their house to make room for a small studio where Uncle Mike could give private dance lessons.

Jason listened politely, but his mind was racing ahead to the talk they would have when they returned to the dorm.

~ * ~

Back at Jackson, Marina reached in the back seat for a briefcase-style bag.

"What's that, Mom?"

"Oh, there are a few things here I'd like you to see. We'll look at them when we get up to your room. We can visit privately there, can't we?"

"Sure. Todd's gone home for the weekend again. His folks live close enough that he can do that as often as he wants. Not like me, huh?"

"His mother and dad are pretty lucky," Andy said, cuffing Jason gently on the jaw. "You could have been close to home, too, but you decided to go halfway around the world."

"Aw, c'mon, Dad. It's not that far!"

In Jason's room, Marina put the bag on his desk, pulled out the chair and sat while Jason went next door and dragged another chair through the bathroom for his father. Andy sat facing Marina, and Jason perched on the edge of his bed. All of a sudden, everyone fell silent. Marina and Andy exchanged glances and then looked down at the floor. Jason looked from his mother to his father, at the serious looks on their faces. *This is probably a good thing*, he thought, *because I have something very difficult to tell them.*

"Mom, Dad … I'm so glad to see both of you. I feel terrible you've come all this way and I have to spoil our visit by telling you something unpleasant."

This is it, Marina thought. *This is where he tells us he knows something that's supposed to come as a surprise to us.*

"It's about Grandpa," Jason went on. "Last week, I heard a story about him and a student of his back when he used to teach here. The gossip was pretty ugly and I've dreaded having to tell you about it, but I think you ought to know."

Marina and Andy exchanged distressed looks.

Now what the hell's going on here? Neither of his parents appeared surprised or even curious, Jason noted. Now wasn't that an interesting reaction?

"That your grandfather and this student had an affair?" Marina asked.

"Uh, yeah, that's about what I heard. The grandmother of a girl in Amy's dorm taught here with Grandpa. She remembered the old campus gossip and passed it on to her granddaughter, no less, when she found out I was enrolled here. At first, I thought the whole thing was nonsense, but it upset me to think people might be still talking. Wait … why do I think you already know about this?"

"We do. Your dad and I made this trip for the express purpose of talking to you about what you apparently already know. We didn't want to discuss this over the phone. It's far too serious a topic to treat lightly. We know how much you adored your grandfather—"

Jason interrupted. "Wait a second. I loved the man I thought I knew, not the cheater he was. I'll never feel the same about him again!"

"This is exactly what we were afraid of," Andy said. "We wanted to tell you about your grandfather and Joanna in a way that might take out some of the sting. We knew you were going to see her and, although we trusted her not to hurt you, we didn't want you to stumble on the truth without hearing about Joanna and your grandfather from us first."

"You *trust* her? You *know* her?"

"We know her," Marina said, "at least I do. I've spoken to her, I mean, not in person but ... wait. Let's start back at the beginning right after Dad died with how we discovered she existed. Maybe that will help you get to where we are now."

Jason sat, open-mouthed, stunned, unable to absorb everything he was hearing. He stood and paced the length of the small room.

"You've known about this how long? Since not long after Grandpa died? You've talked to this woman? Why did you think I didn't deserve to be let in on it? What? Jason's just a little boy? He can't handle truth like this? What was it? Why did you pretend for so long? Why did you lie?"

Before Marina or Andy could reply, Jason grabbed his jacket from the back of the chair and bolted from the room, the heavy metal door clanging as he slammed it on his way out.

Andy started to his feet, but stopped at the touch of Marina's hand on his arm.

"He needs some time to process this," she said. "I think I know where he's heading. Let's give him a few minutes and then we can go to him."

~ * ~

Jason slowed his frantic pace as he neared the little path through the woods. To his right, nestled among the bright trees decorated in what was left of their autumn finery, the university chapel stood, its wooden door slightly ajar. Everyone had mocked it when it was opened in 1960, he remembered reading. Its roof looked like the flying nun's cap or some alien winged creature. Not usually inclined toward churches, Jason had never been inside. Now, he found his feet leaving the path and crossing to the doorway. Inside, a small red lamp glowed from the base of a thin brass chain. Simple wooden pews lined both sides of the room. The floor-to-ceiling stained glass window behind the table that served as an altar flickered with the lamplight and the midday sun outside.

He didn't kneel. Instead, he stood in the center of the aisle, his thoughts disjointed, his emotions roller-coastering from anger to humiliation to rage. Why hadn't he deserved to know the truth? Was this what had been causing such a rift between his parents? He remembered asking Marina if there was something he needed to know and how she had calmly said no. It seemed like months had gone by before his mother had regained a bit of her sparkle. Was the turmoil about this? How did she find out? Was it something Grandpa said?

Thinking back on the times spent on the boat, he realized his grandfather may have been trying to tell him life isn't as perfect or as simple as he would like it to be. Sure, even without admitting to his feelings for another woman, Grandpa had hinted often enough there was a kind of sadness in living, and he always came back to the same theme ... life takes us where we're supposed to be and we need to know there is a plan we are here to fulfill.

Memories flooded his mind. Jared Fowler never made an enemy. He was always kind and considerate to everyone he encountered. Jason could hear the respectful tone of Jared's voice as he spoke about a co-worker or discussed a problem he was having at the theater. Never had Jason heard Jared's voice raised in anger. How could he possibly hope to measure up to his grandfather when his first response to unpleasant news was irrational fury? He needed to do better. And suddenly, he heard his grandfather's loving voice entreat him to forgive and move on. Jason felt a deep sense of peace settle over his heart. Lowering his head, he fought back tears as he backed out of the chapel and turned again toward the quad.

He was surprised at how quiet it was on this part of campus, usually teeming with chattering students. He didn't come upon anyone as he slowly mounted the steps of Kenton Hall. It was almost like everyone had vanished so he could have the campus to himself to work out his feelings. He reached for the door, but changed his mind about going inside and instead sat on the top step.

It's time for me to grow up. What did it matter what happened so many years ago? Who am I to pass judgment on the whys and wherefores of my grandfather's relationship with Joanna Ransome? How arrogant he'd been when he confronted her with such bitter anger and recrimination! He remembered her sad eyes when she told him she had loved his grandfather and he knew Jared would have been disappointed in the way he'd acted.

Looking up, he saw his mother walking slowly up the sidewalk from the woods. He waited until she was sitting next to him.

"I've been a real jerk."

"No, you haven't, Jason. You were angry and disillusioned. So was I when I first started putting the pieces together. I was furious with Dad for lying to us, for hiding such an important part of his life, and especially for dying before we could hear what Joanna meant to him. But as time went on and I learned about her, the kind of person she is and the way she protected Dad, the way she kept the relationship secret so he wouldn't lose our respect or his marriage to your grandmother ... the more I learned about all that, the less anger I felt."

"What *did* you find?"

Marina told him about the photos, the e-mails, the tape and then about having called Joanna to ask that she postpone the meeting with him until after they'd been there.

"I'm sorry you can't listen to the tape," she said, "but I can tell you it's very emotional, Jason, very powerful. I believe she loved him, hon. From what I've learned, she kept their secret for forty years, her entire adult life. And I think he loved her very much, too. I came to respect that and to want to know her, to reach out to her."

"No one else wanted you to, though?"

"Right. Your dad and Uncle Mike, even Aunt Genna, thought it was too dangerous for me to try to bring Joanna into my life. It would have opened the door to your finding out, your grandmother learning Dad never stopped writing to Joanna."

"I was going to ask if Grandmom knew any of this. Did she ever know about Joanna?"

"Yes, a long time ago, right after the affair was supposedly over. She never knew, though, that your grandfather kept Joanna in his life. He risked losing Joanna, in fact he hurt her very badly, in order to keep that façade intact for his family."

"But she forgave him?"

"Yes, she forgave him. She said nothing he could ever have done would make her stop loving him. She loved him, Jason."

"I have to do the same," he said, standing. "I have to understand and forgive. It's what Grandpa would have wanted. Let's not leave Dad alone in the room. Wanna go back?"

~ * ~

Andy met them at the door to the room. "I'm sorry you had to find out everything this way, son. It's partly my fault. I was very hard on your mother when she first started picking up the clues your grandfather left behind. She took a lot of grief from me, Uncle Mike and Aunt Genna. She wanted so badly to make us understand the relationship between your grandfather and Joanna. We only saw the damage that would be done if you and your grandmother got wind of what she'd learned, so we convinced her to forget about Joanna and get on with what needed to be done in our family. When you decided to come to Manning, we didn't think there was any chance you'd encounter the story this way."

"I understand a lot better," Jason said, "and I see what Joanna was probably trying to tell me. She and Grandpa didn't just have an affair, their feelings went deeper and lasted a lot longer, didn't they? You must have been really shocked when you found out."

Marina sighed. "I was at first, honey. After all, the affair between your grandfather and Joanna could have ruined a lot of lives. At the time, neither of them thought about that. In the end, though, your grandfather did the right thing. He stayed with his family and worked things out with Grandmom. Although he and Joanna stayed in touch, he spent his life giving us all so many happy memories. He was just a man, a human being who loved us enough to wrench himself from what he may have wanted more than anything so we could have him with us where he knew he belonged. I don't feel anger; I feel sympathy, sorrow, even compassion. These are emotions that come with understanding and forgiving. I think you're well on your way there. It's far easier to remember Grandpa with love for the good he did than to dwell on any negative things from his past, don't you think?"

Jason didn't reply. Instead, he went into Todd's room and came back carrying a small tape player.

"Todd got this to listen to some audio tapes he needed for a class. I think I'm ready to hear what's on the tape."

Marina saw the tears in Jason's eyes the instant he heard his grandfather's voice. *This hurts him badly now,* she thought, *but perhaps it will help him understand.*

They listened all the way through. It took nearly an hour, but no one grew restless or made a motion to turn it off.

Finally, the last note faded away and Andy turned off the player.

"I see what you mean about the way Grandpa sounded, the way he sang to her. His voice was wonderful, wasn't it, Mom?"

"He sang at our wedding. He sang at the party we had when you were christened. He sang when he worked in the yard. He sang until his lungs wouldn't let him sing anymore. But I never heard him sing like that."

They sat in silence for several minutes.

Jason handed the tape to his mother. "Take this back with you. I guess I only have one more question. Will you ever tell Grandmom about this?"

"No. We don't know how much she knew or whether she suspected Grandpa was in touch with Joanna all these years. We can't risk finding out the hard way. She doesn't need to know anything. This would only be painful for her and she doesn't deserve to be hurt."

Jason paced from one side of the room to the other. He stopped abruptly.

"I haven't been honest with you, either. Last Sunday, when I told you I'd been in the library studying? I wasn't. I went to Brigantine to see Dr. Webber. I found her and I was horrible to her. I acted like a stupid kid and I feel terrible now."

"We know, honey. Joanna called after you left and told me how upset you'd been. She was wise enough to let you go and not try to explain. I'm afraid you wouldn't have been able to accept anything from her."

Jason raised his eyebrow. "Oh, my God! She told you I'd been there? How mean I was?"

"She didn't have to. She simply said you'd had your worst fears confirmed and you took the discovery badly. She wanted to explain to you but she knew that wasn't the time."

"I'm sorry," Jason said. "I didn't mean to hurt her; I was too angry to listen to what she had to say."

"That's okay. Under the circumstances, I'm sure she understood how you were feeling. Anyway, I told her I'd let her know how you were when we got here. Shall we call her? Help set her mind at ease? I'm sure she's anxious to know and, if you'd like, maybe you could apologize at the same time."

"I sure hope you're right, Mom. I hope I didn't totally turn her off and lose the chance to talk with her about Grandpa. I wouldn't blame her if she wouldn't speak to me again."

Twenty-five

Joanna woke Friday morning with a start, stifling a sob. It was the recurring dream, the one she'd begun having about a month ago. This time, it was more vivid than usual, jarring her back to consciousness with a devastating sensation of grief. She shut her eyes tight and put her head in her hands. Oh, this time it was so real!

She and Jared were on the Staten Island ferry. The boat was crowded as always; they were squeezed tightly against the rail, the breeze blowing their hair, the sun beating down warmly, the Statue of Liberty off to their left. In front of them, the skyscrapers gleamed a deep coral in the late afternoon setting sun, the Empire State Building, their Emerald Palace, towering over them all. She was snuggled in the warmth of Jared's arms, and the feeling of contentment was overwhelming. This was the answer to her prayers, the life she wanted to live forever. When the ship docked, they would go back to their hotel and spend the rest of the evening alone.

Tomorrow they would go home, home to the little house they had bought from Dan at the end of the lane in the woods. Marina and Michael would be coming to visit that weekend, so she would quickly make up the two cots they kept for the children and bake a batch of chocolate chip cookies they especially liked.

The happiness was intense. She turned to Jared and raised her face to his. Then everything changed.

Moving slightly away, he gazed at her, his eyes filled with sadness. Suddenly, they were there alone. The people had vanished; the ferry dissolved away. They were in her old apartment and she was begging him not to go, not to leave her alone.

But Jared backed away, releasing her hand as he faded from view ever so slowly, until Joanna couldn't see him any longer. Instead, a seagull fluttered against the window, its wings gently touching the pane. Then it landed easily on the sill, its eyes large and unblinking.

"You are ever in my heart ... nor time nor distance nor silence can ever dim the wondrous memories of what we had or take away from what we have," she heard the bird say with Jared's voice ... words from a poem he had written for her many years earlier.

"And one day, we will be together again. Watch for me, my darling Joanna. Watch for me."

And then the bird flew off, leaving her with such a profound sense of loss and grief she began to cry, heavy deep sobs that brought her back to the present, but with the dream still fresh.

Why now? Why a whole decade since she'd last seen Jared? Until this dream began haunting her, thoughts of him had been sweet and comforting. Now she dreaded going to sleep. Night after night, she awoke in tears, missing him so badly she didn't know what to do.

She crawled out of bed, reached for a handful of tissues and dried her eyes. In the bathroom, she pressed a cold washcloth to her face. Even then, she could see Jared's face slowly vanishing and feel the heavy sorrow closing in on her heart.

"It started with your grandson," she said out loud. She had been doing fine; her life was uncomplicated, filled with family and her writing. Then came her encounter with Jason Buckman and suddenly everything had changed. She found herself constantly thinking about and reliving the past. She was sinking into the morose state she thought she had left behind with the advent of the e-mails before Jared's death.

How ridiculous she had been to think Jason would accept her or listen to anything she wanted to say. It had only taken one face-to-face encounter for her to experience his real emotions.

Joanna felt a bit better after two cups of freshly-brewed coffee and a hot shower. But no matter where she wandered in the house, no matter how high she turned up the stereo, she could still hear Jared's deep voice coming from that infernal seagull. *Am I going mad?* she asked herself. *I can't sit here alone anymore. I need to get out of here.*

~ * ~

"Jo? What makes you call today? Can't stay away even on your day off?"

"No, I thought maybe you were free for lunch. What do you say? Why don't we check out that new café in the Belvedere Hotel ... what's it called? Images?"

"Oh, the one with the wall filled with pictures of old Atlantic City! I've heard a lot about it. Sure, why not? It's Friday and no one's exactly banging down the door. I can take an extra-long break. I'll meet you there in about a half hour."

~ * ~

One of the newer structures in the city, the Belvedere was right in the center of the row of casinos that snaked along the shoreline. Joanna remembered reading in *The Press* that the owners, a large Vegas corporation, were pushing hard to have the huge new parking garage finished to complete the construction of the resort's only non-casino hotel. Since the new convention center had been opened, Atlantic City was desperate for more hotel space to attract the huge trade shows that required hundreds more rooms than were presently available. The variety of shops and restaurants in the Belvedere were beginning to pull in tourists and residents alike, thanks to some daring young chefs and creative, ambitious menus.

Joanna went out to her car, fighting the wind as she struggled to open the door. She had plenty of time to get into town, park the car and make her way to the restaurant. She wondered if she'd see any familiar faces or places among the vintage photos that lined the walls. After all, Atlantic City was where she'd grown up; perhaps some casual photographer had captured her or her friends as they walked the boardwalk or sunned on the beach.

At the top of the Brigantine Bridge, the car shuddered against the force of the wind. Joanna drove into the city through the midtown tunnel. Streams of cars and limos were pouring into town when she came out at the convention center and turned onto Fairmount Avenue for the short ride to the Belvedere. As always, no matter what time of day or night, the streets were clogged and crowded with tour buses and taxis.

"Unchained Melody" began to play on the radio as she pulled into the open-air parking lot next to the new six-story garage where hundreds of workers were bustling about, their white hard hats gleaming in the sun. Her favorite oldies station had the song on its frequent play list. She was amazed at the number of times she heard this or one of "their" other songs in the average week. And every time she heard one, she pictured Jared—Jared, singing to her, Jared bending to kiss her, Jared with that sleepy, dreamy-eyed look. She saw him now, and closed her eyes, smiling at the sight of his face.

A deep rumbling filled her ears, and at first, she thought it was an earthquake. But looking out the front windshield, she saw nothing out of the ordinary. Above her, too far out of her line of vision to offer warning or chance of escape, one entire side of the new garage had broken free from its steel supports and was cascading to the street.

Joanna never saw the large grey chunk of concrete that was hurtling toward her car. She was still puzzling over the vibrations when suddenly everything was dark.

~ * ~

Only a block away, Betty watched in horror as the entire right side of the parking garage tumbled, one floor layering on top of another. She pulled over to the curb and sat stunned, knowing that, had she arrived mere moments earlier, she would have been in harm's way, probably having just parked her car or walking toward the hotel doors.

She picked up her cell phone and quick-dialed Joanna. Best to warn her away from what Betty knew would soon be a massive rescue operation—already she could hear sirens getting close.

No answer from Joanna's phone. Betty felt a chill of fear. Joanna was always on time, often early so as not to keep someone waiting. Betty pictured the proximity of the outdoor lot to the tragic collapse she saw in front of her, felt herself shivering with shock and then ran from her car toward the worst devastation she'd ever witnessed.

Construction workers, bleeding and dazed, wandered around aimlessly, muttering names of fellow crewmembers. Police officers, newly arrived, cordoned off the area, directing traffic onto side streets, waving ambulances and rescue units as close as possible to the scene. She ran to the nearest officer.

"Please, my friend was meeting me at the Belvedere. She might have just pulled into the lot. Is there any damage there?"

"Sorry, lady, I don't know anything about what's going on anywhere except right here. You'll have to wait behind the tape there and we'll try to find out as soon as we can what's going on. I wish I could help but..."

A group of workers walked slowly toward Betty, their clothes torn, everything covered in a light coating of gray dust. Holding each other, they went past, coughing. Again Betty dialed Joanna. Again no answer. A police car stopped at the corner, its lights flashing. Betty recognized Jake Westcott as he got out. A rookie on the force, Jake had been a client at the youth center when he was in his teens. Working with Joanna had turned the young man's life around, and he often stopped by to say hello.

"Jake! Jake!" Betty ran to him, tears streaming down her face. "Jake, I think Joanna might be caught in there somewhere! We were supposed to meet for lunch and you know how she's always early and, oh God, Jake, can you look for her? Can you see if there are any cars trapped?"

Jake held both her arms. "You're not sure, right? Have you tried calling her?"

Betty nodded frantically, waving her cell phone. "She doesn't answer. Oh, Jake, I'm so afraid something's—"

"No point in thinking the worst. Maybe she hadn't gotten there yet. Maybe a thousand things. Hang in here and let me see what I can find out, okay? I'll be back as soon as I can."

Jake retrieved his cap from the car and strode hurriedly into the crowd of fire and police personnel. Betty stood for several minutes watching the clouds of dust swirl around in the stiff breeze. Then she went back to her car, laid her head on the steering wheel and prayed.

Twenty-six

Marina clicked off her cell phone and shoved it back in her purse.

"She's not answering. We can try again later. How about an early dinner?"

"I'm not sure I can eat very much," Jason said. "I'm still shaken up from everything I've heard this afternoon. Guess it'll take some time to absorb it all, huh?"

On the desk, the phone rang loudly, startling Marina. Jason picked up the receiver on the first ring.

"Jason? It's me, Amy. Turn on your television set, hurry ... channel six."

Without asking why, Jason reached out and pushed the button on the small set on his dresser. He looked at his parents and shrugged.

"Amy says turn it on," he said, with the receiver still at his ear.

The trio sat in stunned silence as the on-site reporter described the ghastly accident that had occurred about four hours earlier in Atlantic City. He recited the details that were available ... the sudden collapse of a whole section of the new parking garage ... four construction workers known dead ... one pedestrian being treated for injuries sustained from falling concrete ... three people in cars in the outdoor parking lot in critical condition. One of them had been identified as Atlantic City psychologist Dr. Joanna Webber, on the way to meet a friend for lunch. Freak accident, the reporter called it. Tragic loss of life and certainly the worst construction accident in the city's history. So many injuries ... non-construction casualties were airlifted to Cooper Trauma Center in Camden.

Jason blanched. "Amy? I have so much to tell you, but now's not the time. This is so awful. My parents are here and I'm not sure what we're going to do. Thanks for calling. I'll touch base later."

Marina already had her purse in her hand and was heading toward the door. Andy rooted around in his pocket for the car keys. Jason turned off the television set and followed them. Not a word was exchanged as they left, faces taut with anxiety, their destination certain but unspoken.

From trips to South Street with his friends, Jason knew Camden was directly east across the Delaware river from Philadelphia. Once there, he was sure they would have no problem finding the hospital.

~ * ~

The man at the information desk was hidden behind a newspaper. He looked up at the sound of their approach.

"May I help you?"

"Yes," Marina replied. "We're looking for the trauma unit. A friend of ours was brought in a few hours ago and we're very concerned about her condition."

"Name?"

"Dr. Joanna Webber. She was airlifted from—"

"Oh yes, the Belvedere accident. It's all over the television," he said, manipulating the mouse to scroll down his computer screen. "She's still listed in very critical condition. You can go on over to the trauma unit, but no one but immediate family can get in to see her. Follow this corridor to the end and then turn left. Trauma is straight ahead."

"Very critical condition," Jason muttered. "Oh, my God!"

~ * ~

At the entrance to the trauma unit, they were faced by a set of double doors. "Authorized Personnel Only," said the sign. There was a bell on the wall next to the door and Andy gave it a tentative push.

"May I help you?" A tall, thin nurse wearing an incongruously cheerful multi-colored smock came out into the hallway.

Andy repeated his inquiry about Joanna and their hearts sank as they saw the serious look that came into the nurse's eyes.

"I'm sorry I don't have more encouraging news to give you. We've done everything we can for her now and it's truly a matter of time and how hard she can fight. Her injuries are extensive."

"Is there any chance we could see her?" Jason asked.

"No, I'm sorry, not now. We did allow her son, his wife and grandson in for a few minutes, but even they weren't permitted to stay."

She gestured across the hall. "That's the waiting area. I'm sure they're still there. They would probably appreciate the company. We'll keep you posted if there's any change," she said as she disappeared through the door.

"What do you think?" Andy asked. "How do we explain to her family who we are and why we're here? Perhaps we should find another place to wait, not disturb them right now."

"No," Marina said. "We should go in. Remember? In one of her e-mails, Joanna told Dad her family had always known about him. She said she wanted them to know him as she did. How I wish Dad had done the same for us."

"There's no time for that now, Mom," Jason chided. "Maybe we can help them somehow."

A man paced the floor, running his fingers through his white hair. On a vinyl-covered sofa, a young boy, eyes red from the tears still streaking his face, clung tightly to a woman who was wiping her eyes with a crumpled tissue. She stared up at them as they entered the room.

The man turned, his blue eyes registering his curiosity.

"Mister Webber? I'm Andy Buckman and this is my wife, Marina Fowler Buckman. I'm not sure if that name means anything to you."

Steven walked to them, looking first at Andy, then at Marina and finally at Jason. His gaze softened as it rested on the young man.

"Why yes, of course it does. You're Jared Fowler's family. My mother's spoken to us about all of you. I'm very surprised you're here."

His voice broke and it was obvious he was struggling to gain his composure. "This is Jared's grandson?"

Jason put out a hand, shook Steven's briefly. He hadn't taken his eyes off Brian, who stood close to his mother's chair. Marina concentrated on Steven, mentally searching for any resemblance, anything that might confirm Judith's theory.

She studied the whitish hair so like hers, but the face, round and youthful, had nothing of Jared Fowler in it.

"This is a terrible way to meet," Marina said. "We're so sorry about this. Can you tell us what happened?"

"I'm not really clear myself. Betty—she's the secretary at the clinic where Mom works—Betty said Mom called and they arranged to meet for lunch. They were going to a new restaurant at The Belvedere, a hotel in Atlantic City. Betty was just getting there when she actually saw the decks of the new parking garage fall. She tried to call Mom to warn her away from the area, but there wasn't any answer. A police officer friend of hers told her they'd found Mom's car with massive damage from the falling concrete and Mom unconscious in the driver's seat. The doctors say she has severe head injuries, but they're encouraged that she's still breathing on her own. That's the only piece of good news they can give us."

Jason crossed the room and knelt in front of Abby. He touched Brian's arm.

"Hey, buddy, I'm Jason. I know how worried you must be about your grandmother. I lost my grandfather not long ago and it was the worst feeling in the world. Your grandmother's still fighting, though, and she'll make it fine. We've gotta have faith, right?"

Brian looked up as small tears streamed down his cheeks. "She's gotta make it; she just has to! I love Gran so much."

"Why don't we go out and get a soda, Brian? We can bring some coffee back for your mom and dad, okay?"

"Go ahead," Abby told the boy, a slender youngster with hair almost the color of Jason's.

"Okay," he said, wiping his eyes with the back of his hand. "But we'll come right back, won't we?"

"Sure," Jason said, leading the youngster to the door. "We won't be long."

When the boys had gone, Marina and Andy sat across from Abby, who motioned for her husband to sit as well.

"We don't know how much you know about the relationship between your mother and our dad," Marina began.

"Well, actually, I grew up hearing about your father," Steven said. "It was never a secret there was someone who was very important to my mother, someone she loved very much but whose first loyalty was to his family. It hurt to see her so alone, but Mom's life was her own choice and she seemed content to devote it to helping other people. After my father died in

Vietnam, she never even came close to being involved with another man, although we encouraged her to date. We all hoped she would meet someone to share her life. But she always said she'd already met the one man she was destined to love forever, and no one else could ever measure up to Jared Fowler."

So that was it. Joanna was widowed and never remarried. *Was she waiting for Dad?* Marina wondered.

"You know far more than we do," she said. "Dad never told us about your mother. I learned about their relationship after his death. It was a shock, to say the least. But I was drawn to her from the beginning. When I saw her at the funeral, I wanted to know who she was to my father and then after I learned parts of their story, I felt tremendous compassion for her. What they had must have been very special."

"What brings you here now? Of all times?"

"Actually, we were hoping to visit with your mother. Jason recently learned about her and his grandfather and he had gone to Joanna's home to talk, but the conversation didn't go well. He left a very angry young man. After we talked with him, he said he wanted to go back and make amends. We tried to call her to see if it was all right for us to come, but she didn't answer her phone. Afterwards, we saw the news report on television and drove right here."

"Oh yes," Steven said. "Your son is at Manning. My mother said she'd met him during alumni weekend. What a coincidence."

"Yes, I suppose it is." Marina reached out to hug Abby. "When she recovers, I'd really like to get to know her better."

Abby reached for a packet of tissues in her purse. "Joanna is about the most important person in our lives. I don't know what we'd do if anything happened to her."

The door opened to admit the nurse, a chart in one hand, discarded latex gloves in the other.

"A quick update, Mister Webber. Your mother's vital signs are stronger, although they're still far from stable. She's deeply unconscious, but the fluctuation in her heart rate is encouraging."

"Can we see her again?"

"Not yet. She needs to be absolutely quiet for a while longer. Perhaps in an hour or so. I'll come back later and let you know."

Jason and Brian came back with the drinks as the nurse was leaving.

"Is Gran going to die?"

Steven wrapped his arms around the frightened eight-year-old. "I hope not, son. Her heart is getting stronger, but we can't get our hopes up too high. She's still in bad shape."

"I want to believe what you told me, Jason," Brian said. "You know, that your grandfather will take care of Gran, that he'll keep her safe. I sure hope you're right."

The adults looked at one another in silence as the boys sat close together on the sofa. Marina wondered what that was all about. What had Jason said to Brian? What did he know?

Later, the nurse appeared at the door. She beckoned for Steven.

"Your mother seems to be rallying a bit. She opened her eyes a minute ago for a second. I think it would be all right for you to come in for a few minutes."

"There are three other people here who have come a long way to see my mother," Steven said. "Would it matter if we all went in together?"

The nurse hesitated. "Normally, that wouldn't be allowed, but I don't think a short visit will hurt."

Steven turned to the others and motioned them toward him.

"We can go in, but only for a short time. Mom's opened her eyes and the nurse says that's a positive sign. Maybe knowing we're all here will encourage her to hold on and keep fighting."

The cubicle was tiny, surrounded by curtains and filled with an assortment of machines, monitors and tubes. Steven, Abby and Brian gathered at one side of Joanna's bed, while Marina, Andy and Jason squeezed in at the other.

Joanna's head was swathed in bandages; an IV line ran into her arm. A heart monitor beeped out its regular pulse. She was pale and her eyes were closed.

Brian reached out for her hand. Without thinking, on the other side Jason did the same.

"I want to hug her and tell her I'm sorry," Jason said to no one in particular.

"You still can, son," Andy replied. "Go ahead."

Jason released her hand and leaned down to put his arms around Joanna's unresponsive shoulders. When he laid his cheek against hers, her eyes fluttered and her lips moved soundlessly.

Her eyes opened slightly.

"Jared," she whispered. "Jared. I've been watching for you. The seagull..."

Then she smiled and closed her eyes. The heart monitor continued its steady beeping.

"She's asleep," the nurse said. "I think it would be best if we left her alone."

Brian stood on tiptoes and kissed Joanna's cheek. Steven squeezed her hand. "We're right outside, Mom, when you wake up again."

Abby kissed her finger and placed it lightly on Joanna's forehead. Marina and Andy touched her arm, tears in their eyes. Jason stood unmoving until his father took his arm and guided him out of the room. He knew he'd heard correctly ... the seagull?

In the hallway, Steven turned to the nurse. "What do you think?

"I think you should go home and get some rest, especially your little boy. She may sleep for hours, maybe days. I promise I'll call if there's any change."

"Why don't you and Brian go on home?" Steven said to Abby. "It's been a long day and you guys need a break. You can be back in minutes if anything changes. I'd like to stay for a while longer."

"Promise, Dad? Promise you'll call the minute Gran wakes up again?"

"Promise, Bri. Now go home with Mom and get some sleep. You know Gran wouldn't want you making yourself sick."

Abby and Brian walked toward the door.

"Thanks, Jason, for talking to me," Brian said. "I think you're right. If anyone can help Gran now, it's probably your grandpa."

Twenty-seven

Still thinking of what Joanna had said, Jason realized Brian was talking to him and forced himself to respond.

"Keep the faith, buddy. Good night. I'll see you in the morning."

"We'd like to stay, if that's okay with you," Marina told Steven. "I think you could use some support."

"Of course. It would be good to have you. Thanks."

Steven sat in one of the heavy chairs. Andy sat next to him, with Marina and Jason on the long sofa by the door. Jason stared straight ahead at nothing in particular, his mind cluttered with questions. What was he supposed to know? What was he missing? Exhaustion was written on everyone's face, but so was the determination to stay near Joanna in case they were needed.

"Marina, I'd like to know something about your father," Steven said. "My mother didn't say much except to tell us who you all were and what you did as careers. Occasionally, she shared some of the things in your dad's letters, but mostly she kept them to herself. I was only a kid when they got together for the first time since their separation, but I'll never forget the happiness on her face when she got back from New York."

Marina smiled. "The only things I know about Dad and Joanna are what I've discovered since he died. And that's not a whole lot. I read the last e-mails they exchanged, and I have to admit I was puzzled about some of the references. But that's only because Dad never told us anything about your mother or the time he spent with her. I know they'd met a few times during those years, but not where or when. You probably have a lot more to tell me than I can tell you."

"Well, I'd like to know where you lived, what kind of man your father was, anything, I guess."

"Aside from my dad, Grandpa was the most wonderful man in the world," Jason interjected. "He was kind, helpful and one of the smartest people I've ever known. I guess you could say he was my idol."

"Dad was the kind of person who accomplished great things but didn't want a lot of credit for any of it," Marina added. "He kept a low profile and didn't like having reporters or television people hanging around him. After a play at the theater, he'd slip out the back and let the cast meet the public. He was a very modest guy."

"My mother finally played his tape for us a couple of years ago when she went to New York to give him a copy she had made. I was very impressed by his voice," Steven said.

"Imagine my shock when I put that tape into the player in his car and heard it for the first time," Marina said. "I'd heard him sing for years but never like that."

"Mom said he recorded those songs for her at a little piano bar they used to go to," Steven said. "He gave her the tape for her twenty-first birthday. It's hard to imagine her being that young and already as committed to him the way she was."

"There's something I've been curious about since I read it in one of her e-mails," Marina said. "Do you know anything about an Emerald Palace? Was that the name of the bar?"

"No, the bar was the Downtown Club. You must mean the Empire State Building. That's what they called it. Mom said it was lit in red and green the Christmas they first went to Manhattan together. She talked a lot about New York and how much they loved it."

"Do you know how many times they actually got together during those years?" Jason asked.

"About three or four, I think. Always in New York when your grandfather was in the city. The last time Mom went up was in 'ninety-three and she was pretty upset about Jared's health when she got back. That's when she gave him the tape."

Marina didn't say anything for a few minutes. Finally, she looked down at her fingers, twisted her ring several times.

"Did you know why our parents never got together for good?"

"Yes, I did, and it's always been a source of a bit of guilt for me. I know my mother and dad were married very shortly after your dad decided to stay with you. Mom was lonely and scared and feeling very rejected, she told me, and my dad was part of the circle of friends she hung with at grad school. She never went into detail about what happened exactly, but I got the picture pretty clearly. It was a rebound thing, probably shouldn't ever have happened. But I was on the way, so they got married and tried very hard to make it work. I remember little things, pieces of conversation, a lot of arguing and plenty of weekends spent with Mom's parents. Mom and Dad were clearly unhappy together and looking back at it, I think they would probably have separated anyway if Dad hadn't been drafted and then killed in a helicopter crash his first day in Vietnam."

"Oh, Steven, how terrible for you," Marina said. "How old were you?"

"I was five, so I didn't understand a lot. All I knew was Dad went off to the Army and never came back. Mom and I met his parents for the first time when we took his body home to Ohio, and we were pretty close until they died a few years ago."

"For the first time? When you were that old?" Andy asked.

"Uh-huh. Mom said Dad's parents never accepted their marriage and didn't want to meet her or see me. He tried his hardest to convince them, but nothing he could say ever changed their minds. They carried the guilt over that mistake until their deaths ... all those years separated from their own son and grandson because they were too hard-headed to admit they were wrong."

"I have a picture of you when you were about that age," Marina said. "Dad had it in his desk drawer, and my brother Mike and I found it when we were cleaning up after his funeral. You looked so much like I did at five, I actually wondered for a long time if I had a half-brother I didn't even know about."

"You never said anything about that, Mom," Jason said.

"No, you didn't," Andy echoed.

"I was trying very hard not to admit the possibility. But after I talked it over with Judith, I realized Dad could never have denied his own child, so I put it out of my mind."

She looked at Steven. "Judith is my oldest and best friend. I often unloaded on her as I began discovering things about Dad and your mother. She kept me from making some serious errors in judgment along the way."

"I would have liked having a sister," Steven said. "But I know I'm Philip Webber's son. I'm like my dad in so many ways. He was a real blondie like me and I obviously inherited his penchant for detail. Mom says he'd be very proud that I ended up in architecture. I may look a lot like him but from what I've been told, I'm a more emotional, outgoing person than he was. I guess I got the best of each of them."

"From the program she gave at Manning and the news account on TV, we know your mother was a well-known psychologist," Andy said, "Is she still practicing?"

"No, she retired several years ago, not long after your father-in-law did, as a matter of fact. She volunteers at the youth center in Atlantic City three days a week. That's where she grew up and went to school, so she still feels like it's her hometown."

"I wondered if Dad ever visited her there," Marina said.

"Not as far as I know. The last time she saw him was in New York, unless you count the funeral. That was very painful for her."

"She told you about it?" Andy asked.

"No, not me. Abby encouraged Mom to talk about her trip to Chicago, to open up about her feelings. In a way, it was good, but in another way..."

"I remember when I first saw her," Marina interrupted. "I was curious about who she was ... no one seemed to know her, but as the pieces of memory came trickling back, I realized I'd unknowingly met the Joanna of Dad's letters."

Steven looked down at the floor. When he raised his head, there were tears in his eyes.

"She came back from Chicago a profoundly sad person. She told Abby she'd only gone because Jared asked her to in one of those last e-mails. But seeing all of you, being there at the cemetery when the workers got ready to lower the casket into the ground, all of that weighed very heavily on her."

"I watched her from the car as we drove away," Marina said. "She had a red rose in her hand and I'm ashamed to admit I resented it at the time. I reacted like a little kid who wanted to be the only one to have a special flower for her dad. If I'd been able to think more clearly, I might have realized there must have been some significance behind it."

"Yes, there was. Abby told me your father gave Joanna a red rose when they made their first trip to New York in 'sixty-one."

"I thought it was something like that. I found a matchbook from the Statler Hilton in his car," Marina said. "I bet that's where they stayed."

"Mom never talked much about those early days. What I know came later, after I was old enough to understand. I always admired the fact that she was a successful professional woman with a wide circle of friends. Deep inside, though, there was always an underlying sadness. She would have been supremely happy with your father, but knowing he would never leave the life he'd built in Chicago, the family who thought he was perfect, I guess respecting the image he worked so hard to preserve, she gave in, surrendered her dream and went on with her life. Whatever they saw in one another the first day they met was obviously powerful enough to follow them through the rest of their lives."

Marina's mind was reeling with all the questions she wanted to ask. But as they talked, she felt fatigue begin to take control. Reclining back on the sofa, she closed her eyes.

"Tired, huh?" Jason asked. "Me, too."

The nurse tiptoed into the waiting room. It was very quiet. Everyone was sleeping, the men in their chairs, Marina on the sofa, Jason's head resting on her arm.

Jason dozed lightly. Suddenly, he felt a cool rush of air and a hand on his shoulder.

Jason. Hey, wake up.

He opened his eyes and saw his grandfather kneeling in front of him.

I need you to listen very carefully, son. Joanna's very badly injured. Even if she wakes up, she won't ever be the same or be able to do the things she loves, so I'm taking her home with me. We've waited many years to be together. You've been an extension of me, my boy, and I want to thank you for helping me keep a promise I made a long time ago.

Then he was gone.

Jason bolted upright, grabbing Marina's arm so tightly she whimpered. "What is it, Jason? Are you all right?"

Slowly, he released his grip and looked around the room. Andy's eyes opened; Steven had begun to stir.

Jason stood. "We need to go in to Joanna. Something's happened."

"Why do you say that?" Andy asked.

"Grandpa told me. I saw him."

"Grandpa? You just dreamed it, son..."

"No, Dad, I saw him! It was *him.* He said not to worry, that Joanna was going home with him and he thanked me for helping him keep a promise. I don't understand what he meant by that, but I know from what he said she's going to die."

"Joanna's condition hasn't changed or the nurse would have told us," Marina said. "You must have been dreaming."

Jason moved toward the door. "No, I wasn't dreaming. We need to go to her," he insisted. "Grandpa said so ... please!"

As he reached for the handle, the trauma unit door swung open. The nurse was removing her mask, smoothing her smock. She looked up at him with sympathy in her eyes.

"I'm sorry. I tried to get out here but it happened so quickly there wasn't enough time. Dr. Webber had a massive cerebral hemorrhage and passed away suddenly. There was nothing we could do."

She moved aside and the four of them went into the unit, into Joanna's small cubicle. The heart monitor had been turned off. Joanna's face was unmarred, her eyes closed, her lips lifted in a slight smile.

Steven buried his head on his mother's chest and wept.

After a few minutes, he straightened, wiped his eyes and took a deep breath.

"Thank you," he said to the nurse. "I know you all did everything you could. I need to call my wife and help her find a way to break the news to our son. This will be very hard for him."

The nurse led Steven to a phone at the nurses' station. Marina and Andy touched Joanna's hand gently then walked out, their faces somber. Jason stood motionless, still trying to process what had happened.

"I don't understand everything, Joanna," he whispered. "I just know it was awful of me not to listen to you, not to find out what you could have told me. I hope you and Grandpa are together and can forgive the childish way I've acted. I'm so sorry."

He kissed Joanna's cheek and went to join the others.

~ * ~

Steven was back. "Jason, I think something extraordinary happened here. My mother always taught me never to question things that seem to have no explanation. She said I would ultimately learn whatever I was supposed to know. But given your closeness to your grandfather, I'm not at all surprised he chose to tell you about her. He knew you would listen."

"Grandpa and I talked a lot about things like that. I guess he and Joanna thought a lot alike."

Steven turned to Marina and Andy. "Abby wants you to come to the house. We all need some rest and we live only a few blocks on the other side of the bridge. Tomorrow, we can start planning the arrangements, and I'd also like to drive to Mom's place in Brigantine. Would you like to come with us?"

"Of course," Marina said. "Thanks for including us. We want to be there for you, Abby and Brian."

"We'll need all the support we can get," Steven said. "It's all been so sudden, so unreal. Before we go, I'd like a few minutes with my mother alone."

~ * ~

It was a restless night for everyone. After accepting loaner nightclothes and borrowed toiletries, Andy, Marina and Jason managed a few hours of sleep. They all got up early and dressed to make the drive to Joanna's condo. Steven had spoken to the funeral director before they left, describing the family's needs, and Andy had contacted the airline to change their return flight to Chicago.

They followed Steven's car along the river to the Walt Whitman Bridge, then east on the Atlantic City Expressway. On the radio, local newscasters chattered away continuously about the aftermath of the tragedy at the Belvedere. Already there was finger-pointing as various parties scrambled to find someone or something to blame for the collapse. The high winds had played a small part, said one, perhaps concrete that hadn't had time to set, said another, but more than likely it would take months for the exact cause to be discovered.

~ * ~

Steven opened the door of Joanna's home and they crossed the marble threshold into a shadowed, paneled hallway. A large master bedroom was on the right, a smaller guest room on the left. Beyond that, the den was shrouded in shadows, shutters closed. Next to the computer on the desk was the photo of Jared Fowler in his academic robes.

Jason walked into the room to get a closer look. "That's Grandpa! I've never seen that picture."

"Mom said she snapped it with a pocket camera before your grandfather walked in the commencement ceremony procession the year he left Manning. She had it enlarged and it's been displayed somewhere in this house since the day she moved in."

He handed the photo to Jason. "I know she'd want you to have it."

Steven led Marina, Andy and Jason out of the den into the great room. On the left, the dining room table and chairs were upholstered in pastel to match the sectional and chair in the living area. The galley kitchen, with its gleaming white appliances, was to the right. In front of them, from one side of the room to the other, floor-to-ceiling windows and a sliding glass door opened on the spectacular vista of the shoreline,

Atlantic City's skyline to the right, the vast rolling ocean in front, miles of beach to the left. The dune grass swayed gently in the cool breeze; the surf rolled silently into the sand.

"It's very beautiful," Marina said. "I can see why she loved it here."

"Mom always said she wanted her ashes scattered on the ocean out there," Steven said, looking out the window. "Only we thought it would be many years before we'd have to carry out her wish." He turned away to conceal his tears.

Abby walked out of the den, carrying a large manila envelope and handed it to Steven. He opened it and took out its contents.

"Hey, that's Gran's book," Brian said. "She said I could read it when I get older."

"My mother wrote about her life," Steven said. "She wouldn't let us read it. Claimed it would jinx her if we knew in advance what she was writing. All she would say was she'd written her memories from the time she was a college student until a few years ago when she lost contact with your father. She said she wrote it more as a novel than a memoir, though. 'The Great American Love Story,' she said. Then she would always laugh. She even picked out a pen name so people wouldn't know she'd written it. A few weeks ago, she told us it was nearly complete and she was going to try to get it published. I'll make a copy of the manuscript for you. I'm sure it will give all of us some new insights into our parents' lives."

While the others talked, Jason stepped out of the condo and walked to the beach. Holding the picture of his grandfather, he stood not far from the spot where he had first encountered Joanna a few days earlier. The wind was cold; the waves broke about ten feet from shore. He closed his eyes and said goodbye to her, wishing he'd been able to make amends.

But somehow, he knew Joanna understood, wherever she was. And he was certain that wherever she was, she wasn't alone.

Epilogue

Three Days Later

Brian carried the urn gingerly, his eyes focused on the sand, putting one foot deliberately in front of the other, knowing he carried something precious. Abby's arm was around Steven's waist as they walked onto the beach from the wooden walkway through the dunes. Marina and Andy, Jason between them, followed. Their hearts ached for the suffering Joanna's family was going through. It brought back so vividly another funeral in another place not so long before.

They approached a rock pile jetty, climbed up and walked to the end, while the waves sent bubbles of white froth that beat against its sides. Brian carefully removed the cap from the brass container. He looked back.

"Jason, I want Gran to fly 'way up in the sky, but I'm not tall enough. Will you help me?"

Jason lifted Brian up on his shoulders and held his legs securely. The little boy held the urn as high over his head as he could. Then he shook it. The wind caught the feathery ashes, lifting them over the water, carrying them out to sea. The two families stood for a few minutes, watching, then turned back to the house.

Jason lingered for a moment, thinking of his grandfather and Joanna. Looking into space, he said, "I know you're together, finally happy and at peace." Lost in thought, he passed by two birds as he walked through the dunes, neither noticing nor understanding.

The seagull with the black spot on his head sat on the dune with his mate, watching the people go by. After a few minutes, the two birds called to each other, spread their wings and soared over the building. They flew over the cars and the small group of mourners, then circled and dipped low, almost as if to land. They called to one another again and flew toward the sea. Hearing their musical cries, Jason looked up, squinting against the sun.

"...I love seagulls," his grandfather had told him. "I love how free they are, the way they swoop down and then shoot up into the air so high. Maybe someday a seagull will find you and make sure you get where you need to be."

Jason smiled, his heart light. His grandfather had brought him here. He was where he needed to be. And, having kept a promise he made to Joanna Ransome so long ago, so was Jared Fowler.

Meet Jeanne Howard

Jeanne Howard has been writing since she was old enough to hold a pencil. From poems to essays and now to women's fiction, she has used the power of words to entertain, move and captivate her readers.

Jeanne holds a bachelor's degree in English and a master's in counseling psychology. In 1973, she was co-founder of a successful group of weekly newspapers, which she continued to operate until 1994.

A native of New Jersey, Jeanne is retired after a second career as public information officer for a large suburban school district. She spends her time as executive editor for Wings ePress, Inc., enjoying her cat, Selma, her husband and two grown daughters.

Other Works From The Pen Of

Jeanne Howard

Seasons of Forgetting - Two people, defying the conventions of their time, powerless against the love that refuses to break their connection, pursue a tumultuous relationship spanning four decades.

Dear reader,

I hope you've enjoyed reading this compelling story of love
and loss as much as I enjoyed writing it.

Your opinion is valuable to other readers like you,
who may be looking for books like mine.

Please consider taking a few minutes to post a review,
however brief,
on the site where you purchased this book
or on the Wings ePress web page.

You may also want to visit my author page
at the Wings' website, where you can find
the other book I've written.

Thank you!

Jeanne Howard